"A P[...] STORYTELLER"

—Time

Graham Greene, the greatest of living English writers, chills the mind and the senses in this unforgettable story of a manhunt through the night-filled English woods. Throbbing with sinister violence, THE MAN WITHIN tells of Andrews, a man on the run. In desperate flight from the law and from the smugglers he had betrayed, he knew he would run forever—until he learned that he could not escape himself.

THE MAN WITHIN, Graham Greene's first novel, was unanimously acclaimed by critics as the brilliant beginning of one of the most distinguished literary careers of our time.

"Greene is superb. . . . He evokes the most actual streets, the most vivid skies, and individuals who can have a lacerating reality as they search the labyrinth of their lives."

—Newsweek

"A MASTER CRAFTSMAN . . . THE PREMIER WRITER WORKING TODAY IN THE ENGLISH LANGUAGE."
—Chicago Tribune

THE MAN WITHIN
was published in the U.S.A. by The Viking Press, Inc.

Books by Graham Greene

Novels

Brighton Rock
A Burnt-Out Case
The Comedians
The Confidential Agent *
The End of the Affair
England Made Me *
  (Also published as
  The Shipwrecked)
The Heart of the Matter
The Honorary Consul *
It's a Battlefield
Loser Takes All
The Man Within *
The Ministry of Fear
Orient Express (Original British
  title: Stamboul Train)
Our Man in Havana*
The Power and the Glory
The Quiet American
The Third Man*
This Gun for Hire (Original
  British title: A Gun for Sale)
Travels with My Aunt

Short Stories

May We Borrow Your Husband?
A Sense of Reality
Twenty-One Stories

Travel

Another Mexico (Original British
  title: The Lawless Roads)
In Search of Character
Journey Without Maps

Essays

Collected Essays

Plays

Carving a Statue
The Complaisant Lover
The Living Room
The Potting Shed

Autobiography

A Sort of Life *

* Published by POCKET BOOKS

THE
MAN
WITHIN

Graham Greene

PUBLISHED BY POCKET BOOKS NEW YORK

THE MAN WITHIN

Viking Press edition published 1947

POCKET BOOK edition published May, 1975

Standard Book Number: 671-78881-7.
This POCKET BOOK edition is published by arrangement
with The Viking Press, Inc. Copyright, 1929, renewed, ©,
1957, by Graham Greene. All rights reserved. This book, or
portions thereof, may not be reproduced by any means without the permission of the publisher: The Viking Press, Inc.,
625 Madison Avenue, New York, N.Y. 10022.
Front cover illustration by Alan Magee.

Printed in the U.S.A.

For Vivien

"There's another man within me
that's angry with me."

—SIR THOMAS BROWNE

THE
MAN
WITHIN

PART I

CHAPTER I

HE came over the top of the down as the last light failed and could almost have cried with relief at sight of the wood below. He longed to fling himself down on the short stubbly grass and stare at it, the dark comforting shadow which he had hardly hoped to see. Thus only could he cure the stitch in his side, which grew and grew with the jolt, jolt of his stumble down hill. The absence of the cold wind from the sea that had buffeted him for the last half hour seemed like a puff of warm air on his face, as he dropped below the level of the sky. As though the wood were a door swinging on a great hinge, a shadow moved up towards him and the grass under his feet changed from gold to green, to purple and last to a dull grey. Then night came.

A hedge sprang up before his eyes at the distance of a dozen yards. His confused tired senses became aware of the smell of last year's blackberry leaves wet with past rain. For a moment the scent swathed him in a beautiful content and left him with an ache for time in which to rest here. The grass grew longer be-

fore he reached the hedge, and a little later his feet
were heavy with wet earth and he knew that he was on
a path. It was his feet rather than his mind that knew
it. They made a rambling progress, now in the muddy
centre of the way, now in the grass at the right hand
edge, now scraping the outer fringe of the hedge on
the other side. His mind was a confusion of scents and
sounds, the far hush of the sea, a memory of rattling
pebbles, the smell of the wet leaves and the trampled
marl, the salt sweep of the wind that he had left behind on the top of the hill, voices, imaginary footsteps. They were jumbled together like the pieces of a
puzzle, and they were half forgotten because of his
fatigue and fear.

The fear in his mind told him that paths were dangerous. He whispered it out loud to himself "Dangerous, dangerous", and then because he thought that the
low voice must belong to another on the path beside
him, he scrambled panic stricken through the hedge.
The blackberry twigs plucked at him and tried to hold
him with small endearments, twisted small thorns into
his clothes with a restraint like a caress, as though
they were the fingers of a harlot in a crowded bar. He
took no notice and plunged on. The fingers grew
angry, slashed at his face with sharp, pointed nails.
"Who are you anyhow? Who are you anyhow? Think
yourself mighty fine." He heard the voice, shrill and
scolding. She had a pretty face and a white skin. "Another day," he said, because he could not wait. He had
to leave the town. The last twigs broke and the
night became darker under trees. Through the latticing

of the leaves half a dozen stars came suddenly to view.

He stumbled against a tree and leant for a moment against it, allowing his legs to relax. Freed from some of the weight of his body, they seemed to ache more than ever. He tried to pull himself together and re-member exactly where he was—no longer in Shore-ham but in a wood. Had he been followed? He listened hungry for silence and was rewarded. Had he ever been followed? He had seen Carlyon in the bar of the Sus-sex Pad, but only in the mirror behind the harlot's head. Carlyon had been standing sideways to him and was ordering a drink. Unless Carlyon saw him leave, he was safe. What a fool he had been to leave so sud-denly. He should have gone quietly out and taken the girl with him. Fool, fool, fool, fool, the word droned on in his mind, a sleepy and mechanical reiteration. His eyes closed, then opened with a start, as a twig broke under his own foot. He might have been asleep now in a comfortable bed, all the more comfortable for being shared. She was pretty and had a good skin. He didn't suppose he would have been asleep. . . . He woke again two minutes later feeling cold. He had dreamed that he was again in the bar, looking in the mirror at Carlyon's face, and in the dream the face had begun to turn. But was it only in the dream? He could not stay here and again he began to run, very stum-blingly because of the roots of the trees.

Oh, but he was tired, tired, tired. His wrist was hurting and felt damp and weak, slashed by the thorns in the hedge. If Carlyon had suddenly appeared now in front of him, he would have thrown himself down

on his knees and cried. Carlyon wouldn't do anything.
Carlyon was a gentleman like himself. And one could
always appeal to Carlyon's sense of humour. "Hello,
Carlyon, old man, it's ages since I've seen you. Have
you heard this one, Carlyon, old chap? Carlyon,
Carlyon, Carlyon." "And there shall be weeping and
gnashing of teeth." "How dare you teach my boy that
stuff?" and then he'd beaten her. His father had always talked of him as "my boy", as though his mother
had not borne the pain. The damned, old hypocritical
bully. "Please God, give me a bear." He hadn't wanted
a live puppy, which needed looking after. Am I going to faint, he asked himself? What's this wood doing? Why a wood? Hansel and Gretel. There should
be a cottage soon with a witch in it, and the cottage
should be made of sugar. "I am so hungry," he said
aloud. "I can't wait for Gretel." But inside himself he
knew only too certainly that there was no Gretel. He
and Gretel had kissed under the holly tree on the
common one spring day. Across a faintly coloured sky
a few plump clouds had tumbled recklessly. And then
time and again he was walking up narrow stairs to
small rooms and untidy beds, and walking down again
feeling disatisfied, because he had never found Gretel
there. How curious everything was. And now this
wood. . . . He saw a light glimmering in front at what
seemed an infinite distance, and he began to run, remembering that Carlyon might be somewhere behind
him in the dark. He had to get on, get on, get on. His
feet stumbled, stumbled, and every stumble sent a
shoot of pain up his arm to the shoulder, starting from

his torn wrist, but not a stumble brought the light nearer. It shone mockingly ahead, very small and sharp and immeasurably knowing. It was as though the world had heaved upward, like a ship in a rough sea, and brought a star to its own lamp's level. But as distant and as inaccessible as the star was the light.

He was almost on top of the light before he realised that its smallness was due to size and not to distance. The grey stones of a cottage suddenly hunched themselves up between the trees. To the man raising his head to see the ramshackle bulk, it was as though the uneven, knobbled shoulders of the place had shrugged themselves from the earth. The cottage had but one floor above the ground, and the window with which it faced the wood was of thick glass, slightly tinted, like the glass of liquor bottles. The stones of the place gave the impression of having been too hastily and formlessly piled upon one another, so that now with old age they had slipped, some this way, some that way, a little out of the perpendicular. An excrescence built clumsily upon one end might have been anything from some primitive sanitary arrangement to a pigsty or even a small stable.

He stood and watched it and swayed a little upon his feet. Soon he would go up and knock, but for the moment in spite of weariness and the pain from his wounded wrist, he was engaged in the favourite process of dramatising his actions. "Out of the night," he said to himself, and liking the phrase repeated it, "out of the night." "A hunted man," he added, "pursued by murderers," but altered that to "by worse than death."

He imagined himself knocking on that door. He saw it opening, and there would appear an old white-faced woman with the face of a saint. She would take him in, and shelter him. She would be like a mother to him and bind his wrist and give him food and drink, and when he had slept he would tell her everything—"I am a hunted man," he would say, "pursued by worse than death."

He became afraid again of his own reiteration of the phrase "worse than death". There was little satisfaction in an image which stood upon a fact. He looked behind him once into the dark from which he had come, half expecting to see Carlyon's face luminous there, like a lighted turnip. Then he stepped nearer to the cottage.

When he felt the rough stones warm under his palm, he was comforted. At least it was something solid to have at one's back. He turned and faced the wood, stared and stared, trying to pick out details and to see where each trunk stood. But either his eyes were tired, or else the darkness was too deep. The wood remained a black, forbidding immensity. He felt his way cautiously along the wall to the window and then, standing on tiptoe, tried to peer within. He could perceive only shadows, and the flame of a candle which stood on the ledge inside. He thought that one shadow in the room moved, but it might merely have been the effect of the flickering light. His mind cleared a little and gave room for cunning, and with cunning there crawled in uneasiness. He felt his way very cautiously along the wall towards the door, listening for any sound from the cottage on one side of him and from the wood on the other. It would be like his luck, he thought, his heart giving a sick jolt, if he had stumbled on a smuggler's hole. It was just such a night, he knew, as he would have chosen himself to run a cargo, dark and moonless. Perhaps he had better move on and avoid the place, and even as the thought crossed his mind his fingers touched the wood of the door. His legs were weak as butter, his wrist was sending stab after stab of pain up his arm, and the edge of an approaching mist touched his consciousness. He could go no further. Better face what lay within the cottage than lie defenceless outside with Carlyon perhaps approaching through the wood. The vision of the white-haired old mother had been effaced very completely. He fumbled at the door, but he was unprepared for it to swing readily open, and he fell on his knees across the threshold in a silly sprawl.

He looked up. Clogged and dulled by that ever-approaching mist a voice had spoken to him. "Stay where you are," it had said with a kind of quiet and unsurprised command. Now he saw the other side of the room, wavering a little like a slim upstrained candle-flame, a woman. She was young, he recognised with an automatic leer, and white in the face but not frightened. What kept him still upon his knees, besides the complete physical weariness that made him unwilling to rise, was the gun which was aimed steadily at his chest. He could see the hammer raised.

"I say," he said. "I say." He was displeased at the dead sound of his own voice. He felt that it should be full of the mingled pathos of weariness and appeal. "You needn't be afraid," he tried again. "I'm done in."

"You can stand up," she said, "and let me look at you." He rose shakily to his feet, with a feeling of immense grievance. This wasn't the way for a woman to behave. She should be frightened, but she very damnably wasn't. It was he who felt the fear, with his eye warily watching the gun.

"Now what do you want?" she asked. To his surprise there was no anger in her voice, but a quite genuine curiosity. It annoyed him to know that she was patently the mistress of the situation. It made him even in his weakness want to bully her, to teach her. If only he could get that gun. . . .

"I want a hiding place," he said. "I'm being followed."

"Runners?" she said. "Gaugers? You can't stop here. You'd better go the way you came."

"But I can't," he said, "they'd get me. Look here, I'm on the side of the law. It's not the officers who are after me." His eyes fixed on the gun, he made a step forward, spreading out his hands in appeal, in a gesture which he had often seen made on the stage.

"Keep back," she said, "you can't stay here. Turn round and go out."

"For the love of God," he said. He had picked that expression also from the stage, but the girl could not be expected to know it. It sounded genuine, for his voice was full of real tears. He was tired out and wanted to sleep.

"If you are being followed," she said, as though

speaking to a very stupid child, "you are wasting time here."

"When I get you," he said with sudden fury, "I'll teach you charity. Call yourself a Christian"—his eyes filled with warm sentimental tears at a sudden vision of little grey churches, corn fields, stiles, honeyed distant bells in the dusk, robins in snow. "I'll teach you," he said again. The white serenity of her face infuriated him, "I'll tell you what I'll do to you." With childish petulance he flung his mud at something beautiful and very distant, hated himself and enjoyed his hatred. He described what he would do to her in a brief, physiological sentence, and rejoiced at the flush which it fetched to her face. His outburst brought the mist down closer upon him "You can join your fellows on the streets then," he cried at her, determined to hurt before fainting should make him a powerless, shameful weakling at her mercy. For a moment he thought that she was going to shoot. He was too exhausted for fear now and felt only a vague satisfaction that he had made himself sufficiently hateful to drive her to action. Then the danger passed. "I told you to go," was all she said, "I don't know what you want here."

He swayed a little on his feet. He could hardly see her now. She was a lighter wisp in a world of grey. "Look, he's at the window," he cried with sudden vehemence, and as the wisp moved he lunged forward.

He felt the gun within his hand and forced it upwards, struggling at the same time for the trigger. The girl had been taken by surprise and for the moment gave way.

With the muzzle pointing somewhere at the ceiling, he pulled the trigger. The hammer fell, but there was no explosion. The girl had fooled him with an unloaded weapon. "Now, I'll teach you," he said. He tried to wrench the gun away, the better to get at her, but his right wrist seemed to double up and collapse with the effort. He felt a hand press against his face, and his whole body grew weak, and he stumbled backwards. He hit against a table which he had not seen was in the room, so focused had his eyes been on the danger in front of him. He put out a hand to save himself, for his legs seemed made in numerous joints, which were now all folding in upon each other. Something fell to the floor with a brief dart of gold, like a disdainful guinea, and his fingers were scorched for a moment by flame.

The pain cleared his brain with the suddenness of an unseen hand wrenching a curtain aside. He looked behind him and found himself staring into a heavy bearded face, over which three other candles sent a straying luminance.

"But . . ." he cried, and never knew what he meant to add. He backed away in disgust from the body where it lay in its unlidded and unvarnished coffin. He had never met death before so startlingly face to face. His mother he had never seen in death, for his father had huddled her quickly away in earth with a cross and a bunch of flowers, and his father had been killed in a running fight at sea and dropped unobtrusively over the side, while he was learning to decline *oikia* at his school in Devon. He was frightened and disgusted and sick and somehow ashamed. It was, he felt remotely, indecorous to broil thus over a coffin, even though the coffin were of unvarnished deal. His eyes searched a deepening darkness, flickering with gold points where the candles shone, until they found a face which seemed now white rather with weariness than serenity. "I'm sorry," he said, and then the lights were all extinguished.

CHAPTER II

OVER a toppling pile of green vegetables two old women were twittering. They pecked at their words like sparrows for crumbs. "There was a fight, and one of the officers was killed." "They'll hang for that. But three of them escaped." The vegetables began to grow and grow in size, cauliflowers, cabbages, carrots, potatoes. "Three of them escaped, three of them escaped," one of the cauliflowers repeated. Then the whole pile fell to the ground, and Carlyon was walking towards him. "Have you heard this one?" he said, "Three of them escaped, three of them escaped." He came nearer and nearer and his body grew in size, until it seemed as though it must burst like a swollen bladder. "Have you heard this one, Andrews?" he said. Andrews became aware that somewhere behind a

gun was being levelled, and he turned, but there were
only two men, whose faces he could not see, laughing
together. "Old Andrews, we won't see his like again.
Do you remember the time . . ." "Oh, shut up, shut
up," he called, "he was only a brute, I tell you. My
father was a brute." "Ring a ring a roses," his father
and Carlyon were dancing round him, holding hands.
The ring got smaller and smaller and he could feel
their breath, Carlyon's cool and scentless, his father's
stale, tobacco-laden. He was gripped round the waist,
and someone called out "Three of them escaped." The
arms began to drag him away, "I didn't do it," he
cried. "I didn't do it." Tears ran down his cheeks. He
struggled and struggled against the pulling arms.

He emerged slowly into a grey dispersing mist, cut
by jagged edges. They grew towards his sight and became boxes, old trunks, dusty lumber. He found that
he was lying upon a pile of sacking and there was a
stale smell in the room of earthen mould. A pile of
gardening implements leant up against one wall, and
one upturned lidless trunk full of little shrivelled bulbs.
At first he thought that he was in the potting shed of
his home. Outside should be a lawn and a tall pine,
and presently he would hear the shuffling footsteps of
the gardener. The old man always dragged his left
foot behind him, so that there was no regular cadence
to his steps. They had to be counted like an owl's cry
—one twoooo—one twoooo. How it was that he came
to be lying in the potting shed in the grey light of early
morning Andrews did not question. He knew very well
the unwisdom of questioning it—half indeed he was

aware in what place he lay. I will play a little longer, he thought, and turned over and lay with his face to the wall, so that he might not notice the unfamiliar details of the room, shed, whatever it might be. Then he shut his eyes, because the wall he faced was stone and it should have been wood.

With his eyes shut all was well. He sniffed the warm scent of the mould comfortingly.

The old man would grumble at his presence, complain that he had shifted a hoe, a spade, a fork. Then as certainly as night closed day he would take up a box lid full of seeds, rattle the seeds back and forth with a noise like small quick hailstones and murmur "Winkle dust." Andrews screwed his eyes tighter, sniffed deeper. He remembered how the old man had been standing once beneath the pine at the end of the lawn. He was feeling his chin thoughtfully and staring up at the tapering dark slimness above him. "Three hundred years," he was saying slowly to himself, "three hundred years." Andrews had commented on the sweet elusive smell that came sifting through the air. "That's age," said the old man, "that's age." He spoke with such conviction that Andrews half expected to see him vanish himself into a faint perfume formed out of bulbs and damp turned earth. "They make coffins out of pines," the old man continued, "coffins, that's why you get the smell sometimes where there ain't no pines. Up through the ground you see."

The thought of coffins jerked Andrew's eyes open. He saw again the candle fall and the bearded face looking up at him. It was sheer chance that he had not placed his hand full on that dead stubble. Three years swept past; the present scratched at his nerves. He jumped up and looked round. How long had he slept? What had that girl been doing in the meanwhile? He had been a weak fool to collapse and a sentimental fool to dream into the past. The present called for brisk action if he was to bring himself to safe haven, but remembering all the circumstances of the last few weeks, he wondered with a sick lurch at the heart whether there was any haven to which Carlyon would not penetrate.

In the wall opposite was a window cobwebbed and dusty. By piling two of the boxes together he was able to reach it, and he calculated that he could just squeeze his body through the opening. He was afraid to break the glass, because of the noise the act would cause, and his fingers felt cautiously and timidly at the catch, which was almost welded to its position with the rust of many years. He began to pick at the rust with his nails and by small fractions of an inch he was able to move the catch. The tiny noises he made fretted at his nerves and the very need of caution made him careless. He stood on tiptoe, partly with excitement and a restlessness to be gone, partly that he might get a better purchase on the terribly reluctant catch. With a long drawn out squeak, it twisted and left the window free; at the same moment the noise of a door-handle turning swung him round. He had hardly noticed the door of the room, so certain had he been that it was locked, until now when it opened and the girl stood there. Andrews felt acutely ridiculous balanced upon his boxes. Carefully and slowly, with his eyes fixed on her, he stepped down.

She laughed, but without amusement. "What were you doing up there?" she asked. He felt furious with her at finding him in so ignominious a position.

"I was trying to escape," he said.

"Escape?" she turned the word over on her lips as though it were a novel taste. "If you mean you wanted to go," she said, "there was the door, wasn't there?"

"Yes, and you with the gun," he snapped back.

"Oh that gun," she laughed again, not scornfully this time but with a real merriment, "I haven't an idea how to load it."

He took a few steps towards her and looked less at her than at the open doorway behind her, which led, he saw, into the room of last night's humiliation. He was certain that she was bluffing. She must have more than a coffin and a dead man in that room to give her the courage to face him so calmly—so impudently he styled it to himself. So he advanced a little way, widening his vision of that room beyond.

"You mean that I can go?" he asked.

"I wouldn't stop you," she answered. A note of anger was struggling with amusement in her voice and at last amusement won. "I didn't invite you for the night."

"Don't talk so much," he said angrily and flushed a little when she asked if he were listening for something. For he was listening intently and thought for a moment that he heard the squeak of a board and then again a man's breathing. But he could not be sure.

Suppose she had gone out during the night and found Carlyon . . .

"Look here," he cried, unable to bear the suspense longer, "what have you done?"

"Done?" she said, "done?" He watched her suspiciously, hating that habit she had of turning words over like a pancake, first this side, then that.

"Who have you fetched while I've been sleeping? I know your sort."

"You are a man, aren't you?" she said with sudden vehemence and was met with a purely mechanical leer and response. "Do you want me to prove it?" It was as though the young man's face were a mask to which small strings were attached. She had pulled one and the mouth had opened and the lips had twisted a little at one corner. She felt a brief wonder as to what string would work the eyes that remained watching her suspiciously, a little frightened, completely unresponsive to the lips. Andrews himself was not unaware of those strings that put his speech and mouth in servitude to others. Always a little too late he would try to recall his words, not through any shame in their purport—it would have been the same if they had been spoken in poetry, but because they had been dictated by another. So now that consciousness coming again a little too late made him try to cover up his previous words by others angrily spoken. "What do you mean anyway?"

"Do you think," she said, "a man ever knows a woman's sort? If I believed that," she added, "I'd . . ." she looked at him with an amazed stare almost as though he had spoken the words. "You can go," she added, "there's no one to stop you. Why should I want you to stay?"

That's all very well, he thought. Is it bluff? The girl has plenty of nerve. It seemed unlikely after the way he had broken in the night before that she should not have tried to communicate with someone. And the whole neighbourhood just at present was riddled with runners and revenue men. He was uncertain how he stood with them, and he had no trust, like Carlyon, in his own elusiveness. However, she said he could go and she stood there waiting. What a devil the woman was—forcing him to make a move. He no longer wanted to escape and stumble blindly into an unknown countryside. He wanted to lie down with his face to the wall and drowse. But she was waiting and waiting and he had to move. He moved slowly and softly towards the door, treading suspiciously like a cat in a strange house. When he reached the doorway he flung back the door as far as it would go lest anyone should be hiding behind it, ready to pounce on his turned back. Behind him he heard a laugh and swung round again. He felt tired and harassed and in no mood for mockery. A wave of self-pity passed across his mind and he saw himself friendless and alone, chased by harsh enemies through an uninterested world. Sympathy is all I want, he said to himself. Old white-haired women with kind wrinkled eyes stooped towards him, large laps and comfortable breasts mocked him with their absence. Little pricking tears rose to his eyes. I know I am a coward and altogether despicable, he said to himself with heavy self-depreciation, trying without much hope to underbid his real character, I know I haven't an ounce of courage, that if Carlyon appeared now I'd go down on my knees to him, but all I want is a little sympathy. I could be made into a man if anyone chose to be interested—if someone believed in me. . . . But here his other self took a hand. He was, he knew, embarrassingly made up of two persons, the sentimental, bullying, desiring child and another more stern critic. If someone believed in me— but he did not believe in himself. Always while one part of him spoke, another part stood on one side and wondered "Is this I who am speaking? Can I really exist like this?"

"It's easy for you to laugh," he said bitterly. But am I really bitter, the other part wondered. Am I play acting still? And if I am play acting, is it I who act or another who pulls the strings? But what a Pharisee the other part of him was. It never took control of his mouth and spoke its own words—hard, real, trustworthy. It only stood on one side and listened and taunted and questioned. So now it let his voice go on, genuine or play acting dictated. "You don't know what it feels like to be alone." Watching the face that still smiled at him, not with hostility but with almost a friendly mocking, he became frightened at an unintended reality in his own words. He was indeed alone. Perhaps that other part of him remained silent, not through self-righteousness, but because it had no words to speak. There was nothing in him but sentiment and fear and cowardice, nothing in him but negatives. How could anyone believe in him if he did not even exist?

He was surprised, deep in the maze in which he chased himself, when she answered him. "I've been alone, too, the last two nights. I don't mind the daytime, but I get a bit scared at night now he's dead." She nodded her head towards the room on the threshold of which he stood.

He looked across the room. The coffin still lay upon the kitchen table. The candles were no longer alight, but dropped in weary attitudes of self-depreciation.

"Husband?" he asked. She shook her head.

"Father?"

"Not exactly. He brought me up though. I can't remember my father. I was fond of him," she nodded her head again. "He was kind to me in his way. It's a bit frightening being alone."

It was as though she had forgotten the circumstances of Andrew's coming. They faced each other. She also seemed alone in a somewhat dark wood. She also was frightened she said, but there was a courage that added to Andrew's shame in the candid hand she appeared to stretch through the dark to his companionship.

"It will be worse to-night," she said. "I have to bury him to-day."

"I should have thought," Andrews answered, remembering the stubble on which he had nearly placed his hand, "it would be less—frightening without a body in the house."

"Oh no," she said, "oh no," looking at him with puzzled eyes. "I wouldn't be afraid of him." She came and stood in the doorway beside Andrews and looked

across at the lidless coffin. "He must be terribly alone,"
she said, "but there's the peace of God in his face.
Come, and look," she stepped across the room, and
very reluctantly Andrews followed.

He could see little of the peace of which the girl
had spoken in the face. The eyes were closed, and he
had a sense drawn from the coarse strong skin of the
lids that they must have been hard to shut. At any
moment he felt the strain might become too great and
the lids would turn up with a sudden click like a roller
blind. Round the mouth were little cunning wrinkles
that prowled outwards across the face in stealthy
radiations. He looked at the girl to see if she were
mocking him in her talk of God in connection with
this bearded rapscallion, but she was looking down at
the body with calm and passionless affection. He had
a sudden inclination to say to her, "It's you who have
the peace of God not he," but refrained. It would
sound melodramatic and she would laugh at him the
more. It was only to suit his own ends or his own
self-pity that he allowed himself the pleasure of
melodrama.

It was while he was regarding the face and the tri-
umphant cunning of the lines, growingly conscious at
the same time of the girl's fixity of thought, like a firm
comforting wall beside his won shifting waters, that
he heard faint stumbling steps. It was fear that made
his ears sufficiently acute, the girl behind him had not
moved. He twisted his eyes up from the dead man and
faced her again.

"So you've been keeping me here?" he said. He was

only half aware of the foolishness of his accusation. One reasoning part of him told him that he had been with her since he woke at most a matter of minutes, but reason somehow had seemed lacking in this house since he had entered it and seen what should have been a frightened girl holding him with a calm gun between the yellow tipped candles. And since he had come to consciousness again five or ten minutes before, he had lived over again a boy's life in Devon and had stood, he told himself with a sudden rush of sentiment, between the cunning and yet clumsy earth and the purposeful courage of the spirit. These experiences could not be confined to the small measure of minutes, and so with a sense of real grievance he accused her. "You've been keeping me here?"

"Keeping you?" she said. "What do you mean?" Suddenly the footsteps which had been very faint grew distinct in a stone shifting. Andrews's mind pierced its maze of vague thinking in a flash of fear, and he half ran across the room to the door through which he had entered the night before. A sense of overwhelming desolation passed over him, a wonder whether he would ever know peace from pursuit, and he gave an unconscious whimper like a rabbit snared. The reality of the sound seemed to acquaint the girl with the measure of his fear.

"Don't go out there," she called to him.

He hesitated with his hand upon the latch. The girl was feeling her cheek with the tips of her fingers. "It's only the woman come to tidy the place," she said.

"I mustn't meet her," Andrews whispered, afraid that their voices would reach the path outside.

"If you go out there," the girl said, "you'll meet her. She'll be coming from the well now. Better go back where you slept," and then as he moved across the room, "no." A slow flush crept from her neck across her face.

"What's the matter now?" he asked angrily.

"If she discovers you—hiding—she'll think—"

"God, you're respectable," he said with a resentful amazement. It was as though the calm spirit that had watched the dead man had become tarnished by the latter's own earthy cunning. Some yellow sunlight, clear and cold with frost, struck across the room from the window and fell across her face, belying the dull good sense of the words she spoke.

"No, but you can't," she said. "It's not as if you were in any danger."

He came close to her and put his hands upon her arms and pulled her close to him. "Listen to me," he said, "I am in danger. I'd rather kill that old woman whoever she is than be talked about in Shoreham. I'm a coward, do you see, and it would be easier to kill her than the man who'd be after me. Now will you let me hide?" He loosened her and she pushed herself away from him. "There must be some other way," she said. She suddenly began to speak rapidly. "You are my brother, do you see? You arrived last week hearing that he was dying because you didn't like me to be alone." She grimaced a little as though at a bad taste.

A splash of water from an overfull pail interrupted

her. Footsteps sounded almost at the threshold of the door. "You must invent things," she said. "What more is there? I must have forgotten—"

"What shall I call you? Your name?" Andrews whispered rapidly, as with a high squeak that latch of the door rose.

"Elizabeth," she said, "Elizabeth."

The door opened and it seemed incongruous after the panic that the footsteps had evoked to see only an old woman with a pail of water which went slip slop over the brim and splashed upon the floor. She was a little stout old woman who gave the impression of being very tightly pulled together by a great number of buttons that strayed from their normal positions and peeped out from interstices and side turnings in her voluminous clothes. She had small eyes and very faint, almost indistinguishable eyebrows. Her hair was some of it white and some of it grey and through it wandered stray strands of very pale metallic gold which looked unnecessarily flippant on an old head. When she saw Andrews standing by the girl she put down the pail on the floor and preened her mouth to whistle until it appeared but one more addition to her collection of buttons. She did not actually whistle but hovered delicately upon the point, while her eyes, which changed from surprise to questioning and last to a somewhat sly amusement, seemed to whistle instead. Under her unembarrassed amused stare Andrews fidgeted and longed for his companion to speak.

At last the old woman, waiting no longer for an invitation, entered. Her eyes having taken in the pair of them were no longer interested. She placed the pail down on the stone floor and then with an old and very dirty rag began to scrub. She had cleaned but a small space when she found it necessary to pull aside the table on which the coffin lay, and this she did with a complete and to Andrews an amazing unconcern. Her eyes had taken in all they desired to see, but her thoughts remained amused. She suddenly chuckled and hastily beat the water in her pail and coughed to hide the sound.

The girl smiled towards Andrews and, with a small pout of the lips that said quite plainly, "now for it", spoke. "This is my brother, Mrs. Butler," she said.

The voice that came from the figure kneeling on the floor was startlingly unexpected. It consorted, not with the white or the grey hairs, but with the too metallic yellow strands. It was soft, almost young, just avoided beauty. It was like a pretty sweet cake that had been soaked in port wine. It would have been lovely, if it had had the certainty of loveliness, but it was damped all through.

"Well now, I didn't know that you had a brother, Miss Elizabeth," it said.

"He came a week ago when he heard Mr. Jennings was dying," the girl went on.

"And so a brother should." The old woman wrung out her cloth into the pail and sat back unexpectedly on her heels. Her eyes were not soft like her voice but as sharp as they were small. Both Andrews and the girl became conscious of their stiff, unreal attitudes, standing a little apart from each other waiting for nothing. "You had all the looks in your family, Miss Elizabeth," Mrs. Butler said. "Your brother doesn't look very strong—or perhaps he's tired." A giggle began to form like a soap bubble in either eye. It grew under almost visible constraint, until at last she let it loose to bound gaily round the room. Then she soaked her cloth again and began to scrub furiously as though she would daunt that spirit of rude flippancy. "And what's your name, sir, if you don't think me rude?"

"Why, the same as my sister's," Andrews replied, trying to sound amused and at his ease.

"I meant your Christian name, sir?" she went on, making rapid progress across the floor.

"Oh, Francis, of course. Hasn't my sister spoken of me?" In the space between a sentence and a sentence, he had had time to watch the sunlight mould the girl's face, give lightness to its somewhat heavy lines, smooth its perplexity into peace. A dark Elizabeth, he thought, watching her hair, how strange. He began to enjoy himself, the burden of his fear had dropped away and left him in the middle of a childish game in which there was no harsh reality. "Elizabeth," he said, "have you never spoken of me to Mrs. Butler? I take it very ill, I really do. And I away at sea imagining that you thought of me."

"Why, are you a sailor, sir?" Mrs. Butler said, not troubling to raise her eyes from the arc of floor in which her small fat arms swung. "I shouldn't have thought it."

"But then I'm a bad sailor," he continued his eyes

on the sunlight or that part of it that lay across Elizabeth's face. He was determined to make her smile. "When I heard how—he was dying, I left my ship. I thought my sister would want someone else beside you to protect her. You can't imagine, Mrs. Butler, how often I've read of you under the stars." He stopped. He had won his smile.

And yet now that he had won his smile, he was ill at ease. It reminded him, perhaps, of all hopeless and unattainable things—not desire then, for he was too weary for desire, but for civilisation. Civilisation meant for him the enjoyment of quiet—gardens and unboisterous meals, music and the singing in Exeter Cathedral. These things were unattainable because of Carlyon. Of the others he had no fear. They could not, he felt, escape from their environment—a rough, cursing, drinking life. He could escape from them in drawing-rooms, but in the middle of however quiet a tea, however peaceful the lazy shadows of the fire, however soft the talk, the door might open, Carlyon enter.

Mrs. Butler cleaned on, her buttocks swaying rhythmically to the circular movements of her arms. He saw her suddenly as a hostile spy from reality, though it was not so that he would have phrased it. His fear was too sharp for abstractions. But unexpressed in conscious thought, he had felt of this house as of a cottage in a fairy-story. He had stumbled on it in a wood when blurred with sleep. It had given him shelter and a sense of mystery; it had not belonged to the world which he had known, the constant irritation and strain of the sea nor to the fear of the last few days.

But Mrs. Butler had come from the town that morning. In crannies of her ears still lurked the sounds from which he had fled, the waves, fishwives' voices, rattle of carts, "Mackerel, fresh mackerel," gossip in the market, "Three of them escaped."

Mrs. Butler had left the door open and through it he could see clearly in sunlight that which, when he came, had been obscured by weariness and night. He had thought of this cottage as alone in the middle of a wood. Now he could see that it stood at the edge of a mere coppice. Above the trees like a blister was the down over which he had come. "What's that?" he said at a sound, unable to keep all sign of fear from his voice.

"Why, it's only a cart," the girl answered.

"A cart?" he cried and walked to a window. It was true. This cottage hidden, as he had thought, in a forest lay within a hundred yards of the high road. It was useless to tell himself that a high road was his safest place, that Carlyon, probably by now with a price upon his head, must equally fear the open. He was superstitious on the subject of Carlyon. He could not imagine Carlyon in hiding.

"A sailor?" said Mrs. Butler, her eyes fixed on the floor. "There's sailors and sailors. There's some as don't like these gaugers, but I say as 'ow they be only doin' their duty. They be paid for it same as me on this floor. And they get the worst of it most every time. Look at Tuesday."

"What time's this funeral?" Andrews asked, turning his back on Mrs. Butler with abrupt brutality. He was very conscious that behind his back she had raised an astonished head and was eyeing him with shrewd consideration. The girl he found had moved to the door and he followed her with a sense of relief, glad to leave behind, though only for a little, Mrs. Butler's curiosity and her pretty, damp voice. "What time's this funeral?" he repeated.

"They'll be fetching him," she said, "at eleven," and her simple sentence cleared away the last illusion of isolation. Time was here in the cottage. Clocks ticked and hands went round as everywhere else in the world. He had a sense of time rushing past him, rushing like a Gadarene swine to destruction. Time squeaked at him as it passed at an increasing pace down a steep slope. Poets had told him over and over again that life was short. Now for the first time he knew it as a vital fact. He longed for peace and beauty, and the minutes were flying by, and he was still a fugitive, with mind muddled, obscured by fear of death.

"Shall we be alone?" he asked, his voice a mixture of longing and apprehension.

"Alone," she repeated in a low voice, so that her voice might not reach through the splashing of a damp cloth to Mrs. Butler's ears. "No, we shan't be alone. You don't know these country people. I hate them," she added with unexpected intensity. "This is a show to them. They'll flock to it, but I shan't feed them. They'll expect to be fed. They haven't been near me since he died, and I'd have welcomed anyone for a bit of company in the evening. They never came when he was alive."

"What do you mean?" he raised his voice in unthinking fear. "A crowd of them?" He took hold of her wrist. "If you've planned this," he said.

"Need you be a fool as well as a coward?" she answered in an off-hand tired fashion. "Why should I plan anything? I'm not sufficiently interested in you." She released her hand and moved out of doors. "I don't know why I've helped you as much as I have," she added with a small shrug.

He followed still suspicious. He felt unreasonably grieved that this cottage was not the lonely woodland house, which he had imagined. "Don't take credit for that," he said. "I forced you to it."

She did not look at him. Her hands were on her hips and she stared at the down over which he had come with a small wrinkle of perplexity. She seemed to be trying to puzzle out the reason behind her acts. "It was not fear," she said, but it was not to him that she replied. "It would be a fool who'd be afraid of you," she said and smiled as though at an amusing memory. "I suppose I was tired of being alone."

CHAPTER III

"AND though after my skin worms destroy this body, yet in my flesh shall I see God; whom I shall see for myself, and mine eyes shall behold, and not another."

The priest was tall and thin and stooping and he

suffered from a running cold. He snuffled between each phrase as he took long, loping strides through the graveyard. It was a raw day and he appeared anxious to get through with a dreary business. Between every phrase he snuffled and at the end of every sentence he gave a hasty furtive wipe at his nose with a corner of his surplice that blew out in the wind like a banner. He strode, not concealing his hatred of the cold, but those that followed after, a large straying band of intense villagers, walked as slowly as he allowed them, seemed almost to hold him back by the flapping end of his surplice. They refused to be cheated of a funeral. Their cheeks and noses were scarlet and their eyes sparkled like frost and peered avariciously after the wooden coffin.

It means nothing to them at all, the girl thought with acidity, sonorous words floating with strange lightness for their bulk over her head. They were here because a funeral was something to see, because, when rightly managed, it meant beer and cakes and because the long eddy of words that gathered together at regular intervals to rise and burst in a great ninth phrase ("Lord, let me know mine end and the number of my days: that I may be certified how long I have to live") made them feel important. She would not give them beer and cakes, for she had been fond of the spirit that had inhabited the body carried before them. Yet because she had had no love for the body itself, which when she was small had beaten her and when she grew older had made strange crude gestures blindly towards her and repelled her, she felt unmoved. She was accustomed now to the absence of the cursing, unhappy, perplexed spirit. She had loved that with a quiet steady warmth. It had fed her and sheltered her and she was grateful, and when towards the end she had seen it putting up the best fight it was able against its own groping, sneering body, she had pitied it.

"For I am a stranger with thee; and a sojourner as all my fathers were. O spare me a little that I may recover my strength: before I go hence and be no more seen."

Andrews stirred a little. They were the first words that had reached his consciousness since the fear of many persons had dumbed his heart. He was afraid when the villagers had arrived, the women to inspect the corpse and the men to look in vain for beer. Each new face had been a stab of anxiety and when unrecognised a faint relief, until the steady alternating currents of fear and comfort had lulled his mind asleep. He had been helped, turning his back on the chattering women, by the sight of the sea mist that poised itself for a moment on the top of the down over which he had come. Blown by a breeze behind, too faint to disperse it, it tottered for a moment drunkenly on the edge, and then fell in swathe after swathe into the valley. Its coming brought a sense of secrecy and of what he knew at heart was a false security. His unconsciousness held nothing but a dim irony and a perception of farce. He was the brother of the chief mourner, but the ceremony was to him only a solemn mummery. The man they put into the ground and for whom all these persons sang at intervals in a dreary whine was unknown to him and meant nothing more to him than the sudden sight of a bearded face and the dart of a fallen golden star.

The girl—Elizabeth—his sister (it was hard to remember that she was his sister) had remained silent in the midst of a swiftly running current of voices. When the undertaker's man had turned down the lid of the coffin there had been a little scurry of strange women-folk to catch a last glimpse of the "deceased". Then she had shown her own sign of feeling. She had turned to face them as though she would push them back and her mouth had twisted into an angry word which she did not speak. Then she gave a small gesture with her fingers addressed to herself. She stood aside and the undertaker's man shut the coffin lid, casually as a man shuts a book. There was no air of finality about it, even when he drove in the nails. Andrews saw a little group of women whispering in a corner. They looked and whispered, and fear momentarily pierced his unconsciousness. He looked around him and imagined all faces turned towards him. The men disappointed of beer had nothing to do but talk and look curiously at the interior of the cottage, which they had never before entered. The women sniggered a little among themselves at the bareness and poked furtively at a chair here and a table there and made comments under their breath. Andrews thought that they were speaking of him. The men shuffled uneasily and stood massed together and fidgeted with their feet. They were annoyed with their wives for having brought them where there was no refreshment. Most of them had small farms and there was plenty of work they might have been doing. For want of other employment they looked cornerwise and carefully at the girl. They had seen her about many a time in the lanes but had been afraid to speak to her. There had been rumours—that she had been the dead man's mistress, his natural child, a dozen contradictory tales, which united to put her outside the pale of "Good day," comments on the weather or the crops, or even a nod of the head. Now death made her approachable and a little envied. They spoke of her slyly to each other in whispers, not so much to keep their comments from her as to keep them from their wives, comments on her appearance, on her potentialities as a bed-fellow, on the fun she may have offered to the man now dead. Andrews thought that they spoke of him.

With an effort he pulled his will erect. He saw himself standing on one side, an obvious stranger, uninterested and apart. He called "Elizabeth" with forced ease across the room. He had vague ideas of convincing them that he was her brother. She paid no attention, and he could think of no more to say. His will subsided slackly. ("For I a stranger with thee; and a sojourner as all my fathers were.")

Standing there in a misty graveyard beside the dark Elizabeth, Andrews felt his first flash of sympathy towards his father. Once his father had visited him at school. Andrews was in the gravel playground. It was in the interval between two lessons and he was hastily revising some Latin grammar. He had looked up and stared with amazement at the unexpected sight of his father, a tall, heavy man with a big beard clumsily dressed, crossing the gravel with the headmaster. The headmaster was small, quick and neat with birdlike motions. His father was shy, embarrassed, conscious suddenly of his own coarse bulk. He had said, "I was passing through and thought I'd come and see you." He stopped, not knowing how to continue and stood shifting from one foot to the other. "Happy?" he asked. Andrews had the instinctive cruelty of a child. He remembered his father at home, domineering, brutal, a conscious master, not chary of his blows to either child or wife. "Very," he said. His voice filled with artificial pleasure and he pronounced his words with artificial neatness. "We are doing Horace this term, father," he said, "and Sophocles." The headmaster beamed. His father murmured incoherently that he must go now, disappeared across the gravel, his heavy boots sounding self-consciously.

Andrews did not know then what kept his father away from home for short and frequent periods of blessed peace. He never knew the cause of that particular unfortunate visit. Perhaps he was on his way to the coast and a sudden realisation that his career must end sooner or later in death made him anxious to see his only idea of immortality. The voyage which followed must have reached its normal, successful end, for a few weeks later, when holidays fetched Andrews home, his father was there, dominant, easily aroused, as ready as ever with the whip, which he seemed to keep more for his family than for his hounds. A year later, while the child was at school and the father at sea, the mother died with the serene faithfulness of a completely broken will.

The shambling priest was reading the lesson in a meaningless drawl muffled by the mist and his increasing cold. The words meant no more to him than did the dead man. It was a mechanic ritual less conscious than the act of brushing teeth.

"I speak this to your shame but some men will say, how are the dead raised up? And with what body do they come? Thou fool that which thou sowest is not quickened unless it die."

The coffin had been carried from the cottage in a farm cart. Elizabeth beside him he had walked into a wall of white that at every step melted before him and closed behind him. The villagers and their wives followed after, their footsteps sounding no lounder than the drip of misty rain that fell from trees and bushes along their road. The silence was greater for the regular small tap tap of feet and drip drop of water. They could see the back of the cart which they followed but not the horse that drew it. Andrews looked behind him and saw a ghostly platoon. Faces and hands thrown forward in front of invisible bodies appeared and disappeared. He felt suddenly that all danger had been remitted until the funeral was over. Disembodied faces, hands that swam unattached in a white sea could not hurt him. He longed—not passionately, his mind was too asleep for passion—but with a small elusive ache that they would never reach the graveyard. This ache had crept into his sleep and also a sense of friendship with the girl who paced slowly beside him. He was asleep and longed a little that he might not awake. In his sleep one lay with him who would be gone when there was daylight in the brain.

They reached the burying place, and as the service went on fatigue grew and threatened to strip away his unconsciousness. He became aware that somewhere, as yet outside his mind but ready, opportunity given, to leap within, lay the fear to which he had grown accustomed. He held it at bay outside himself, but the struggle, as the minutes passed and the priest's voice droned on, grew more intense.

They had taken the coffin to the edge of the grave, and the service must be drawing to an end. The priest's voice grew rapid like the feet of a horse when its head is turned to home, faster and faster with the faintest trace of excitement at the thought of food and a rest from journeying: "O holy and merciful Saviour thou most worthy Judge eternal, suffer us not at our last hour for any pains of death to fall from thee." They had lowered the coffin into the grave and began laboriously to shovel earth upon it. Spades slipped on the ground which was hard with cold. To Andrews the falling clods were a measurement of time, recording the vanishing moments of his peace. He would be happy to stand in the cold and the mist through eternity watching the shovelling spades. Fear was pressing in upon his mind. He could not keep it outside himself for long.

Bundles of mist disintegrated. A low chatter of voices began replete with the blessing which had just been pronounced and moved towards the grave. Farmers stood in a ring and stared with interest at a hillock of earth judging its points. The women watched the chief mourner. By the rules of village life Elizabeth should now break down. Then after a brief struggle for the privilege one would put her arm round the girl and weep with her. Later they would be asked to accompany her back for refreshment. Their suspicions regarding Elizabeth's birth and her moral character were confirmed when she abruptly turned her back on the grave.

She said to Andrews in a voice like frozen straw. "For God's sake get rid of these people. I don't want them. I don't want them." The mist opened a little, closed again and she was gone.

Andrews stood alone. He wanted to turn and run and put a wall of mist between him and that gathering of amazed eyes. Loneliness and fear were like the emptiness of hunger to his belly. If he took six steps away he would be lost to all the world in a blanket of white wool. He could find a childish comfort, bury his head beneath the bed-clothes and fear no more the creaking of old furniture, deep in a darkness within a darkness. Why should any man be plagued as he had ever been plagued, with all the instincts—desires, fears, comforts—of a child and yet possess the wisdom of the man? In these moments of crisis he felt physically drawn in two—an agonising stretch of the nerves. One part of him said, "Hide yourself in this mist. You will see no one and nothing can hurt you. You will be comforted." The other part said "Fool! How they would

talk." He was the girl's brother. He must act a little
longer as her brother. That was the only safe way.

He said to them—yet not to them but only to those
amazed and offended eyes, "My sister's upset. Forgive
us if we don't invite you back. She must be alone for
a little. You will understand that it has been a great
shock." Very unconvincing and stiff his voice sounded
to himself. He watched for any relaxation of the inquiry in the ring of eyes. Then he waited no longer but
walked away. He stumbled as he went on a stone,
which had fallen before its time from a gravedigger's
spade.

When he had walked a dozen yards he struck against
an iron railing and the chill of the metal brought him
part of the way towards consciousness. He felt his
way along the rail gingerly with the tips of his fingers,
finding relief in the slight pain he suffered from the
stinging cold. When his feet, groping through an invisible gap, felt the broken ruts of the road beneath
them, he waited. He had but to follow it half a mile to
his left hand, so he calculated, to come upon the lights
of the cottage. Yet there was no possible excuse to return. He should be thankful for the shelter of a night
and the bare charity that had left him free. Bare charity
enough, he thought, growing slowly aware of hunger.
He had had no food for more than fifteen hours. There
was a little breeding left in him under the double influence of fear and hunger, but the small relic made
him unwilling to thrust himself back as an unwanted
guest. That she would accept him with an uninterested
acquiescence deterred him. If she would only meet him

again with resistance, he would be happy to seize shelter by force. He knew how easily he could work himself into a righteous anger and forget himself. It's this damned Christianity, he thought, or else not enough of it. He would welcome her as an enemy, or as a friend who would pity him and understand his fear. It was her cold neutrality he hated.

With unexpected resolution he turned his back on the way he had come that morning and half ran as it were into an obscure future. The more he thought of the girl the more he hated her and pitied himself. If I had been a cat, he considered, she'd have given me something to eat. That he had not been offered food was the idea that now grated on his mind. The thought of her became so hateful, such an incarnation of inhuman indifference, that he nearly turned back to find her. He wanted to give her pain, beat her, make her cry out. She doesn't know what it is to be alone and frightened, he thought. If I had been a cat . . . A tree brushed his face with a branch of wet twigs; even inanimate nature seemed to treat him with casual scorn. "I can't be a coward, not altogether a coward," he pleaded in a carefully hushed whisper. It needed courage to write that letter and go on living with them. And it was on the side of justice, he added, before his mind could murmur of jealousy.

He became aware after a little of an uneasy feeling, which was not fear, nor shame, nor hunger. It would be dangerous to return, he said to himself. I can get clear away from the neighbourhood while this fog lasts. He walked on a little further, but hesitatingly.

Carlyon's quick, he thought. He'd search every shelter. I'm safer in this fog walking. When hunger forced itself again upon his notice he comforted himself illogically. After all there's other shelter besides that cottage. He discovered that it was comforting to speak aloud. The small sound of his own voice was companionship in this white darkness and at the same time muffled by the fog, it was not loud enough to be overheard. He began to imagine fresh shelter: impelled by an empty stomach he returned but less convincingly to the thought of kindly old women. But there was something lacking in these dreams that had not been lacking the previous day. There was an ache in his mind as well as his belly, although he refused to take note of it. There was something very dissatisfying about the kindliest welcome which he imagined, but how could he recognise a fact, too ridiculous for expression, that he was homesick for the cottage in which he had spent a few uncomfortable hours? He fought hard against that realisation, and even quickened his step as though to remove himself out of the influence of a malign enchantment. In his struggle, for about the first time in the last three days, he forgot his danger and his fear. He did not even notice that he was walking uphill and that the fog was thinning very gradually in front of him. If he had ears to hear, his own speech would have come to him with startling loudness in comparison with its previous imprisonment.

"A cat," he said, "she'd have given a cat food," but anger was disconcertingly confined to his voice. For as far as he knew the girl had had no food herself. He dwelt on the idea of a cat as constantly as he was able, but that image of inhumanity began rapidly to be scored over by fresh lines of thought, struggle as he would to preserve it intact. He remembered how she had led him to the dead man, awakening thus a brief feeling of intimacy between himself and her, and he remembered her words about the peace of God.

Andrews's character was built of superficial dreams, sentimentality, cowardice, and yet he was constantly made aware beneath all these of an uncomfortable questioning critic. So now this other inhabitant of his body wondered whether he had not mistaken peace for inhumanity. Peace was not cowardly nor sentimental nor filled with illusion. Peace was a sanity which he did not believe that he had ever known. He remembered how once, becalmed at sea day after endless day, he had grown to loath the water's smooth unstirred surface as a symbol of a hatefully indifferent deity. And yet in the weeks of storm that followed he had longed to regain that quality which he began to regard as peace.

It was the sun shining on his eyes that woke him to the surroundings and an immediate knowledge of danger. He had been walking up hill and now emerged from the thickest fog as from a tunnel. It stood concrete at his back like a white wall. In front of him only faint floating wisps softened hedgerows, projecting boughs, the sun's rays. It was not, however, the mere abstract fear of light which startled Andrews. A tall man, with dark hair uncovered by a hat stood in the middle of the road. His back was turned and his hands

were clasped behind him. Andrews could not mistake
the light poise of the legs and shoulders that seemed
to symbolise a spirit on tiptoe. He had been walking
so fast up the hill that when he suddenly checked himself he nearly stumbled forward on his hands and
knees. Although he had spent the last three days in
almost continuous fear of Carlyon, now when the moment he had dreaded seemed to have arrived, his first
instinct was not that of flight. It appeared incredible
that he should so fear Carlyon, the man to whom he
had turned continually for companionship in an alien
and brutal life. He was only saved from stepping forward and touching Carlyon's elbow by the sight of the
man's hands. Their clasp was tense, trained. They were
the hands of a man holding himself as still as he was
able in order to listen. Andrews half shifted a foot and
the shoulders in front of him stiffened. He remembered
a remark that Carlyon had once made to him, prompted
by a sudden friendliness, "I'd know your step, Andrews, in a thousand." He could see quite clearly the
strange ugly face of Carlyon as it had looked at him
then shaded with an abstract tenderness. The face was
a little swarthy, and very angular. A low brow belied
the intelligence within. It would have been a crude, almost criminal face if divorced from the quick but
heavy body and the eyes which seemed brooding always on indefinable things, save when they lit with a
kind of contempt at the body which housed them. The
face had once been described as that of a chivalrous
ape.

The hands like the hands of an ape would be strong.

Andrews, moving as softly as he was able, took three steps backward and was swallowed in the mist. He waited listening with a racing heart; the sound of its beats he felt would drown any noise there might be. He could no longer see Carlyon and therefore he was certain that Carlyon could not see him. The anxiety that pecked at his nerve was the uncertainty whether or not Carlyon had recognised his tread. He waited, afraid to run, because in doing so he would be forced to turn his back.

No sound came, except a gentle, reiterated drip from a bough behind his right ear. He tried to persuade himself that Carlyon had heard nothing, and yet he could not banish the image of the tightly clenched hands. His mind changed tack and protested that even if Carlyon had heard and recognised his tread there was no cause for fear. Carlyon had, after all, no reason for supposing that he, Andrews, had been the cause of a certain disastrous fight. Carlyon was his friend. "My friend, my friend, my friend," he repeated to try and soothe the panic of his heart.

Minutes must have passed before a sound broke the stillness. It was not a sound which Andrews had expected to hear. It was that of a low whistle, no louder than a man unconsciously might give in amazement. Andrews had counted six louder heart beats when the whistle was repeated. Then there was silence. Andrews very cautiously withdrew himself to the side of the road and a little further into the mist. His movements sounded terribly loud to his own ears. He bent forward and listened. A vague orange glow showed where

the tunnel of mist came to an abrupt end. A few yards
beyond stood the invisible Carlyon. Andrews did not
believe that he had shifted so much as a foot.

Andrews bent a little farther forward. He thought
that he could hear a gentle whisper. He shivered. There
was something uncanny in the thought of Carlyon with
sad, apelike face standing very still with back turned
and tensed clenched hands, whistling and whispering
to himself. For a moment Andrews wondered whether
his friend (he found it impossible even in flight and
fear to think of Carlyon other than as a friend) had
been driven mad by the events of the last few days. He
wanted to advance out of his tunnel and take Carlyon's
arm. He thought, as he had often thought before, how
different everything would have been, if Carlyon had
been his father. Last night in the dark of the wood and
far from Carlyon he had feared him. Now in more imminent danger he was torn between his fear, precipi-
tate, unreasoning fear, and a friendship that was almost
a grudging, soured love.

Andrews believed afterwards that in another moment
he would have stepped out and greeted Carlyon, but
as he stared into the orange glow, fear was given an
opportunity to assert itself over friendship. A shadow
for an instant striped vertically the glow and vanished
again without a sound. Someone had entered the mist.
Andrews cowered back against the hedge and listened.
There was complete stillness. Andrews felt certain that
somewhere within a few feet Carlyon also was listening, striving perhaps to catch those heartbeats which
sounded so betrayingly loud. Then a stone was kicked

and rumbled slowly a little away down the hill. A second shadow broke the glow and disappeared.

It was probably this second, more careless shadow, that Andrews next heard feeling along the hedge, with the noise of a small breeze through stubble. Progress was slow in a pathetic effort to be silent, pathetic with the pathos of a hippopotamus treading cautiously on dry twigs. The pathos, however, did not appeal to Andrews, who realised very clearly that in a few minutes he would inevitably be discovered. He could not fly without betraying himself, and his only hope was to step soundlessly into the middle of the road. But where was the first shadow, Carlyon? It needed a courage he was not accustomed to exercise to remove his back from the friendly firmness of the hedge and place himself defenceless in the road. He feared that if he moved he would come in contact with Carlyon. Only the slow pressure of necessity symbolised by the cautious crackling in the hedge creeping closer to him at every moment forced him at last to move.

The two paces which he took into the road seemed soundless even to himself, but he was not comforted. He felt completely exposed. Although he could see nothing, he felt, standing there ridiculously with slack, impotent arms that anyone could see him. He thought he could hear them coming towards him and had a wild longing to cry out to them "Stop, stop, stop, please stop." There was a game which he had played at school, where one boy, too often himself, stood with back turned counting ten, while the other boys advanced to touch his back. Andrews had perhaps forgotten, but he had never lost, the strain of waiting, hurriedly counting, for a hand to fall upon his back. So now he began to count in haste "one, two, three, four, five, six, seven, eight, nine, ten" as though there might be some remission for him at ten. He did not know why he counted and there was no remission.

He had a knife he remembered, in one pocket, but he could not remember which, and he did not dare to look. He was afraid even to raise a hand, lest it should make a sound in passing through the air. He let his arms hang limply at his side, like the arms of a doll empty of saw-dust. After a considerable time the rustle in the hedge ceased. Somewhere behind a whispering began, too faint for him to catch a word. Then there was a rustle in the hedge on the opposite side of the road, more rapid, almost perfunctory. Then that too ceased and the whispering returned and hovered elusively in the mist. Sometimes he thought it came from his right side, sometimes from his left, at other times from behind him. It grew more rapid, seemed to beat desperately up and down, like a lost bird in a room. He began to think that he could distinguish words. Several times he imagined his own name "Andrews". Hope stirred in his heart that Carlyon would give up the search and take his escape for granted. As though to confirm this hope the whispers grew more and more careless. He could distinguish phrases. "Somewhere here," and "I'd swear to his step."

After an interval Carlyon's voice blew like a melancholy wind through the mist. "Andrews," it said, "Andrews." And then "Why are you frightened? What's the matter with you? It's Carlyon, merely Carlyon."

The fascination of the voice! It seemed to hold for Andrews everything which he so much desired—peace, friendship, the end of a useless struggle. He wanted to say, "Here I am, Carlyon," and lie down there in the mist and sleep; and wake to find Carlyon sitting beside him talking to this and that with brooding kindliness, drowning the nauseating fatigue of danger, the acrid smell of smoke, the monotony of winds with the cool beauty of his voice. Above the eternally reiterated clatter of feet on deck, the beat, beat, beat of flapping canvas, the curses, movement, scurry, unrest; below Carlyon's ape-like face transfigured with peace—

> Ye have been fresh and green,
> Ye have been filled with flowers,
> And ye the walks have been,
> Where maids have spent their hours.

"Andrews, Andrews," with a soft melancholy. "I must not, I must not," he said to himself, sobbing hysterically and yet with an effort retaining silence, though the effort was a tearing pain in throat and chest. "That's over." Over for ever friendship, poetry, silence at the heart of noise; remained fear and a continual flight. And he had intended to win peace.

Carlyon, he realised, had not spoken now for many moments. He was surrounded again by silence save for the drip, drip, drip of the laden bough. Space that had closed in on him during the sound of the voice call-

ing spread away again on every side. He was alone in
a wilderness of white mist hopelessly barren of companionship. He waited listening for a little while longer
and then stumbled back into the mist the way that he
had come. He thought that Carlyon had been de-
ceived or had given up the search. It did not occur to
him that Carlyon might wait quietly and listen to find
the direction which he took. Andrews ran crookedly
along invisible ruts with a slow strange lightening of
the heart.

CHAPTER IV

HE became aware of the cottage again by the red glow
of a hidden flame, which penetrated a little way into
the white blanket of mist, with a promise of warmth
and calm companionship and food. Fear had not dispelled his hunger, it had but overlaid it with a more
fierce emotion. Now with the slow return of peace he
remembered what his belly desired. He was not angry
nor frightened now, only a little ill at ease. He advanced cautiously, with one arm of his spirit raised to
ward off a blow.

Through the window he peered into a room deprived of daylight. A large fire burnt with a kind of
subdued ferocity and its red rays, instead of bearing a
light, split blacker pools of darkness in the room. Only
in a small semi-circle before it was a space cleared,

and the dark pushed back from there formed a more sombre and concentrated wall on the further side. Squatting on the floor in the cleared space Elizabeth knitted with a metallic flash—flash of needles like sparks from a gaseous coal.

Her figure started so distinctly from the shadows, distorted though it was by the glass, that Andrews did not realise that his own face was veiled. He tapped with fingers which he intended to sound gentle and reassuring. She looked up and remained staring at him with a mixture of fear, perplexity and doubt, and let the knitting fall upon her lap. He smiled but was unaware she could not see his smile, or glimpsed at most a vague grimace from almost invisible lips. He tapped again and saw her lift whatever it was she had been knitting to her breast and tightly press it to her. How slim, he thought, as she rose and stood (a dark Elizabeth, he wondered again) where the flicker of flames played up and down her body like the dazed, groping fingers of a lover. Her hand pressed so hard on her breast that it appeared to be reaching for the heart to hold it and still its beats. Only then did Andrews realise that she could not see him clearly, and that she was afraid. But at the moment when he prepared to reassure her, the small quiver of fear left her lips and she passed from the zone of the firelight and advanced to the window through the shadows.

He heard her fingers feeling not very certainly for the catch. Then the window swung open and he stepped away. "Is it really you back?" she whispered, and he could not tell from her voice whether she was afraid or glad.

"Yes, yes," he said, "it's me."

She said, "Oh, you," in a flat, disappointed tone. "What do you want?" He became afraid that she would again shut the window, leaving him in the cold, deprived of the tossing fire.

"Won't you let me in?" he asked. "You needn't be afraid," and when she laughed ironically, he began to speak rapidly. "I did all that you told me," he said. "I got rid of all those wretched villagers."

"Was it necessary to come here to tell me that?" she asked.

"I want shelter," he said with despairing simplicity. He heard her leave the window and unbolt the door. "Come in then if you must," she called to him.

He came and moved at once to the fire, his momentary sentiment drowned in the mere desire to be warm, to drink heat with every pore of his body. He felt that he could with small encouragement have lifted the burning coals and pressed them to his breast. He twisted his figure into odd distorted shapes, so that every part of him might receive a blessing from gracefully gesticulating hands of flame.

"Have you any food?" he asked. With the cold acquiescence which he had feared she went and fetched a loaf of bread, and would have placed it on the table had he not stretched out his hands for it. Still crouching over the fire he broke off portions with his fingers. Only when his hunger was partly satisfied something uneasily stirring in his mind made him apologise.

"I haven't had food for fifteen hours," he said. "I was hungry and cold out there. It's good of you. . . ."

She came into the circle of firelight. "There's no reason why I should shut you out," she said. "I've been alone. You are better than no one, even you."

Warmed by the fire, hunger quenched by bread, he began to grow jocular.

"You oughtn't to find any difficulty in getting company," he laughed. "And who was it you expected to find outside the window?"

"We've buried him," she said. "I don't suppose that he'll return."

Andrews looked up in astonishment at a pale, set face, touched with a reluctant grief. "You don't mean," he asked in awe-struck astonishment, "that you thought. . . ."

"Why shouldn't I think that?" she asked, not with indignation but with candid questioning. "He's only a few days dead."

"But they don't rise again," Andrews said in the kind of solemn whisper which he had used as a boy in the school chapel.

"Their spirits do," she answered, and her white, still face continued to question him.

"Do you believe in all that?" he asked, not in mockery, but in a curiosity tinctured with longing.

"Of course; you can read it in the Bible."

"Then," he hesitated a moment, "if men are not quite dead, when we bury them, we can still hurt them, make them suffer, revenge ourselves."

"You must be bad," she said fearfully, "to think of that. But don't forget that they can hurt us, too."

She came up to the fire and stood beside him, and he shifted a little under the clear, courageous gaze of her eyes. "I'm not afraid of you now," she said, "because you are just a person I know, but when you came last night you were a stranger and I was afraid. But then I thought to myself that he," and she pointed to the table as though the coffin still lay there, "would not let me be harmed. He was a bad man, but he wanted me, and he'd never let anyone else get me."

"I never meant any harm to you," Andrews muttered, and then added with a convulsive pleading: "It was only fear that made me come. You other people never seem to understand fear. You expect everyone to be brave like yourself. It's not a man's fault whether he's brave or cowardly. It's all in the way he's born. My father and mother made me. I didn't make myself."

"I never blamed you," she protested. "But you always seem to leave out God."

"Oh, that," he said. "That's all on a par with your spirits. I don't believe in that stuff. Though I'd like to believe in the spirits, that we could still hurt a man who is dead," he added with a mixture of passion and wistfulness.

"You can't if they are in heaven," she commented.

"There's no danger of that with the man I hate," Andrews laughed angrily. "It's curious, isn't it, how one can hate the dead. It makes one almost believe your stuff. If they are transparent like the air, perhaps we breathe them in." He screwed up his mouth as though at a bad taste.

She watched him curiously. "Tell me," she said, "where have you been since we buried him?"

He began to speak with resentful anger. "I told you it was only fear that drove me to you last night, didn't I? Well, I don't want to trouble you any more."

"And fear brought you back again?"

"Yes—at least not entirely." Looking down at her dark hair, pale face and calm eyes seemed to infuriate him. "You women," he said, "you are all the same. You are always on your guard against us. Always imagine that we are out to get you. You don't know what a man wants."

"What do you want?" she asked and added with a practicality which increased his meaningless anger. "Food? I have some more bread in a cupboard."

He made a despairing motion with his hand, which she interpreted as a refusal. "We get tired of our own kind," he said, "the coarseness, hairiness—you don't understand. Sometimes I've paid street women simply to talk to them, but they are like the rest of you. They don't understand that I don't want their bodies."

"You've taught us what to think," she interrupted with a faint bitterness breaking the peace of her mind.

He took no notice of what she said. "I'll tell you," he said, "a reason why I came back. You can laugh at me. I was homesick for here."

He turned his back on her. "I'm not making love to you. It wasn't you. It was just the place. I slept here and I hadn't slept before for three days." He waited with shoulders a little hunched for her laughter.

She did not laugh and after a little he turned. She had been gazing at his back. "Aren't you amused?" he asked ironically. His relations with her seemed necessarily compounded of suspicion. When he first came he had been suspicious of her acts . . . and now he was suspicious of her thoughts.

"I was wondering," she said, "whom you were frightened of and why I like you." Her eyes wandered down his body from face to feet and stayed at his right heel. "You've worn your stockings out," she said simply, but the way in which she turned the words on her tongue till they came out with a rounded sweetness gave to their simplicity a hidden significance.

"They are not of silk," he said, still seeking for disguised mockery.

She held out a hand which she had kept pressed to her side. "Here is a stocking," she said; "see if it will fit you."

He took it from her as cautiously as if it had been a strange reptile and turned it over and over. He saw that it had been newly darned and remembered how he had seen her from the window working in the fire-lit space.

"You were mending this," he said, "when I came to the window." She made no answer and he examined it again. "A man's stocking," he commented.

"It was his," she replied.

He laughed. "Do your spirits wear stockings?" he asked.

She clenched and unclenched her hands, as one nervously wrought up by another's stupidity. "I had to do something," she murmured rapidly as though her breath had been nearly exhausted by a too long and fatiguing race. "I couldn't just sit." She turned her back on him and walked to the window and leant her forehead against it, as though seeking coolness or perhaps support.

Andrews turned and turned the stocking in his hand. Once at the window Elizabeth's figure was motionless. He could not even catch the sound of her breathing. A gap of shadow separated them, and the flickering of the flames made useless but persistent attempts to cross it. He was shamed by the patient obstinacy of their compassion, and was temporarily rapt from his own fear, hatred and self-abasement, touched for a lightning instant with a disinterested longing for self-sacrifice. He would not cross that bridge of shadows, for he feared that if he touched her he would lose the sense of something unapproachably beautiful, and his own momentary chivalry would vanish before the coward, the bully and the lustful sentimentalist to whom he was accustomed. For that instant his second criticising self was silent; indeed he was that self.

He was on the point of making some stumbling gesture of contrition, when the coward in him leaped up and closed his mouth. Be careful, it cautioned him. You are a fugitive; you must not tie yourself. Even as he surrendered to that prompting he regretted the surrender. He knew that for a few seconds he had been happy, with the same happiness, but stronger, as he had gained momentarily in the past from music, from Carlyon's voice, from a sudden sense of companionship with other men.

The mist which had been white was turning grey. The real dark was approaching, but it made no apparent difference to the room. Andrews, feeling the comfortable warmth of the fire behind him, wondered how Carlyon was fairing in a colder and surely more alien world. And yet was it more alien? Carlyon had the friendship and the trust of his two fellow fugitives. He was not alone. The old self-pity began to crawl back into Andrews's heart, as he watched the girl's motionless back.

"Can we light some candles," he asked, "and make this room more cheerful?"

"There are two candlesticks on the table," she said, keeping her forehead pressed to the window, "and two on the dresser. You can light them if you like."

Andrews made a spill from a playbill, which he found in his pocket, and lit it at the fire. Then he passed, from candle to candle making little aspiring peaks of flame pierce the shadows. Slowly they rose higher and small haloes formed round their summits, a powdery glow like motes in sunlight. Cloaked from all draughts by the surrounding mist they burnt straight upwards, tapering to a point as fine as a needle. The shadows were driven back into the corners of the room where they crouched darkly like sulking dogs rebuked.

When Andrews had lit the last candle he turned and saw that Elizabeth was watching him. Joy and grief were both moods able to pass lightly across her face without disturbing the permanent thoughtfulness of her eyes, which seemed to regard life with a gaze devoid of emotion. The candles now tipped her face with gaiety. She made no reference to her short surrender of grief, but clapped her hands, so that he stared at her amazed by this rapid change of mood.

"I like this," she said, "we'll have tea. I'm glad to have someone to talk to—even you," and she moved to the dresser and began to take out plates, cups, a loaf of bread, some butter, a kettle which she filled and put upon the fire. With proud and reverent fingers she drew a caddy from the dresser, handling it as reverently as gold casket.

"I haven't had tea," he said slowly, "like this since I left home . . . I've wanted it though." He hesitated. "It's queer that you should be treating me like this, like a friend."

Pulling the only two chairs which the room held up to the fire, she regarded him with sombre amusement. "Am I treating you like a friend?" she asked. "I can't tell. I've never had one."

He had a sudden wish to tell her everything, from what he was fleeing and for what cause, but caution and a feeling of peace restrained him. He wished to forget it himself and cling only to this growing sense of intimacy, of two minds moving side by side, and watch the firelight gleam downwards into the dark amber of the tea.

"It's strange," he said, "how often I've longed for a tea like this. In a rough, hurrying sort of life with men, one longs sometimes for refinement—and tea seems to

me a symbol of that—peace, security, women, idle talk
—and the night outside."

"A loaf of bread," she said, "no jam, no cakes."

"That's nothing," he brooded over the thick china
cup, which he held awkwardly with an unaccustomed
hand.

"Why are you here?" she asked. "You don't belong.
You should be a student, I think. You look like a man
who day-dreams."

"Doesn't even a student need courage?" he questioned bitterly. "And I'm not a dreamer. I hate
dreams."

"Is there anything you care for or want?" she
watched him as though he were a new and curious animal.

"To be null and void," he said without hesitation.

"Dead?"

The sound of the word seemed to draw his eyes to
the window, which stared now on complete darkness.

"No, no," he said, "not that." He gave a small shiver
and spoke again. "When music plays, one does not see
or think; one hardly hears. A bowl—and the music is
poured in until there is no 'I', I *am* the music."

"But why, why," she asked, "did you ever come to
live like this?" and with a small gesture of her hand
she seemed to enclose his fear, his misery, his fugitive
body and mind.

"My father did it before me," he replied.

"Was that all?" she asked.

"No, I was fascinated," he said. "There's a man I
know with a voice as near to music as any voice I've

ever heard," he hesitated and then looked up at her, "except for yours."

She paid no attention to the compliment, but frowning a little at the fire nipped her lip between small sharp teeth.

"Can't he help you now that you are in trouble?" she asked. "Can't you go to him?"

He stared at her in amazement. He had forgotten that she was ignorant of his story and his flight from Carlyon, and because he had forgotten, her remark came to him with the force of a wise suggestion. "Andrews, Andrews," an echo of a soft melancholy voice reached him. "Why are you frightened? It's Carlyon, merely Carlyon." The voice was tipped always with the cool, pure poetry which it loved. Why, indeed, should he not go to Carlyon and confess the wrong he had done and explain? That voice could not help but understand. He would go as the woman who had sinned to Christ, and the comparison seemed to him to carry no blasphemy, so strong was the impulse to rise and go to the door and go out into the night.

"Is it of him you are frightened?" she asked, watching the changes in his face. He had thought her voice also near to music, and now he sat still, watching with a strange disinterestedness the two musics come in conflict for the mastery of his movements. One was subtle, a thing of suggestions and of memories; the other, plain, clear-cut, ringing. One spoke of a dreamy escape from reality; the other was reality, deliberately sane. If he stayed sooner or later he must face this fear; if he went he left calmness, clarity, instinctive wisdom for a vague and uncertain refuge. How would Carlyon greet his confession? Carlyon was a romantic with his face in the clouds, who hated any who gave him contact with a grubby earth. Andrews remembered suddenly, his mind still drifting between the two differing musics, another Carlyon, a Carlyon who had shot one of his own men in the back, because on a cargo-running night the man had raped a young girl. No trouble followed, for the man had been a coward and unpopular in a crew of men, who with all their faults and villainies, had the one virtue of courage. Andrews remembered Carlyon's face, as he stepped back from the dark bundle where it lay on a beach silvered by the moon. The thoughtful eyes which peered from the ape-like skull had been suffused with disgust and a kind of disillusionment. They had re-embarked with the utmost speed, lest the shot should have aroused the revenue men, but Carlyon was the last to enter the boat. He came with evident reluctance like a man who had left a lover on land, and he had indeed left a lover, whom he did not see again for many weeks, a dear and romantic illusion of adventure.

"Andrews, Andrews," the voice had lost its charm. That music was spell-less, for Andrews remembered now that it was with the same soft melancholy regret that Carlyon had spoken to the offending smuggler. Pointing out to the sea he had said, "Look there. Can you tell me what that is?" and the man had turned his bank to scan a waste of small ridges, which formed, advanced, fell and receded, and continued so to form, advance, fall and recede, as his eyes glazed in death.

"I can't go to him," he said aloud.

"But if he came to you? . . ." she asked, as though she intended to make up a quarrel between two schoolboys on their dignity.

"No, no," he said, and suddenly rose with a poignant, stabbing sense of fear. "What's that?" he whispered. Elizabeth leant forward in her chair listening. "You are imagining things," she said.

With unexpected brutality he struck her hand, as it lay on the table, with his fist, so that she caught her breath with pain. "Can't you whisper?" he asked. "Do you want to tell the whole world there's someone here? There, didn't you hear that?" And this time she thought that she could hear a very faint stir of gravel no louder than a rustle of leaves. She nodded her head slowly. There's someone moving on the path," she murmured. The hand which he had struck stiffened into a small and resolute fist.

"For God's sake," Andrews muttered, staring around him. She jerked a finger at the door which led to the shed where he had slept the previous night. He half ran to it on tiptoe, and as he looked back, he saw that she had again taken up the stocking which he had dropped unused upon the floor. The red glow of the fire struck upwards and tinged with colour her serene, pale face. Then he closed the door and stood in the dark of the shed, giving occasional rapid shivers like a man in a fever.

The next sound he heard was Carlyon's voice. Its suddenness pierced him. He had expected at least to have been given warning, and time to brace his knees and heart, if by no more than a knock or the click of a lifting latch.

It penetrated to him through keyhole and crack, kindly and reassuring. "Forgive me," it said. "I'm completely lost in this fog."

Countering the deceptive music with its own clear tone, Elizabeth's voice struck against Carlyon's like sword against sword. "Why didn't you knock?" it said.

Had she realised Andrews wondered, listening intently in the dark, that this was the man he feared. He searched a frightened mind in vain for some way of warning her. He could imagine Carlyon's ape-like face gazing at her with a disarming frankness. "One can't be too careful around here," he said. His voice sounded a little nearer as though he had come over to the fire. "You are not alone?" he asked.

Andrews put his hand to his throat. Something had betrayed him. Perhaps as he stood like a blind man in the dark she was giving away his hiding place soundlessly with a wink, a lift of the eyebrow. He had a momentary impulse to fling open the door and rush at Carlyon. It would at least be man against man with no odds, he thought, until the unsleeping inner critic taunted him: "You are not a man." At least a coward can have cunning, he protested, and kneeling down on the floor, he put his eye to the keyhole. It was a moment before he could find the position of the speakers. Elizabeth was sitting in her chair, hand thrust in the stocking, calmly looking for holes. She is over-acting her calmness, he thought fearfully. Carlyon stood over her watching her with an apparent mixture of reverence and regret. He made a small motion toward the two cups, which stood with brazen effrontery upon the table.

She finished her search of the stocking and laid it on her lap. "I am alone," she said. "My brother has just gone out. He is not far," she added. "I can easily call to him, if you don't go."

Carlyon smiled. "You must not be afraid of me," he smiled. "Perhaps I know your brother. Is he a little over the middle height, slightly built, dark, with frightened obstinate eyes?"

"That's not my brother," Elizabeth said. "He is short and squat—and very strong."

"Then I am not looking for your brother." He picked up one of the cups. "He must have been here very lately," he said. "The tea is hot. And he left in a hurry with his tea unfinished. Curious that we did not meet." He gazed round the room with no attempt to hide his curiosity.

"That is my cup you have," Elizabeth said, and added with sarcasm; "Will you allow me to finish it?"

Andrews kneeling by the keyhole put up his hand to ease his collar as Elizabeth's lips touched the cup and drained what he had left. A strange loving cup, he thought bitterly, but his bitterness vanished before a wave of humility which for one moment even cleared his mind of its consciousness of fear. He had been kneeling to gain a view of the room beyond, but now in heart he knelt to her. She is a saint, he thought. The charity and courage with which she hid him from his enemy he had taken for granted; but to his muddled unstraight mind the act of drinking from the same cup came with a surprising nobility. It touched him where he was most open to impression; it struck straight at his own awareness of cowardice. Kneeling in the dark not only of the room but of his spirit he imagined that with unhesitating intimacy she had touched his lips and defiled her own.

"I didn't meet your brother," Carlyon repeated, still with a touch of regretful tenderness.

"There is another door," she said without hesitation. Carlyon turned, and to Andrews watching through the keyhole their eyes seemed to meet. His humility and trust vanished as quickly as they had arisen. Carlyon made a step towards the door. She's betrayed me, Andrews thought, and with fumbling panic-stricken fingers he sought for his knife. Yet he did not dare to open it, even when he had found it, lest the click should make itself heard through the closed door. Carlyon seemed to be starting straight at him. It was incredible that he could not see the eye which watched him through the keyhole, yet he hesitated, nonplussed perhaps as Andrews had been by the girl's courage, thinking she must have help somewhere, that there must be a trap laid. Then she spoke again carelessly and without hurry, leaning forward to warm her hands at the fire. "It's no use going there," she said. "He locked the door as he went out."

For the man in the dark there was a moment of suspense, while Carlyon hesitated. He had only to try the door for all to be discovered. Finally, he refrained.

In part perhaps it was because he feared a trap, but his chief reason must have been that embarrassing streak of chivalry which would not allow him to show openly his doubt of a woman's word. He turned away and stood in the middle of the room in almost pathetic perplexity. If he had known beforehand that there was a woman to be dealt with, he would have sent one of his companions to the cottage in his place, the small, cunning cockney Harry, or the elephantine Joe.

She regarded him with faint amusement from his receding forehead and deep sunk eyes to the strange contrast of his small lightly poised feet. "You are very muddy," she commented and cast a pathetic glance towards the floor, still fresh and clean from Mrs. Butler's scrubbing.

"I am sorry," he said, "very sorry. The fact is. . . ."

"Don't trouble to invent a lie," she murmured abstractly, her attention seeming to wander to the glowing heart of the fire. "You are looking for someone. Anybody can tell that. Unless you are flying from someone like the other man."

"The other man?" he leant a little forward with excitement, and Andrews once again prepared himself for betrayal. The act of drinking from his cup, which had filled him with such humility, seemed now to underline what he considered the vileness of her treachery.

"The man you described," she said, "the frightened, obstinate man."

"He's here?" Andrews could hardly catch Carlyon's

whisper. Carlyon's right hand had hidden itself in an inner pocket.

"He slept here last night," she said.

"And now?"

"He went with the morning, north, I think, but I don't know."

"Yes, that's true," Carlyon murmured. "He nearly ran into me, but escaped again in this wretched fog. He may return here then."

She laughed. "I don't think so," and pointed to the corner where the unloaded gun stood. "Fear," she added, "and shame."

"And your brother?" he asked with a sudden, quick remnant of suspicion.

"He was not here last night, but I warned your friend that he would be here to-night. Shall I warn you?" she added.

"I am not afraid," Caryon answered, "nor ashamed."

She looked again at his muddy clothes. "But you too are flying," she asked, "from something?"

"From the law," Carlyon replied with unhesitating frankness, "not from my friends—or from myself," he added with brooding thoughtfulness.

"Why all this fuss?" she asked, her eyes, kindled in the red reflected glow of the fire, gazing up at him with passionate sincerity and condemning, in an equal judgment, his mud, his flight, his search.

He watched her with fascination and with a kind of difficulty, as though trying to cling with his eyes to some bright object obscurely shining at the bottom of a dark and deep well. "He's a sort of Judas," he said softly and reluctantly.

"He didn't seem to be a man with money," she said. "Are you certain?"

"No. But if I could meet him, I should know in a moment. He hasn't the courage to hide anything." He shivered slightly as a cold draught insinuated itself under the door.

"You are cold," Elizabeth said. "Come to the fire." He looked at her for a moment as though amazed at her friendliness and then advanced to the fire and let the heat and flame stain his hands a red gold. "Why can't you leave him alone? she asked. "Is he worth the trouble and risk?"

Out of their deep sockets Carlyon's eyes peered cautiously, as though he wondered how far it was possible to make this serene stranger understand. "I knew him very well," he said hesitatingly. "We were friends. He must have known me well. Now I hate him. I'm certain that this is hate."

Her voice touched him like a slow warm flame. "Tell me," she said.

He looked at her again with that impression of amazement slowly welling up from a dark, deeply hidden source. "You have a lovely voice," he said. "It is just as though you were ready to play music to any stranger. You know who I am?" he asked.

"One of the Gentlemen," she said, and waited.

"So was the man who was here last night. We were friends. I told him things I would not tell anyone now

—what things I loved and why. And after three years with us he betrayed us to the law."

"Are you sure of that?"

"Someone must have done," he said. "Six men are in gaol on a charge of murder. There was a fight and a gauger was shot, poor devil. Four of us escaped; the two men who are with me, and Andrews, who has done his best to avoid us. And when did he escape? Before we were surprised. I'm certain of that. Why is he afraid of meeting me? I know he is." His eyes, having taken a sad, suspicious gaze at the world, seemed to hide themselves yet deeper in his skull. "You will not understand," he said, "how he has spoilt everything. It was a rough life, but there seemed something fine in it—adventure, courage, high stakes. Now we are a lot of gaol-birds, murderers. Doesn't it seem mean to you," he cried suddenly, "that a man should be shot dead over a case of spirits? What a dull, dirty game it makes it all appear."

She looked at him with pity but not with sympathy. "It must have been that all along," she said.

He shrugged his shoulders. "Yes, but I didn't know," he said. "Should I thank him for my enlightenment?"

She smiled at the tendrils of the fire uncurling themselves and folding again in bud. "Is a man's death and your dream broken worth all this fuss?" she demanded with voice raised a little as though she would carry her protest against man's stupidity beyond the room and out into the shrouding mist and night.

"You are so sane," he said sadly. "You women are

all so sane. A dream is often all there is to a man. I think that you are lovely, good and full of pity, but that is only a dream. You know all about yourself, how you are greedy for this and that, afraid of insects, full of disgusting physical needs. You'll never find a man who will love you for anything but a bare, un-filled-in outline of yourself. A man will even forget his own details when he can, until he appears an epic hero, and it needs his woman to see that he's a fool. Only a woman can love a real person."

"You may be right," she said, "though I don't under-stand most of it. I once knew a man, though, who so forgot his own details as you call them, that he believed himself a coward and nothing else."

"That's less common," Carlyon answered. "Women generally show us up to ourselves and we hate them for it. I suppose that man would love the woman who showed him up."

She suddenly dropped her seriousness and laughed. "Poor man," she mocked, "and you hate this friend of yours because he's shown you up. What a fool you are to waste your time on such a hate."

He made a small motion with his hands towards the fire, as though he wished to seize its light and heat, and bear them to his brain. "Yes," he said. "I hate him," and then waited, with his eyes peeping, as it were beseechingly, from his low skull in a longing to be con-vinced of his own futility and of his own hate.

"But what, after all, could you do if you met him?" she protested.

"I should make sure that I was right," he answered, "and then I should kill him."

"And what would be the use of that?" she asked.

He edged a little away from her and threw back his head, as though he were protecting something infinitely dear. "There would be no use," he said, "no use, but I have a mission."

He saw her lift her eyes full of a pleading friendship. "You are in danger of something worse than the law," she said.

He looked at her with suspicion. "Why all these arguments?" he asked. "Did you like the man?" He eyed her with regret and disgust as he would have done a lovely picture soiled with ordure. "Did you get fond of him in a night?"

"No," she said simply. "But I have lived with hate since I was a child. Why don't you escape from the country? If you stay you'll only injure yourself or else something you never intended to harm. That's always the way."

He took no notice of her words, but watched her face with curiosity and fascination. "If I could take you with me," he murmured, "I should have with me peace and charity. Have you noticed," he said softly, his eyes peering like a dog's between the bars of a cage, "how in the middle of a storm there's always a moment of silence?" He half raised his arms as though he were about to protest at the necessity which drove him back into the storm, and then let them drop in a kind of tired despair.

"You are free," she whispered, her eyes watching

him not through bars but through the gold mist which the flames of the fire shed, "you are not bound."

He shrugged his shoulders and said with a resentful carelessness. "Oh, there's no peace for me." He turned on his heel decisively, but he had taken only three steps to the door, when he came back.

He did not look at her but said with a touch of embarrassment:

"You say he went north?"

"Yes," she said.

"Of course. I know that," he commented. "We nearly met." He shifted a little on his feet. "I don't know your name," he continued. "I don't want you to come to any harm. If he should come back, you mustn't shelter him or warn him."

"Is that a command?" she asked with gentle mockery.

"Yes," he said, and then added in stumbling haste, "but I will beg you, too. You cannot be mixed up in this. You don't belong to our world, noise, hate. Stay with peace."

"Are the two so separate?" she asked.

He listened with his head a little on one side and eyes half-closed, like a man in the presence of a faint music. Then he covered his eyes for a moment with his hand. "You muddle me," he said.

"Are they so separate?" she repeated.

"Let them remain separate," he said vehemently and bitterly, "you can't come to us, and it's too easy for us to come to you."

"Where are you going?" she asked.

"To look for him," he answered. "I'll find him. I know him too well to lose him."

"And he knows you," she added.

Carlyon came nearer to her again. "Was he laughing at me the whole time," he asked, "while we were friends? He's a coward and cowards are cunning. I told him all the things I liked. I read him things, shared what I loved with him. I can only make him forget what I told him by killing him," he added with an incongruous pathos.

Elizabeth said, "Were they as secret as that?"

He backed away from her suspiciously, as though he feared that she too had designs on his most intimate thoughts. "I've warned you," he said abruptly. "I won't bother you any longer. You had better not tell your brother that I have been. I don't wish any harm to him either." He turned and walked very quickly to the door, as though he were afraid that some word might delay him further. When he opened the door a cold draught filled the room with smoke and mist. He shivered a little. As he closed it he shut away from himself the sight of Elizabeth's face, its serenity troubled by a faint and obscure pity.

CHAPTER V

ANDREWS put the closed knife back into his pocket. The dark which had been cold to him grew warm with friendliness. He was overwhelmed with a immense gratitude, so that he was unwilling to open the door and remind Elizabeth of his presence. She was as unapproachable to him in this mood as a picture, as holy as a vision. He remembered his first entrance to the cottage and his last sight of her before he sank exhausted, the pale resolute face set between two yellow flames.

Quietly as though he were in the presence of a mystery he turned the handle of the door and remained on the threshold unresolved and diffident. She was standing by the table cleaning the cups and plates which they had left.

"Is that you?" she said, without looking up, "put these in the cupboard," and when he had obeyed her she returned to the fire and bending down to poke the coals murmured with a half-amused asperity, "A couple of fools."

Andrews shifted from one foot to another. He found, faced by this devastating matter of factness, an inability to utter his thanks. He plucked nervously at a button and at last burst out in a tone almost of resentment, "I'm grateful."

"But what's it all about?" she asked spreading out her hands in a gesture of humourous perplexity. "I hate mysteries," she added, herself mysteriously brooding behind dark eyes flecked only on the surface by an amusement.

"Didn't you hear what he said?" Andrews replied and muttered in so low a tone that Elizabeth was forced to lean forward to catch his words, "a sort of Judas."

"Do you expect me to believe all that he said," she stared at Andrews in wide-eyed, innocent amusement. "He's your enemy."

"Would you believe what I said?" he asked with angry foreknowledge of the answer.

"Of course," she said. "Tell me."

He watched her in amazement, all his sentimental melodramatic instincts rose up in him to take advantage of the occasion. O, the blessed relief, he thought, to stumble forward, go down on my knees to her, weep, say "I am tired out. A hunted man pursued by worse than death." He could hear his own voice break on the phrase. But as he was about to obey those instincts, that other hard, critical self spoke with unexpected distinctness. "You fool, she'll see through that. Haven't you enough gratitude to speak the truth?" But then, he protested, I lose all chance of being comforted. But when he looked at her, the critic won. He stood where he was with hands clasped behind his back and head a little bent, but eyes staring intently, angrily for the first sign of contempt.

"It's all true," he said.

"Tell me," she repeated.

"It's not a story which would interest you," he protested, in a vain hope of avoiding further humiliation.

She sat down and leaning her chin on her hand watched him with a friendly amusement. "You must earn your night's lodging with the story," she said. "Come here."

"No," he clung as a desperate resort to a position in which he could at least look physically down upon her. "If I must speak, I'll speak here."

He twisted a button round and round till it dangled loosely on its cotton stalk. He did not know how to begin. He shut his eyes and plunged into a rapid current of words.

"We were running spirits from France," he said. "and I betrayed them. That's all there is to it. I wrote to the Customs' officer at Shoreham and gave a date and an hour and a place. When we landed the gaugers were waiting for us. There was a fight, but I slipped away. It seems that a gauger was killed." He opened his eyes and gazed at her angrily. "Don't dare to despise me," he said. "You don't know why I did it, my thoughts, feelings. I'm a coward, I know, and none of you can understand a coward. You are all so brave and quiet, peaceful."

She took no notice of his angry outburst, but watched him thoughtfully. "I wonder why you did it?" she answered.

He shook his head and answered in a kind of deep hopefulness, "You wouldn't understand."

"But why," Elizabeth asked, "did you ever start smuggling? You are not made for that work."

"My father was a smuggler," Andrews said. "A common, bullying smuggler, but damnably clever. He saved money on it and sent me to school. What was the use of having me taught Greek, if I was to spend my life like this?" and his hand in its vague comprehensive gesture included the bare room, the cold night, his muddy clothes and fear. He came a little nearer to the fire.

"I will tell you why he sent me to school," he said, leaning forward as though to impart a confidence. "It was so that he could brag about it. He was proud of his success. He was never caught and they never had any evidence against him. His crew worshipped him. I tell you he's become a legend on this coast. I've never dared to say these things about him to anyone but you. And all the time I was at sea, I could see how they wondered that such a mountain could bring forth such a mouse."

"Why do you hate your father so?" Elizabeth asked, "is it because of this?", and with her hand she imitated the comprehensive gesture which he had **made** a minute before.

"Oh, no," he said, "no." He watched her with a despairing intentness and a hopeless longing for some sign of comprehension. He pleaded with her not as an advocate to a jury but as a prisoner already condemned to his judge. "You can't understand," he said, "what life was like with these men. I could do nothing which was not weighed up with my father and found wanting. They kept on telling me of his courage, of what he would have done, what a hero he was. And I knew all the time things they didn't know, how he had beaten my mother, of his conceit, his ignorance, his beastly bullying ways. They gave me up in the end," he said smiling without any gaiety. "I was of no account. They were kind to me, charitably, because that man was my father."

"But why, why," she asked "did you ever mix yourself up with them?"

"That was Carlyon," he said softly, wondering whether the twisted feeling at his heart when he uttered the name was love or hate. It was at any rate something bitter and irrevocable.

"The man who was here?"

"Yes," Andrews said. "My father was killed at sea and they dropped his body overboard, so that even when he was dead, the law had no evidence against him. I was at school. My mother died a couple of years before. I think he broke her heart, if there's such a thing as a broken heart. He broke her body anyway." Andrews's face grew white as though from the blinding heat of an inner fire. "I loved my mother," he said. "She was a quiet pale woman who loved flowers. We used to go for walks together in the holidays and collect them from the hedges and ditches. Then we would press them and put them in an album. Once my father was at home—he had been drinking, I think— and he found us. We were so busy that we didn't hear him when he called. He came and tore the leaves out of the album and crumpled them in his fists, great unwieldy fists. He was unwieldy altogether, large, clumsy, bearded, but with a quick cunning brain and small eyes."

"Why did your mother marry him?" Elizabeth asked.

"They eloped," Andrews said. "My mother was incurably romantic."

"And when your father died?"

"That was more than three years ago," Andrews continued in a tone as tired as though he were speaking of three centuries. "I was finishing school, and Carlyon brought the news. I was glad. You see it appeared to me to mean the end of fear. My father used to beat me unmercifully, because he said it would put courage into me. I think he was a little mad towards the end. My mother's death frightened him, for he was superstitious. When I heard that he was dead, I thought it was the beginning of a life of peace."

"And why not?" Elizabeth asked. "Why this?"

He bent his head sullenly. "I was alone," he said. "I wasn't sure what to do. Carlyon asked me to come back with him and I went." He raised his head and said fiercely, "Can't you understand? You've seen the man for yourself. There's something about him . . . I was a boy," he added as though he was an old man discussing a far distant past. "Perhaps I was romantic like my mother. God knows I ought to be cured of that now. He was brave, adventurous and yet he loved music and the things which I loved, colours, scents, all that part of me which I could not speak of at school or to my father. I went with Carlyon. What a fool I was. How could I be such a fool?"

She screwed up her mouth as though at a wry taste. "Yes, but the betrayal?" she said.

He drew himself up, moving a little away. "I don't expect anyone to understand that," he said. He gave a momentary impression of great dignity, which he spoilt by an immediate capitulation. "You can't realise the life I came to," he said. "There were storms and I was sea-sick. There were periods of night-long waiting off the coast for signals which did not come and I could not help showing my nerves. And there was no hope of any change, of any peace at last except death. My father had left his boat and every penny he had saved to Carlyon. That was why Carlyon came to me in Devon. He was curious to see the neglected son, and then I suppose he took pity on me. I believe he liked me," Andrews added slowly and regretfully with another painful twist at the heart.

"I thought my father was dead," he continued, "but I soon found that he had followed me on board. The first member of the crew I met as I was hauled, pushed behind and pulled in front, on to the boat, was Joe, a fat, big, clumsy, stupid creature, a prize bull of a man. 'You'll soon get your sea legs, sir,' he said to me, 'if you are your father's son.' They worshipped my father, all except a wizened half-witted youth called Tims, whom my father had made his personal servant. My father, I suppose, had bullied him. He used to watch me slyly from a distance with a mixture of hatred and fear until he realised that I wasn't 'my father's son', when he began to treat me with familiarity, because we had both suffered from the same hand." Andrews paused, then began again with an exaggerated irony which did not disguise his own sense of shame. "They all soon realised that I wasn't like my father, but they remained kind and only told me about six times a day what my father would have done in such and such a case. I used to take refuge with Carlyon. He never mentioned my father to me."

Andrews had been speaking calmly, but with a strained note in his voice. Now he lost control of himself. "If I'm a coward," he cried, "haven't I a mind? Wasn't my brain of any use to them that they should treat me like a child, never ask my opinion, have me there on sufferance only, because of my father and because Carlyon willed it? I'm as good as Carlyon. Haven't I outwitted the fool now?" he ejaculated in hysterical triumph, and then fell silent before Elizabeth's quiet passivity, remembering how she had lifted the cup to her lips and filled him with humility, as he crouched in the dark. Now he wished that she would speak, accuse him in so many words of ingratitude, rather than arraign him in silence before peaceful eyes. He grew resentful of her silence and fidgeted with his hands. "I've shown them that I'm of importance now," he said.

Elizabeth raised her hand to her head as though she felt an ache there. "So it was hate again," she said in a tired voice. "There seems to be hate everywhere."

Andrews stared at her in amazement. On what had seemed the illimitable peace of her mind had appeared the cloud small as a man's hand. For the first time a sense reached him of an unhappiness which was not his own. Watching the white face propped up on small clenched fists and touched only on the surface by the fire's glow, he grew indignant with the world, with the dark which surrounded them, with fear, uneasiness, anything which could mar her perfect happiness. "She is a saint," he thought, remembering with a heart still half inclined to sentimental tears of gratitude the manner in which she had saved him from Carlyon.

He came a little nearer very cautiously, with a desire quite alien to his nature not to intrude on a sorrow which he could not share. "It is the dead man," he thought and became aware of a feeling of despairing jealousy. "It's true then," his second self whispered, "always hate."

"No," he said out loud, speaking partly to her and partly to that other self, "not here. Hate's not here," and when she looked up at him with a puzzled frown, he added, "I'm grateful." The poverty of his words! He grew aware of himself as a large, coarse body with soiled clothes and burst out indignantly, "It's not fair that you should be touched by this." Suddenly in spirit he stretched out both hands to his own critic and begged him to take control, if only for a few minutes, of his actions. He said to Elizabeth, "It's my fault. I know that. Perhaps it's not too late. I'll go now—this instant," and he turned hesitatingly and looked with shuddering distaste at the cold night outside. There was a suitable dwelling place for hate and there he would take it, leaving again in security this small warm room and its white occupant. Yet he did not want to go. It was not only that outside Carlyon and his two companions sought him, but that inside he would leave someone who seemed to carry far behind her eyes, glimpsed only obscurely and at whiles, the promise of his two selves at one, the peace which he had discovered sometimes in music.

He stood shamefully hesitating, the strength of his resolution exhausted in his words. "You needn't go," she said. "You haven't done me any harm," and seeing that he had not been affected by her unenthusiastic statement she added reluctantly, "I don't want you to go."

Andrews looked round at her. "Do you mean that?" he asked.

"Oh, it's not your fascinating self," she said, with gentle mockery. "But I'm tired of being alone. I haven't even the body with me now."

"No, but the spirit?" he burst out, wilfully misunderstanding her words, seeing her body as a fragile and beautiful casing, which just succeeded in enclosing her lightly poised spirit that spoke in turn with mockery, friendship, sorrow, laughter and always with a pervading undertone of peace.

She did not understand. "I don't know where that is," she said. "It will keep me safe anyway. I've said he was jealous, didn't I? If you were drunk and full of lust," she added with an outspokennness which startled Andrews, "I should be safe."

"Yes, from anything of that kind, perhaps," Andrews said, "but from death?"

Elizabeth laughed. "Oh, I never thought of that," she said. "When I'm old will be time enough."

"How wonderful," Andrews said thoughtfully, "to live like that without fear of death. You must be very brave. You are all alone here." He had completely forgotten his resolution to go, and now with sudden but not offensive familiarity he sat down on the floor by her feet and let the fire light up the wonder in his face to a warm glow. To Elizabeth it seemed that the lines with which fear had falsely aged his face were smoothed away, and it was a boy's face which watched her with a boy's enthusiasm. She smiled. "Not bravery but custom," she said.

He leant forward towards her, watching her face intently as though he were unwilling to miss the least shade, the smallest movement of the hidden muscles, the slightest change in the colour of what he began to consider in his heart were faultless eyes. "I've told you my story," he said. "Tell me yours. You say that I can stay the night here and it's too early for sleep."

"It's not an interesting story," Elizabeth said. I have always lived here. I've never been further away than to school at Shoreham."

"And that man—who's dead?" Andrews asked, again with the puzzling twinge of jealousy.

"I was here first," she said, as though she claimed like Venus priority over death. "I was born here, I think, but I can't remember who my father was. I think he must have died or left my mother. What money there was came from my grandfather, a rich farmer as wealth is considered in these parts. As for the rest my mother took in lodgers, when she could get them, and when she failed, there was a little less to eat, that was all."

"And that man?" Andrews repeated again with a stubborn boyish intentness.

She smiled. "You are very interested in him," she said. "He was one of my mother's lodgers. He worked at Shoreham with the Customs, a clerk in the office. That didn't make him popular in this neighbourhood, where, as you must know, everyone has a cellar and everyone is at the beck and call of the Gentlemen. He was an outcast, the more so as he lived out here away from his own kind in the town. That puzzled me for a a long time. He never knew anyone, partly from choice, partly from necessity. The strange thing was that he was able suddenly to retire with enough money to live on for the rest of his life.

"I remember the day. I was about ten years old. We lived a very close life, you know, in this cottage. This was our only living-room. Above here are two rooms," and she pointed to a small door on the left of the fireplace. "My mother and I slept in one, and Mr. Jennings—that was the name we knew him by—in another. He would be in to breakfast and supper and we ate with him down here. But after supper, because he was a quiet, brooding man who did not seem to care for company, we would take any work we had to do upstairs to our bedroom. I don't know what he did all by himself but think and perhaps sleep in a chair by the fire, but sometimes I would wake in the very middle of the night and hear him going to his room. Perhaps he was one of those poor people who find it hard to sleep. You saw his face. Don't you think there was something sleepless about it?"

"It was a cunning wicked face, I thought," Andrews said.

"Oh, no," Elizabeth protested, without anger. "He was cunning perhaps, but he was not wicked. He was kind to me in his own way," and she brooded for a moment on the past with a frown of perplexity.

"Well, one night," she said, "after supper we were rising as usual to go upstairs, when he asked us to stay. It seemed astonishing to me, but my mother was quite undisturbed. She was a fatalist, you know, and it made her very serene but altogether unpurposeful. We stayed sitting there, I impatient to know the reason, but my mother apparently entirely uninterested. She took up her work and began to sew, as if it had always been her custom to work in this room. After a while he spoke. 'I've been very comfortable here,' he said. My mother looked up and said, 'Thank you,' and went on with her sewing. Her answer seemed odd to me. I felt that he should have thanked her, not she him."

"Was your mother pale and lovely?" Andrews asked, "with dark hair and quiet eyes?"

"She was dark," Elizabeth said, "but plump and with a lot of colour in her cheeks."

"You have colour in your cheeks," Andrews said thoughtfully, not as though he were paying a compliment but as though he were dispassionately discussing an inanimate beauty, "but it is on white background, like a flower fallen on snow."

Elizabeth smiled a little, but paid no other attention to him. "Mr. Jennings," she said, "bit his thumb-nail—a habit with him—and watched my mother suspiciously. 'You'll die one day,' he continued. 'What will happen to this cottage then?' I watched my mother in a still fright, half expecting her to die there and then before my eyes. 'It will be sold,' she said, 'for the child here.' 'Suppose,' Mr. Jennings said, 'you sell to me now,' and then, because he thought my mother was going to make some amazed comment, he continued very hurriedly, 'I will give you your price, and you shall stay on here with your child as long as you like. You can invest the money to the child's advantage. I am very comfortable here, and I don't want the risk of being turned away when you die.' It was astonishing the quiet way in which he assumed that she would die first, although they were both much of an age. I don't know whether he could see, but she died within the year. Of course, she had taken the offer."

Something rather the reflection of sorrow than sorrow itself crossed Elizabeth's face, and she went on with her story with an air of hurry and a somewhat forced abstraction. "He seemed hardly to notice that my mother was dead," she said. "I stayed and cooked his meals as my mother had done and swept the floors. For some weeks I was afraid that he would turn me out, but he never did. Every week he gave me money for the house, and I never had to touch what my mother left me. He no longer went to work and he would spend his time in long walks along the top of the downs or in sitting beside the fire reading the Bible. I don't think he ever read it consecutively. He would open it at random and put his thumb on a passage. When what he found pleased him he would read on, and when it displeased him he would fling the book aside and go for another of his long walks, until he came back tired and weary looking like a beaten dog. He very seldom spoke to me.

"It was a very lonely life for a child and one day I picked up my courage and asked whether I could go to school again. He wanted to know how much it would cost and when he found out how little it would be he sent me off and even gave me a note to the mistress, asking that they should pay particular attention to Scripture. From that time on he paid me more attention. I would read to him in the evening and sometimes even argue small theological points."

"What a strange, staid child you must have been," Andrews said.

"Oh no," Elizabeth laughed protestingly. "I was like all children. There were times of rebellion, when I would disappear down into Shoreham to play with other children or go to an entertainment, a circus or a fair. At first he would not notice my absence, which was humiliating, but after I had begun my Bible readings he grew more particular and sometimes beat me. Sometimes, too, at meals I'd look up and find him watching me."

Again Andrew felt that absurd twinge of jealousy. "How could he be satisfied with watching you through those years?" he broke out.

"I was a child," she said simply in final answer and

then added slowly, "He was very much taken up with his soul."

Andrews laughed harshly, remembering the little cunning line around the mouth, the stubbly untidy beard, the coarse lids. "He must have had need," he said. He longed to be able to shatter any feeling of friendship or gratitude which Elizabeth might still feel for the dead man.

Her eyes sparkled and she raised her chin in a small belligerent gesture. "No one could have called him a Judas," she said.

Andrews knelt up on the floor with clenched fists. He was filled with a childish personal animosity for the dead man. "I have not a penny in the world," he said. "I ask you—what have I gained? Is this so much? But he—where did he get his money?"

"I learned that later," Elizabeth said quietly, her voice falling like the touch of cool fingers on a hot, aching brow. "He had cheated his employers, that was all. One day I opened the Bible at random as usual and began to read. It was the parable of the unjust steward. I felt, though I was looking at the page and not at him, that he was listening with unusual intentness. When I reached the point where the steward calls his lord's debtors and says to the first: How much dost thou owe my lord; and he says: a hundred barrels of oil; and the steward says: Take the bill and sit down quickly and write fifty; when I reached that point Mr. Jennings—I never called him anything else—gave a sort of gasp of wonder. I looked up. He was staring at me with a mixture of fear and suspicion. 'Does it say that there,' he asked, 'or are you making it up?' 'How could I make it up?' I said. 'People gossip so,' he answered, 'go on,' and he listened hard, sitting forward a little in the chair. When I read 'And the Lord commended the unjust steward, for as much as he had done wisely,' he interrupted me again. 'Do you hear that?' he said, and gave a sigh of satisfaction and relief. He watched me for a little with his eyes screwed up. 'I've been worrying,' he said at last, 'but that's at an end. The Lord has commended me.'

"I said, 'But you are not the unjust steward,' and added with a trace of conceit, 'and anyway this is a parable.'

"Mr. Jennings told me to close the Bible and put it away. 'It's no use talking,' he said, 'you can't get over scripture. It's strange,' he added. 'I never thought I was doing right.'

"He told me then, sure in the Lord's approval, how he had earned the money on which he had retired. All the time that he was a clerk in the Customs he was in receipt of an income from certain seamen, who had not the courage to become regular smugglers. They would declare about three-quarters of the amount of spirit they carried, and Mr. Jennings would check their cargo and turn a blind eye on what they had not declared. Can't you imagine him," she said with a laugh, "picking his way delicately among the cases of spirit, noting carefully a certain proportion? But unlike the unjust steward for a hundred barrels he would write seventy-five, and if that particular captain's payments to him were in arrears, he would even put down the full hundred as a warning. Then he would go home and open the Bible at random and read perhaps some terrifying prophecy of hell fire and be in a panic for hours. But after he had heard the parable of the unjust steward he never asked me to read the Bible to him again and I never saw him open the Book. He was comforted and perhaps he feared to find a contradictory passage. He was cunning, I suppose, and wicked in his way, but he had a childish heart."

"Was he as blind as a child?" Andrews asked. "Couldn't he see that you were beautiful?" He knelt with clenched fists before her with eyes half shut as though he were battered by contrary winds, by admiration, wonder, suspicion, jealousy, love. "Yes, I am in love," he said to himself, with sadness and not with exaltation. "But are you, are you, are you?" the inner critic mocked him. "It's just the old lusts. This is not Gretel. Would you sacrifice yourself for her? You know that you wouldn't. You love yourself too dearly. You want to possess her, that is all." "Oh be quiet and let me think," he implored. "You are wrong. I am a coward. You cannot expect me to change my spots so soon. But this is not the old lust. There is something holy here," and as though exorcised the critic fell again into silence.

Elizabeth smiled wryly. "Am I beautiful?" she asked, and then with a sudden, vehement bitterness, "If it's beauty which makes men cease to be blind as children, I don't want it. It only means unhappiness. He was unhappy at the end. One day a year ago—it was just before my eighteenth birthday—I rebelled more than usual against the loneliness of life here. I disappeared in the morning early before he got up and left his breakfast unmade. I didn't return till quite late at night. I was really frightened at my own action. I had never broken away quite so drastically before. I opened the door of this room very quietly and saw him asleep in front of the fire. He had made himself some supper, but he had hardly touched it, and the poverty and untidiness of it touched me. I nearly went across to him and apologised, but I was afraid, so I slipped off my shoes and got to my room without waking him. It must have been after midnight. I had just taken off my clothes, when he opened the door suddenly. He had a strap in his hand and I could see that he meant to beat me. I snatched at a sheet from my bed to cover myself. He had a very angry look in his eyes, but it changed in one moment to amazement. He dropped the strap and put out his hands. I thought he was going to take me in his arms and I screamed. Then he lowered his hands and went out, slamming the door. I remember that I picked up the strap and fingered it and tried to feel thankful that I had not been beaten. But I knew that I would have been grateful for a beating in place of the new uneasiness."

"Do you mean," Andrews asked, "that you are not yet twenty?"

"Do I look more?" Elizabeth asked.

"Oh no, it's not that," he said. "But you seem so wise—understanding. As if you knew as much as any woman who had ever been born and were yet not bitter about it."

"I have learned a lot in the last year," she replied. "Perhaps before I was rebellious, unwise, but wasn't I younger?" she asked with a sad laugh.

"No, you don't belong to any age," Andrews said.

"Don't I? I think I belonged to an age then—my own age. I was eighteen and frightened of him, but not with an clear idea of what he wanted. I held him off with tricks, played on his fear with quotations from the Bible, and when one day—or rather one night—he told me with a complete, and I think brutal, candour what he wanted me to do, I told him with equal directness that if he forced me to do it, I should leave him for ever. Oh, I had begun to grow up terribly quickly. You see, I traded on his desire for me and by my emphasis on the word 'force', gave him to understand, without another word said, that one day I might come to him voluntarily. And so I held off, narrowly, always with a sense of danger, till he died."

"Then you won," Andrews commented with a sigh of relief which he did not trouble to hide.

"And what a triumph!" she said sadly not cynically. "He had been good to me, kept me in food and clothing from a child without any idea that one day I should be a woman. And when for the first time he wanted something from me in return more than mere cooking or Bible reading I refused. I showed my disgust and I think that at times it hurt him. And now he is dead, and what would it have mattered if I had given myself to him?"

"Then there would have been two Judases in Sussex," Andrews said with a wry smile.

"Would it have been a betrayal?" she thought aloud. "It would have been turned to a good purpose, surely?"

Andrew put his head between his hands. "Yes," he said, in sullen sorrow, "there's the difference."

She watched him for a moment, puzzled, and then stretched out her hand in vehement protest. "But I didn't mean that," she cried; "how could you think it?" She hesitated. "I am your friend," she said.

The face which he raised to her was like that of one dazed and stunned by an unexampled good fortune. "If I could believe that . . ." he murmured in halting, incredulous tones. With a sudden lightening of the spirit he put out his hand to touch her.

"Your friend," she repeated warningly.

"Oh, yes," he said. "I am sorry. My friend," and he dropped his hand to his side. "I don't deserve even that." For the first time his words of self-humiliation were not repeated mockingly by the critic within. "If there was some way I could retrieve . . ." he gave a small, hopeless gesture with his hands.

"But is there none?" she asked. "Couldn't you come forward and deny all that you had written to the officers?"

"I can't unsay a man's death," he said. "And if I were able, I don't believe that I would do it. I can't go back to that life—the sneers, the racket, that infernal sea, world without end. Even in the middle of this fear and flight, you've given me more peace than I've known since I left school."

"Well, if you can't undo what you've done, follow it out to the end," she said.

"What do you mean?"

"You were driven to the side of the law," she said. "Stay there. Go into the open and bear witness against the men they've caught. You have made yourself an informer, at least you can be an open one."

"But you don't understand." He watched her with fascinated, imploring eyes. "The risk."

Elizabeth laughed. "But that's the very reason. Don't you see that by all this nameless work of yours, this flight, you've made the whole pack of them, that mad boy, better men than you are."

"They were always that," he murmured sadly under his breath, his head bowed again so that he might not see her firelit enthusiastic eyes.

She leant forward excitedly towards him. "Which one of them," she asked, "if he was an informer would come forward in open court, make himself a marked man and bear the risk?"

He shook his head. "No man in his senses would." He hesitated and added slowly, dwelling on the name with that puzzling mixture of love and hatred, "except Carlyon."

"Well then," she said, "go to Lewes, go to the Assizes, bear your witness and you will have shown yourself to have more courage than they."

"But I haven't," he said.

"You hesitate and hesitate and then you are lost," she replied. "Can't you ever shut your eyes and leap?"

"No, no," Andrews said. He got to his feet and moved restlessly about the room. "I can't. You are trying to drive me and I won't be driven."

"I'm not driving you. Why should I? Is there nothing in you which would welcome the open?"

"You don't understand," he cried with a sudden fury. His sentimental melodramatic self, which longed for deep-breasted maternal protection, stood with its back to the wall and uttered the old cry with a sharper despair. For he knew that something in him was answering the appeal, and he was afraid. "I can't, I can't, I can't," he said.

"But think," she said, her eyes following him in all his movements, "to escape from this . . ."

He stopped suddenly and turned directly to her. "This!" he said. "But this is Paradise." He came a little nearer. "If I was to stop hesitating and leap," he continued hurriedly, "I could do better than go to Lewes."

"Do better?" she repeated with a slight trace of mockery.

"Why do you always repeat words like that," he said angrily. "It's maddening. You sit there cool, collected, at peace. Oh I'd hate you if I didn't love you."

"You are crazy," she said.

He came nearer. "Suppose I take your advice," he spoke angrily, as though he did indeed hate her, "not to hesitate any longer, I want you. Why shouldn't I have you?"

Elizabeth laughed. "Because you will always hesitate," she said. "I've tried. I give you up."

"That's why I won't touch you, is it?" Andrews's breath rose into a sob, as he felt his last defences crumbling, and over them straddling a new and terrifying future. "You are wrong. I'll prove you wrong. I'll go to Lewes." The word Lewes coming so out of his mouth frightened him. He struck one more hopeless blow against the threatening future. "Mind," he said, "I promise nothing else. I'll go to Lewes and see. I don't promise to go into court."

Elizabeth gave a little sigh of weariness and rose from her chair. "You have a long walk before you to-morrow," she said. "You must sleep." She watched him and the faint suspicion in her glance pleased him. He took it as a sign that she was already partly convinced. He grew suddenly proud and confident in his decision and was happier than he had been for many years. "I will sleep where I slept last night," he said.

She went to the window and pulled the curtain across it. "The fog has gone," she said. "The sky is quite clear and I can see six stars." She opened the little door beside the fireplace and stood on the bottom step of the small flight of stairs.

"Good night."

"Good night."

PART II

CHAPTER VI

ANDREWS woke to a surge of gold light. He lay for a little in unconsciousness of anything save warmth. Somewhere a long way outside his mind disturbing facts nibbled like a brood of mice. But he kept them on one side and with eyes fixed upon that golden stationary wave hypnotised himself into a vacancy of mind. Yet the mice must have continued their nibbling, for suddenly and overwhelmingly reality burst in upon his consciousness. I am leaving here, he thought, I have promised to go, and he thought of Lewes as a dark and terrifying enemy, lying in wait for him to trip him up and fling him backwards into death. But I need do no more than go to Lewes, he told himself. That is all I have promised. And he wondered, in that case, whether he could not break—evade he called it —his promise altogether. But then I can never come back, he said, and it seemed to him an overwhelming, an impossible loss to lose for ever Elizabeth—or rather the sound of her voice, which wrapped him in peace.

He got up and shook himself hopelessly, like a rumpled dog just escaped from a pond who knows his master intends to drive him back into the water many times more. I will go to Lewes, he thought, but I will leave again before the Assizes open. He tried to calculate what day of the month it was. He had dated his letter to the Shoreham Customs, he knew, on the third of February and a week passed before the betrayal was made absolute. On the night of the tenth they had tried to run a cargo, for the last time. Then this was the fourth day of his flight, and only a few days before the Assizes opened. He must not wait in Lewes long. Too many local people would come in to watch the smugglers' fate—or triumph, as likely as not, with a local jury to try them. Every man is against me, he thought. None are on my side save outcasts and the hoard of strangers who will come from London. Judge, counsel, officers. Must I always stand alone on one side? And his heart protested against the necessity which drove him from his present shelter.

The room where Elizabeth and he had told their stories the previous night was empty. He looked round for some scrap of paper on which he could write his gratitude, but there was none, nor had he any pen or ink. He did not dare to go up to where she slept, feeling that if he saw her face again he could not leave her. And yet to go without a word or sign seemed impossible. He felt in his pockets. They were empty, save for some ancient crumbs, hard as shot, and his knife. He stared at his knife hesitatingly. His heart told him to leave it as a gift which might help her, a sign that he was grateful; his mind told him that very soon in Lewes he would need it. He opened the blade and stroked it. It was clean and sharp and on it, very roughly engraved, a schoolboy's first experiment with acids, was his name. It's my only weapon, he thought. It's of more use to me than to her. What could she use it for but toasting and cutting bread? I shall be defenceless without it. Leave it for that very reason, his heart appealed. A sacrifice. But to his fingers running along the blade it was so comfortingly sharp.

I'll leave nothing, he decided. After all she is driving me into this risk, and he moved to the door. Leaning in one corner beside it was the gun, with which she had overcome him. He remembered her laugh, "I haven't an idea how to load it." Suppose that Carlyon —but Carlyon would do nothing against a woman. There could be no danger for her, and yet he felt uneasy. He returned with lagging, unwilling steps to the table, and suddenly, drawing the knife from his pocket, plunged it into the wood, so that it stood there quivering like an arrow. I can get another in Lewes, he told himself, and he shut the door of the cottage behind him. But it is far to Lewes, he thought, robbed suddenly of four sheltering walls, alone in a bare, chill, hostile world.

The morning was cold and sharp and sunny. The bare coppice at the edge of which the cottage stood was bathed in a slow yellow surge. Above it lay the down over which he had come two nights before in scurrying terror. His danger now was greater than ever, for was he not pledged at last to visit Lewes? And yet his fear was not so great. Before it had drowned reason. Now through contact with one firm spirit his reason was predominant. He knew that this was only for a time, that his full blinding cowardice would return, but he would make the most of this respite by deciding on his course of action. His quickest route to Lewes was by road, and quickness he desired. Like a runner in a relay race he wished to touch but the fringes of Lewes and retire, his duty fulfilled. The sooner he reached the town, the sooner he could escape. But though the road was the quickest route, he was very unwilling to trust to it. He imagined himself as a clear-cut conspicuous figure thrown up against a white, bare road, and behind every hedge the possibility of Carlyon or his two companions. No, by way of the downs was longer, but safer. There, if he could be seen, he could at least see others with equal clearness. And the down would take him by Ditchling Beacon and Harry's Mount to the very threshold of Lewes. He could lie out on the last slope until dark came. He glanced at the sun with hate, his heart desirous of that dark.

On the slopes of the down the grass grew in long tufts, so that each foot that fell was clogged as though it had been plunged in treacle. When he reached the summit Andrews was out of breath and he lay down to rest. He wondered what hour it was. The sun seemed to indicate late morning, for as he faced inland it shone nearly full upon his back. We have both been tired, he thought, and have slept long, and he was glad that he had not wakened her. The down all around him was empty and refreshingly safe, and though danger might be lurking in the world below, it was dwarfed

by distance. Somewhere twelve miles away lay Lewes,
but for a little he need have no care of that. He was
perched high up upon a safe instant of time and he
clung hard to that instant, drowning all thought in
mere sensation, the sight of the country unrolled like
a coloured map below him, the feel of warmth creeping from neck to spine. In that long wash of sun, which
left the moon an indistinct wraith in the transparent,
fragile blue, lay a first hint of spring, and in the breeze,
salt from the Channel, hidden from sight by yet another ridge of down, gorse-laden, prophesying green.
There was no green yet in the coppice, which lay like
a band of soft brown fur fringing the hill, but green
crept cautiously, afraid still of an ambush from winter,
into the flat ploughed fields below, advancing from
pastures where small white sheep were grazing. Dotted
across the distance were toy farms, which displayed
how far from the isolation he had imagined was the
cottage where Elizabeth slept. Along a white road a
scarlet cart crawled like a ladybird along the rim of a
leaf. The Surrey hills peered through a silver veil, as
though they were an old man's face, austere, curious
and indestructibly chaste. A cock a mile away crowed
frosty clarity and a lamb bewildered and invisible
cried aloud. The turf on which he lay was fresh with
the previous rain and mist, yet crisp with salt from the
sea.

At the sound of a horse behind him Andrews turned,
his mind again harried by fear. There was no cause.
Some unknown farmer from the lands below, riding
with uncovered head, passed across the brow of Ditch-

ling Beacon, the horse stepping high and delicately, in
the manner of a great lady conscious of a crowd. With
ears pricked it watched its rider out of the corner of
one desirous eye, heart yearning for the gallop, and
was gone. The olive green slopes lay bare once more
to the spring, which came as Jove to Danae in a
shower of gold. A mile of grass and thirty miles of
sea were carried in the breeze down over Plumpton
and Ditchling and on past Lindfield and Ardingly to
fade only before that quiet, impassive silver veil. Save
for the passing wind and the small dots of moving men
and cattle safely far, the world was motionless. Above
a round blue dewpond a singing bird floated in the
air like a scrap of charred paper, too light to stir.

She will be awake now, he thought, and coming
down the stairs into the kitchen. I wish I had stayed
to thank her. Will she realise what the knife means?
He watched the cottage intensely, and as though it
were a signal of remembrance to him upon the down
a puff of white smoke emerged from the single chimney, hung whole for a moment in the sky and then was
broken into fragments. Some the sun caught, so that
they seemed like a drift of birds, wheeling and flashing their white underwings. He found in the crevice of
his mind, where childhood harboured, the faint memory
of a pictured saint, a young girl with pale, set face,
round whose head a flock of doves turned and twisted.
He rebuked the uneasiness which had made him leave
his knife. She says there is a God, he thought, and no
God could help but guard her. Yet what strange ideas
of guardianship gods had, for those who were most

their own they often paid with death, as though the failure of life itself was not a breach of guardianship. Andrews instinctively stretched out his arms, as though he would gather the white birds to his breast, as though, if he had indeed been given the power, they would not have dissolved into the flecks of smoke which they were.

I would rather trust a devil to look after his own than a god, he thought, for there seemed to him nothing more final and irrevocable than death. It did not occur to him that Elizabeth's death might be irrevocable only to him and his desire. Thinking of the devil, he thought too of the stubbled face of dead Mr. Jennings. Perhaps he would guard her, as she believed, through the crude force of jealousy. If love survived the body, as church people believed, why not also jealousy, spilt like a bitter wine into the unhoused spirit? Keep her, he implored, till I return, not noticing the paradox of his appeal. He would return the next day or the day after, having fulfilled the letter of his promise.

It was hard to leave this point of the down, where he could watch the cottage. He wanted by the intensity of his gaze to pierce the walls, make a breach through which, even if he were still robbed of sight, the slow sound of her feet might come to him.

"I will return," he said out loud, but the inner critic who had been still for so long roused himself as though at a challenge and taunted him. You coward, what use? What are you that she should look twice at you? At least a fool, he protested, who may be running himself into a trap for her. The mocker spoke suddenly as though in the heart itself, denuded for the once of reproach. Would she not be worthy of the full risk? Then if you come back you bring her something of value. Yes, but that "if". There was the rub. I was born a coward, he protested, and I will live a coward. At least I have shown these fools that I must be reckoned with, and rising and turning his back on the cottage, he began to walk rapidly in the direction of Lewes, as though he would outpace an image moving at his side of a girl's face set between candles, the mouth twisted with the wry taste of a betrayal.

Yet his quick walk soon slackened, for the day was warm, and he was in no hurry to reach Lewes. He paused here to watch the valley and the light on a small squat church, there to drink with a herd of black and white cows at a dewpond on the downs, bright blue from the reflected sky as though it were part of an illuminated Missal. The cows raised their soft eyes, too drowsy for suspicion, and then made room for him. They were contented and at peace and so for a short while was he. But at every reiterated summit on the downs his heart filled with apprehension, lest below him he should see the object of his journey, and filled again with blessed relief as he gazed before him at the inevitable slopes rising in the distance to yet another crest. At the edge of one such summit he heard voices and dropped cautiously into a narrow gorge of chalk, the cold walls on either side gleaming like blue icicles. The voices, however, belonged only to two dark-skinned gipsy youths, trotting intently over the rise followed by a couple of flippant black puppies, who jumped over each other and rolled in the grass mocking their master's serious purpose. Andrews asked the boys whether he was on the right way to Lewes, and they nodded their heads, watching him with the same dark drowsy peace as had the cattle. Then, like all else, they left him to comforting solitude. The minutes and the hours passed him almost unnoticed. He even forgot his fear of reaching the final summit, so inevitable the relief seemed. He was aware only of the warm day dying when he was no longer able to rest so long upon the slopes before chill gripped him.

Slowly the moon which swam far out over the Surrey hills grew more distinct, breasting a tide grown darker blue with the approach of evening. Somewhere out by Hassocks the sun sank level with the downs, which lay, barred with the last parallel gold rays pointing to Lewes. Up Harry's Mount he climbed, his fear forgotten, and reaching its crest looked down with shocked surprise on Lewes, crouching in the valley like a fierce remnant of old winter.

He stood and watched, sick and suddenly tired at heart, half ready to perceive it stretch out an arm to sweep him down. This is the end then, he thought. Must I go down and talk with people again, and be everlastingly careful? Tears of the old self-pity pricked his eyes. There's no rest for me in England, he thought. I'd better go to France and beg. It was not the begging, however, which raised his heart in instant revolt at the suggestion, but the idea of ceding once and for all sight and sound of Elizabeth.

The sun dived with sudden decision into night from the edge of a distant down. The faint gold powder which had strewn the air was brushed away leaving a still, transparent silver. Andrews walked back and forth with puzzled straying steps that he might keep warm till a deeper darkness came. He looked every now and then at the castle which dominated Lewes from its hill. When it should be cloaked from sight he would go down. It seemed an endless while and it was very cold. The prospect of returning that night the way he had come, his promise fulfilled, grew uninviting. Besides what welcome would he get from Elizabeth after so literal a fulfilment? There could be no great danger, he persuaded himself, in staying one night in Lewes. He knew from experience that there were many inns, and fortune could hardly deal so ill with him as to bring him face to face with anyone he knew. Carlyon would not dare to enter Lewes when the Assizes were so imminent and the town full of officers.

The shadows had fallen over the town and he could no longer see the castle, save as an indistinct hump or a shrugged shoulder. He began to walk down by a path longer than it had seemed in the silver light. By the time he had reached the first straggling houses, darkness was complete, pierced here and there by the yellow flicker of oil lamps, crowned by dingy pinnacles of smoke from the lengthening wicks. Cautiously he made his way into the High Street, and stood for a while in the shadow of a doorway, probing his mind

for the position of the various inns. There were few
persons about in the street, which was like the deck of
a sleeping ship lit by two lamps, fore and aft, and on
each side a sudden fall into a dark sea. Opposite him
two old houses leant crazily towards each other, almost touching above the narrow lane called Keerie-
St., which dived chaotically into the night—a few confused squares and oblongs of inn signs, six steep feet
of cobbles and then vacancy. Out beyond, but he
could not see, was Newhaven and the Channel, France.
Even there lay no complete freedom for him. Along
the coasts were scrubby little men, with squinting eyes,
hard wrists and a sharp mispronounced knowledge of
the English coinage who knew his face well and Carlyon's better.

His shoulder falling from force of habit into a self-
pitying droop, Andrews moved further down the
street. Here and there shops were still open, and their
lit windows showed old white-bearded men peering at
their ledgers with little lines of content around their
eyes. Never, not even at school nor under the pain of
the smugglers' hardly veiled contempt, had Andrews
felt so alone. He passed on. Two voices speaking
softly in a doorway made him pause. He could not see
the speakers. "Come to-night," "Shall I? I oughtn't
to." "I love you, love you, love you."

Andrews, to his own surprise, smote the wall against
which he stood with his fist and said aloud with a
crazy fury, "You damned lechers," walked on weeping with anger and loneliness. "I'll be drunk if I can't

be content in any other way," he thought. "I've still enough money for that, thank God."

With sudden resolve he dived down a side street, stumbling at its unexpected steepness, and came to rest with unerring instinct at the door of an inn. Two windows were cracked and stuffed with rags, the sign was long past the possibility of repair. Of the goat, which was the inn's name, remained only the two horns, as though a mocking warning to husbands not to enter. Loneliness and the desire to forget his loneliness drove away even the instincts of fear and caution, and Andrews flung the door carelessly open and stumbled, eyes red and blind with childish tears, within. The air was thick with smoke, and a roar of human voices, each trying to drown the others and make its opinions heard, smote him in the face like a wave. A tall thin man with small eyes and a red flabby mouth, who was standing by the door, caught his elbow. "What do you want, son?" he asked and immediately began to shoulder his way through the throng, calling out to an invisible potman, "Two double brandies for a gentleman here," and presently re-emerged with what he sought, and vanished again with his own quota leaving Andrews to pay. His brandy drunk, Andrews looked round the room with a clearer mind. He chose a small, respectable man, who stood alone, asked him to join him in a drink. Looking deprecatingly at the empty glass in Andrew's hand, the stranger replied that he would not mind a glass of sherry.

Andrews fetched it and himself revived by fresh brandy began to question his new acquaintance.

"I'm looking for a night's lodging," he said. "I suppose that won't be easy now. The town will be full for the Assizes?"

"I can't tell that," the man replied, eyeing him a little askance as though he feared that Andrews was about to ask him for money. "I'm more or less a stranger here myself."

"And these Assizes," Andrews considered, "what are they for anyway? To bring money to the tradespeople. There's no need for such a fuss to hang a few poor skunks."

"I don't agree with you at all——not at all," said the little man sipping his sherry and eyeing Andrews suspiciously. "Justice must be done in the proper order."

"Yes, but what is the proper order," Andrews asked, raising his voice so as to be heard above the din around him and at the same time signalling to the potman that his glass was empty. "Surely the crime and then retribution."

"You must prove the guilt," the stranger said, turning the sherry gently on his tongue.

"Isn't it proved well enough without a judge and jury?" Andrews's caution vanished still further out of sight at the stinging touch of a third glass. "They were caught by the revenue in the act and you can't dispose of a dead body."

The stranger put down his glass of sherry carefully on the edge of the table and eyed Andrews even more curiously. "You are referring to the smugglers and the alleged murder?" he asked.

Andrews laughed. "Alleged!" he cried. "Why, it's patent."

"No man is guilty until he is proved so," the little man commented as though he were repeating a well-learnt lesson.

"Then you must wait till Doomsday in this case," Andrews murmured, with a sudden bitter sense of divine injustice. He who was innocent suffered persecution, while they . . .

"You could not form a jury in Lewes which would convict them." He waved his hand round the inn parlour. "They are all in it," he said, "for fear or profit. If you scarched the crypt of Southover Church you'd find barrels there, and the parson winks an eye. Do you think he wants to lose his whole congregation or perhaps be whipped at one of his own pillars? If you want to stamp out smuggling you must do away with the idea of justice. Have another drink."

"I will wait a little if I may," the stranger moved his position, so that the full light of the oil lamp fell on Andrews's face. The act thrust suspicion into the other's mind. "I must be careful," he thought. "I must have no more to drink." And yet he was certainly not drunk. He saw his surroundings with perfect clarity, and his thoughts were more than usually vivid. He had longed for human companionship and now he had it, and the desire to fling his arm round the shoulder of the little man opposite him was nearly overmastering. He had so longed to talk to someone, who knew nothing of his past, who would treat him with neither kindness nor contempt, and consider his words with the same respect as he would show to those of any other man.

"You will take another glass?" the stranger said stiffly and shyly, as though unaccustomed to the procedure of standing drinks.

"What is your name?" Andrews said quickly, with a feeling of pride at his own cunning.

"Mr. Farne," the other replied without hesitation.

"Farne," Andrews said slowly. He pondered the name. That it was an honest one he could not doubt. "Thank you," he said, "I will."

When he had drunk, the world seemed a fairer place than it had seemed for a long while. There was companionship in it and Mr. Farne, who listened to him without mockery and never once reminded him of his father.

"Perhaps you did not know my father?" he asked hopefully.

"I had not that pleasure," said Mr. Farne.

Andrews laughed. Mr. Farne was an ideal companion, for he was a wit. "Pleasure!" he grimaced. "You can't have known him."

"What was his name?" Mr. Farne asked.

"The same as mine." Andrews retorted, with a laugh. It seemed to him that he had combined in a sentence of four words the quintessence of witty retort and of caution. For clearly he must not disclose his name to Mr. Farne.

"And what is that?" asked Mr. Farne.

"Absolom," Andrews mocked.

"I am sorry, but I am a little deaf . . ."

"Absolom," Andrews repeated. Mr. Farne, the sweet simpleton, was taking him seriously. To prolong the excellent joke he searched his pockets for a scrap of paper and a pencil, but could find neither. Mr. Farne, however, supplied both. "I will write my name down," Andrews said. He wrote "Absolom, son of King David."

Mr. Farne's laugh suddenly ceased. He stared at the scrap of paper in front of him. "You make very curious capital letters," he said.

"Long tails to them," Andrews answered. "I was always fond of women." He stared round him. "Isn't there a woman in this place that's worth looking at?" he called angrily. "There's no one here, Mr. Farne," he said, "let's go into the town."

"Women do not attract me," Mr. Farne said coldly.

"There's one that would," Andrews stared at him with serious melancholy eyes. "Have you ever seen a saint surrounded with white birds? And yet a woman you know that could give a man pleasure. But she's too good for that. You mustn't laugh. I mean it. I call her Gretel. I don't believe that any man will ever touch her."

"You are a very strange young man," Mr. Farne said deprecatingly. Andrews was arousing attention. They were being stared at. A few men were pressing close, while a fat woman began to laugh shrilly and continuously.

"You don't believe me," Andrews said. "You would if you saw her. I'll show you though. Give me that pencil and paper and I'll draw her."

A tall loose-jointed man with a scrubby beard began to clear a circle on a table. "Look, folks," he said, "here's an artist. He's going to draw us a woman, a peach of a woman."

"Where's the paper and the pencil?" Andrews asked.

Mr. Farne shook his head. "Here is the pencil," he said. "I can't find the paper. It must have fallen on the floor."

"Never mind, dearie," the fat woman called. "Here George, get us some paper," she implored the potman.

"Any paper will do," Andrews cried, exhilarated by the attention he had aroused.

They found him an old envelope and crowded close; Mr. Farne, however, stood a little apart. Andrews knelt down at the table and tried to steady his hand. "Now, nothing indecent, mind," the potman called across with a laugh.

"Here, give the boy a whisky on me," said the fat woman. "There, that will clear you, dearie. Now, show us your little friend."

Andrews drained the glass and picked up the pencil. Clearly in front of him he saw Elizabeth's face, white, set and proud, as he had seen it first, when she pointed the gun at his breast. He knew that they were mocking him, but he had only to show them that face for them to fall quiet and understand. He held the pencil awkwardly in his fingers. How should he begin? He had never drawn a picture in his life, but when he could see her there so clearly, it must be easy. He would draw the candles first with their yellow flames.

"She's a bit of a stick, isn't she, dearie," said the fat woman, "where are her arms?"

"She wants more than arms," the loose-jointed man winked and grinned over Andrews's head and made obscene gestures with his fingers. "Give him another drink."

"That's not her," Andrews said, "those are candles. I'm going to start her now." He made a few strokes with the pencil and then, putting his head upon his hands, burst into tears. "I can't," he said, "I can't. She won't come here." Her face was going away from him very far off. Soon only the glow of the candles would be left. "Don't go," he implored aloud.

He heard them laughing round him, but with his head bowed and eyes shut, he tried to bring back that vanishing image. Good god, he thought, I can't even remember how her hair curls. I must be drunk.

"Never mind, I'll stay, dearie," said the fat woman, bending over him with a giggle, her whisky-laden breath driving like a fume of smoke between his eyes and what he sought.

Andrews jumped to his feet. "I don't know what's the matter with me," he said unsteadily. "Haven't had anything to eat to-day," he swayed a little on his feet. "Bring me some sandwiches." He felt in his pockets and found nothing there. He had spent his last penny. "No, don't," he said and moved towards the door. A vague feeling of shame suffused his mind. He had tried to bring Elizabeth into this company and he had been fittingly punished. This laughter soiled the thought of her. "Be quiet, damn you," he cried.

The cool air of the streets went to his head as though it were another glass of spirits. The pavement surged under his feet and he leant back against a wall, feeling sick and tired and ashamed. He closed his eyes and shut out the vision of the rolling street.

Mr. Farne's quiet, sedate voice spoke through the dark. "You are a very foolish young man," he said, "to drink on an empty stomach."

"O leave me alone," Andrews flung out his hand in the direction of the voice.

"You had better go and have some food," Mr. Farne said.

"All right, but leave me."

"Have you any money?" Mr. Farne persisted.

"No, damn you. Mind your own business." Andrews opened his eyes and scowled at Mr. Farne, who stood watching him with a puzzled face.

"I meant no harm," said Mr. Farne. "Will you dine with me, Mr. Absolom?"

Against his own inclination Andrews laughed. The gullible fool really believes, he thought, that I am Absolom. "I'll come," he said, "if you don't mind holding my arm, my legs are weak. Hunger takes me like that."

He found himself walking down the High Street, held upright by a steady arm. Outside a public house three Bow-street runners in red waistcoats watched their passage with superior contempt. "This town's full of robin red-breasts," he commented with a grimace.

"The Assizes," said Mr. Farne. They stayed for a moment outside a square building above the window of which a fat female justice held the inevitable scales. "Here," Mr. Farne said, "is where your friends the smugglers will be dealt with."

Andrews shook off his arm and turned to face him. "What in hell do you mean," he said, "by my friends? They are no friends of mine."

"A figure of speech only," Mr. Farne protested.

"You may hang the lot for me," Andrews exclaimed, sobered for the moment by suspicion.

"We hope to," said Mr. Farne gently. He put his arm round Andrews's shoulder. "I am lodging just opposite The White Hart," he said. "Will you dine with me there?"

Andrews looked down at his muddy clothes. "Drunk and dirty," he said, and added with a laugh a little self-consciously forlorn, "and damnably hungry."

"I have a private room," Mr. Farne encouraged him. "They do a good steak," he added softly.

"Take me to it," Andrews said. He put his hand to his head in a sudden longing to clear it. What was he doing dining with this Mr. Farne? Who was Mr. Farne? What had he said to him? "I must be careful," he thought, and at the sound of that word, which seemed to have haunted him for weeks, his desperate longing for peace returned, a peace which would be empty of caution and deception and in which he could draw back to him that image which drink had obscured. "I'm tired," he said aloud.

"You can sleep here," Mr. Farne said, nodding towards the inn on the other side of the road.

In a despairing dream Andrews was led across the

road and into a dimly lighted hall. "If they'll let me
sleep here to-night," he thought, "to-morrow I'll return over the downs." He remembered the afternoon
sun and the blue dewpond at which he drank watched
by the lazy cows and on the other side of the downs
Elizabeth sat alone before a fire mending a dead man's
stocking. Mr. Farne was leading him up a dark stair-
case, and in the ancient mirror at its head he saw a
dirty, bedraggled youth stagger towards him. "What
charity to shelter that," he thought.

Mr. Farne gently turned the handle of a door and
ushered Andrews in. The door closed behind him.
"Forgive my disturbing you, Sir Henry," Mr. Farne
said.

CHAPTER VII

A TALL, thin man with sharp pointed face sat at a
table laid for dinner. He had been at most picking at
the food, for he raised not from his plate but from a
stack of papers beside it a pair of dark, tired eyes.
From a high forehead the hair receded in a grey curling
wave.

It was not at him that Andrews stared, but at the
lady who sat with him and who now gazed at Andrews
with a particular challenging air that he knew well
from pothouse women. She was pretty and richly
dressed with a small red pouting impertinent mouth and
curious eyes.

"What is it, Mr. Farne?" the man said, while the woman, resting a round chin on two small fists, stared steadily at Andrews in frank amazement.

Andrews put a hand on Mr. Farne's shoulder and steadied himself. "Invited to dinner," he said, "but I really thought Mr. Farne would be alone. Not dressed for company. I'll be going," and removing his hand, he turned to the door.

"Stay where you are, my man," Mr. Farne said sharply. Andrews stared at him for a moment in amazement, so changed was that gentle voice. "My man." That was what one called a servant. "Look here," he said, anger rising slowly through a brain dizzy with drink, "who do you think you are talking to? Just because you know I haven't a penny. How dare you 'my man' me?" He clasped and unclasped his fingers, exercising them before they should play their part in shaking Mr. Farne. Mr. Farne paid no attention, but crossed to the man at the table and began to whisper.

"Suppose that *I* called you 'my man'?" the woman said in a soft, rather sugary voice. She reminded Andrews of a young and desirable Mrs. Butler.

"For heaven's sake, Lucy," her companion murmured, "can't you keep your fingers off any man?"

She shrugged her shoulders and pouted at Andrews. "You see," she said, "what a bear he is? Can't you imagine what it's like living with him?"

Andrews, catching sight above a low-cut dress of fine shoulders and the beginnings of two firm young breasts, smiled back. I must be very drunk, he thought.

Here was a young and easy woman. O, to have a clear brain.

"Will you come and sit down here, Mr. Absolom?" the man with the tired eyes said, and Mr. Farne pulled out a chair opposite the girl. Andrews sat down and found a glass of muscatel at his hand. He sipped a little. "It's good of you," he said and repeated his earlier statement, "not dressed for company." He scowled at Mr. Farne who had taken a chair on his other side nearer the door. "Introduce me," he said.

"This is Sir Henry Merriman," Mr. Farne said. The named seemed somehow familiar to Andrews. "Your good health, Sir Henry," he said and spilt a little wine on the table cloth. Mr. Farne fidgeted.

"And I," said the girl opposite him, smiling maliciously at Mr. Farne, "am the not very respectable appendage of Sir Henry. Mr. Farne does not approve of me. Mr. Farne, you know, is a regular churchgoer."

"Hold your tongue, Lucy," said Sir Henry sharply. He raised his glass to Andrews. "And your health, Mr. ——," he stopped and waited. The eyes were dark rimmed, as though he spent too few of his hours in sleep. Somewhere very deep in them lay a sharp gleam like a candle shining at the end of a succession of long, dim halls.

"Mr. Absolom,'" Andrews said.

Sir Henry laughed courteously. "Yes, but your real name?" When Andrews did not answer, he asked with an air of polite, indifferent inquiry, "Is it perhaps Mr. Carlyon?" The candle was growing larger

and brighter. It was being carried forward by an unseen hand through the long dusty chambers.

Oh, but this was comic, Andrews thought. To be
mistaken for Carlyon of all people. He began to laugh
so loudly and uncontrollably that he found it hard to
answer. "No, no, not Carlyon," he spluttered.

Straight on top of his own words came Sir Henry's.
"But you know Carlyon?" The air of indifference had
gone. Something urgent and fanatical had taken its
place. The voice cut through the mist of drink straight
to Andrews's understanding. "What do you mean?"
he cried. He got unsteadily to his feet. "I'm going. I
won't stay here to be insulted. Of course I don't know
him. What should I know a damned smuggler for?"
He put his hand to his head and cursed himself. He
was not so drunk that he did not know that he had
betrayed himself again. Drink and hunger had confused
him. He was no match for sober wits. "I'm going," he
repeated.

"Sit down," Mr. Farne said sharply. He rose and
locked the door. Andrews watched him in amazement
and then sat down. They were too much for him.

"Lucy, you'd better go to bed," said Sir Henry.

She made a grimace at him. "I won't be sent to
bed," she said. "I'll either stay here or go down to
the bar and find some company."

"Oh stay then," Sir Henry replied, as though too
tired to argue. He turned to Andrews. "Now, young
man, you may as well tell us everything. We are
friends. We only want to help you."

"This is a free country," Andrews protested mechanically, "you can't keep me here if I want to go."

"Why no," Sir Henry said "but there is nothing to prevent my handing you over to the police."

"Oh, I don't fear that," Andrews answered. "On what charge?"

"Smuggling," said Mr. Farne, "and murder."

"Why should you give us that trouble?" Sir Henry continued. "You are innocent, I know, of the second charge."

"Well, then, why can't you leave me alone?" Andrews muttered with sulky tearfulness.

"I am here," Sir Henry said with unexpected energy, "to hang these murderers. You want that, too, don't you?"

I must be careful, Andrews told himself, give away nothing. "I don't know what you mean," he said aloud.

Mr. Farne sniffed impatiently and Sir Henry fidgeted with his fingers. "You informed against these men," he said. "An anonymous letter to the Customs," he looked up at Andrews with contempt and curiosity.

"Why do you say I did it?" Andrews asked.

"Oh, there's no doubt. No doubt at all." He spread a dirty envelope on the table. "Absolom, son of King David. Look at this capital A and this K. You gave yourself away finely, my friend. I have your letter to the Customs in my pocket. You wrote it with your left hand, but you can't destroy those twirls and twists."

"All right," Andrews gave a gesture of surrender, "I'll admit it. Only give me something to eat."

"Go and find a waiter, Lucy," Sir Henry said, "and tell him to bring up a steak for Mr. ——."

"Andrews."

"And tell him also that he must find a bed in the hotel. Mr. Andrews is staying here for the next few days."

They did not speak to him again, until he had eaten. He felt then not only refreshed but clearer in the brain. He was caught, and deep beneath his superficial fear, he was thankful. The initiative had been taken out of his hands. He was being driven remorselessly along the right road, and it was no use to struggle any more. He glanced surreptitiously round him. Mr. Farne was reading and Sir Henry was deep in his papers, his long, white, unringed hands moving nervously in rhythm with his thoughts. The girl was dozing in her chair. He watched her with greedy interest. "What fun can she get out of that man?" he thought. "He thinks of nothing but his work. He can't make her wriggle as I could." For one moment he was perturbed by the thought of Elizabeth. She was more desirable and more lovely, but infinitely more distant. "It's hopeless," he thought. "What's the use of thinking of her?" He could not believe that she was intended for any man and least of all for himself. Besides it was because of her that he found himself here and why should he not take the fun when he must needs take the risk? Here was someone who was not too good for him, formed of the same lustful body and despicable heart.

She opened her eyes and found him watching her.

She smiled. "We must find some clean clothes," she said. "I'm sure Mr. Farne would lend you some of his. They are very sober of course. Mr. Farne is a churchgoer." Mr. Farne jumped out of his chair and walked with little irritated steps towards the window, where he stood, his back turned to them, watching the High Street with a forced interest. "Mr. Farne and I have never been true friends," she said, her small lips twisting at the corners with annoyance that there should be any man who did not desire her and contempt that Mr. Farne should be so lacking in what she considered manhood.

Sir Henry looked up from his papers. "Go to bed, Lucy," he said with asperity.

She watched him mischievously. "And you?" she said.

"I am busy," he said.

Her face was momentarily touched with a very faint tenderness. "You are not going to work again all night, Henry?" she asked. "You must get some sleep."

He said, "I'm all right," with a slight tone of astonishment, as though he were surprised at an unaccustomed anxiety. "Go along now. I've got a lot of work to do before to-morrow."

She got up, but before she went to the door, paused for a moment at the table. "You are overworking," she said.

He smiled. "It's my career. Besides, I particularly want to win this case."

"You'll kill yourself sooner or later," she said.

"O you needn't be afraid," he said drily and impatiently. "I'll find you a new keeper first."

She flushed and glanced at Andrews with an angry smile. "I can find one for myself at any time," she replied.

"I should not advise you to choose Mr. Andrews," Sir Henry said with an amused smile, as though he were watching an angry and ridiculous child. "Mr. Andrews lacks means." She went out and slammed the door behind her.

Andrews was confused, but not this time with drink. He felt as if he had come suddenly out of a mysterious windswept silence into a place of hurried noise and movement and crowds. A temporary homesickness for the cottage and Elizabeth was banished by Lucy's smile, which promised "fun". If she intends to play me off against this man Merriman, he thought, I'm game. Drink no longer blurred his brain, but it had left a small restless feeling of desire and a strong belief in his own fascination. He longed to follow Lucy out of the room.

"Look here," he said, "what do you want with me?"

Sir Henry looked up. "Are you sober now?" he asked.

"I was never drunk," Andrews said angrily. "Only hungry."

"Well, then, what I want is to see you in the witness box. I'm leading for the Crown. If you are not a witness you must see for yourself that there's only one other place for you."

"What use am I to you?" Andrews protested. "I'd gone before the fight began."

"That doesn't matter," Sir Henry said. "All I want is your evidence that these men landed, that you were with them when they landed."

"But the risk?" Andrews said.

"You should have thought of that when you sent the letter. But I'll do my best for you. I'll have you watched as long as you stay in Lewes. You can remain at this inn. I've had a room taken for you. Afterwards it's your own look-out, but you'll have the whole of England to drop into. You exaggerate the risk. I advise you, however, after this to give up smuggling." He looked at Andrews curiously. "I can't imagine why you ever started. You talk like an educated young man."

"I can read Latin and Greek, if you call that education. I haven't been taught how to live. What can I do when this is over?"

Sir Henry tapped the table impatiently with his fingers. "You are a lucky find for me," he said. "There's no cause to be grateful to you, but I'll give you some introductions in London when this trial is over. You ought to be able to get a job as a clerk. But you had better act honestly in the future or you'll end where I hope your companions will end."

"Don't prate to me," Andrews cried, "about honesty. You are not risking your life in this trial as I am. You are paid for it."

"Don't be impertinent," Mr. Farne returned from

the window. "You are doing this to save your own skin, not for justice."

"For neither, I think," Andrews replied, his anger dispelled by the vision of Elizabeth raising his cup to her lips. But I can never return there, he thought. When this is over I must clear out. I don't suppose I shall ever see her again. The thought was a sharp pain, which made him clench his hands and long for the relief of tears. Deliberately he turned his back in mind upon the cottage and shut out all sight and sound and remembrance of it, and fixed instead his eyes upon the danger in front of him which he must be cunning to evade. In this quiet room over the High Street, in the presence of the two barristers, all fear of violence seemed absurd. The peace which he had experienced the night before was like a dream, and into a dream nightmare could easily enter. But now he was awake, amid real surroundings, among calm, ordinary people, and it was impossible to believe that he was really hunted by a sudden death. His flight seemed no longer to be necessarily eternal. When this was over he would go to London and leave the past behind and live like an ordinary man, working daily for his bread. I shall be able to buy books, he thought, his heart leaping, and go in and listen to the music at St. Paul's and the Abbey. The streets would be full of cabs and the pavements crowded with people. He would walk here and there and be no more conspicuous than an ant in an ant hill. It would be a pain to be so happy, he thought, and then realised that that ache was not a prophecy of bliss but of vacancy. He put his head on his hands.

What will be the use, he wondered, with my life empty of her for ever? When it was warm, he would want her to be with him to bask in the warmth and when cold to crouch with him over the fire. Always in his brain when he woke would be the thought, she is only a few hours away. Go and see if she is in the cottage. She may have moved or be lost or be dying or hungry or lonely. And every morning fear would struggle with the thought and win. There could be no more peace for him in that constant struggle than in flight. What then am I to do? he asked himself with a tired gesture of the hands.

The two barristers were speaking to each other, ignoring Andrews.

"And Parkin?" Mr. Farne said. "What do you think of Parkin?"

"He's the best judge the prisoners could have. He's a conceited windbag who likes to hear the sound of his own voice. If there's one honest man on the jury Parkin will alienate him by his snobbery or else confuse him by the length of his summing up. Farne, you ought to be going to bed. You've got a long day in front of you and the best part of the evening too if I know Parkin. He'll sit till there are no more candles to burn."

"And you, Sir Henry?" Mr. Farne asked with a trace of anxiety.

"Oh I, Farne, I've still a little more work to do. I need less sleep. I'm older. Farne, shall we get a conviction?"

"Not unless you get some sleep, Sir Henry."

"I don't know why you are all worrying like this—you and Lucy. Farne, will there ever be a time when a jury can be trusted to give a verdict according to the evidence in a smuggling case? It makes one tired of justice and long for martial law."

"Don't say that, Sir Henry. Justice is justice. What about this man, Sir Henry? Do you want him any more to-night?"

They are treating me like a servant again, Andrews thought, but his anger had no time to rise before it was quenched by Merriman's tired, courteous tones. "A waiter will show you to your room, Mr. Andrews," he said. "Sleep well. To-morrow we face the guns." He passed his hand across his face as though he were trying to remember all those things which are necessary to the comfort of men to whom work was not the great and most abiding pleasure. "If you are thirsty, Mr. Andrews," he said, "order what you like." Mr. Farne grunted disapprovingly, and holding open the door waited for Andrews to pass through.

"I should advise you to drink no more to-night," he said, when they stood in the dark passage without. "Good night."

Andrews watched his small trim figure in its dark clothes move down the passage, turn a corner and vanish from sight. "To-morrow we face the guns." He had not expected to be called upon so soon. Panic buffeted against his resignation to fate. I could slip out of the hotel to-night, he thought. But what then? An endless repetition of last week. And if he stayed? Danger will at least be plain and in front of me, he

considered, fear nevertheless catching at his throat.
His mouth and lips were dry. It would be easier to
decide what he should do over a glass. He moved to
the stairhead and became aware of a candle flame
moving up towards him. But it was not the flame itself he saw but its reflection in the large mirror at the
sharp turn of the stairs below him. The candle passed
and he became aware of Sir Henry's companion visaged
in the glass. Her body was indistinct, owing to the dark
blue velvet of her dress which fell almost to her small
feet and then trained off into the darkness behind. The
white face with its red, vivid lips stared back at itself
with an expression of anxiety. The candle was lowered
a little way in a long gloved hand and shone on lovely,
exquisitely sloping shoulders and the fall of the young
breasts. The face leant forward and stared cautiously
from the mirror at the invisible reality before it. So
close must the girl have been, although hidden from
Andrews's eyes by the turn of the stairs, that a mist
from her breath marred the image. A hand appeared
and brushed it away, with a cautious secretive movement. Andrews stepped down the stairs, and the image
startled moved back out of the mirror, but round the
corner he came on the living person.

"Looking at yourself?" he said with a forced, embarrassed laugh.

"To see whether I am beautiful," she answered challengingly.

"You needn't do that," he said.

"Are you a judge?" she asked.

"I've known a lot of women," Andrews said boastfully, "but none as lovely as you—in face," he added with a sudden sense of loyalty to Elizabeth.

"Or in body?" she said, flashing the candle from her head to feet.

"Nor in body," he repeated reluctantly.

"But then you are so young," she came a little nearer to him. "An older man would not think so."

Andrews thought of the man working, working, working above his head. "Are you in love with that old man?" he asked.

She leant against the baluster. "How do I know?" she murmured. "He's been kind to me. I've been with him for three years. But he's getting more and more tied up in his work. He'll turn me off soon, I expect. No, I'm not in love with him, but after three years one has a sort of fondness for a man."

"It must be a dull life for you," Andrews said.

"You mean," she laughed, "that you want to make love to me." She looked him up and down between narrowed lids. "It would be dull if I troubled to be faithful. You are staying in the hotel, aren't you? We must really find you some clean clothes."

Andrews shifted his gaze a little. "I shouldn't trouble," he said and began to move down the stairs. She watched him closely and shrewdly and then barred his passage. "Where are you going?" she asked.

"Only to have a drink."

"And aren't you enough of a gentleman to ask me to join you?" Her voice was mocking with an aftertaste of suspicion. "All right. Come along," he said. He did not look at her as they descended the stairs, but told himself over and over again that his position was too serious to think about "fun", that he must come to his decision to go or stay uninfluenced by the restless prick of desire which grew on him at every step.

She led him into a room where a fire still sent out desultory tongues of flames at lengthening intervals. It was empty. All the other visitors had gone to their rooms. She rang for a waiter and gave an order and he returned with a glass of port and a glass of whisky.

Andrews watched her as she sipped the port. "Your lips are the lovelier colour," he said.

"Pretty," she laughed, and turning to the fire stirred it with her foot so that shadows were driven into life and danced across her face. "Tell me, why did you betray those men?"

"You wouldn't understand," he said with conviction. "It was jealousy of a dead man and because I was despised by them."

"It doesn't sound sense to me," she said, "but I suppose you got something out of it."

"Fear."

"Is that all? I'd have made certain of something more. And Henry's putting you into the witness box to-morrow? I shall come and see. You mustn't be as reticent as you are with me." She looked at him more closely. "You are going aren't you?" she asked.

"Of course," he said abstractedly. She stepped back from the fire, glass in hand, to his side, so that his leg felt the shape and touch of her thigh beneath the velvet. His reason gave way beneath a sudden access of desire. He took her in his arms and kissed her lips and throat and breast, and as she remained unresisting with the passivity of the women whom he had met in common bars, his own desire grew, his hands strayed about her, till finally he stepped aside panting and half way to tears.

"You are a funny boy," was all she said.

He damned himself for a swine as he thought of Elizabeth. But that was all over and why should he not have fun where he found it? That other air is too rarefied for me, he thought. Let me stick in my own sty.

"I want you," he said aloud.

She leant a little towards him. "And you expect me to fall into your bed at your wish?" she said. "You'd be a funny choice for me, wouldn't you? A penniless smuggler, who's betrayed his fellows. And a mere boy." She smiled. "That's the one attraction," she murmured, with an appraising glance. "You have a cool impertinence. I feel half inclined—— It must be this damned spring weather beginning." She came close to him and suddenly pressed her lips on his mouth. They tasted sweet with port. "How he bores me with his work," she said. "When all's said there's only one amusement while one's young."

Andrews's lips and mouth felt dry with excitement. "Can I come up with you?" he asked.

She pouted her lips. "No, not to-night, I'm sleepy. Not inclined."

Desire and caution could not live at one time in Andrews's brain. "You won't see me again," he said.

She laughed at him. "Do you think that I mind? One doesn't discriminate in spring. It would be fun to hook Mr. Farne. Do you think that these sober church-going people behave like everyone else? But I doubt if the trial will be over to-morrow."

"I'll be gone to-morrow," he said.

She looked up in quick suspicion. "You mean you are running away?" she asked.

"Why should I stay? It only means danger for me."

"But Henry?"

"What on earth is he to me?"

She watched him thoughtfully. "He's set his heart on winning this case," she said.

"Is that where his heart is?"

"Oh, I may hate him for it," she exclaimed, "but it's great anyway. I shall be leaving him soon. I want excitement. I shall grow old too quickly with him or else he'll find me out. But I'd like him to win this case. He has worked so hard for it."

"Well, let him win it without me."

"Listen," she stood in front him with small chin raised challengingly in the air, "you can have me—to-morrow night, if you'll pay for me. And the payment I want is your evidence for Henry. You can boast afterwards that you've got me at a cheaper rate than any other man has done."

"Too high," he said.

"How can you tell?" she answered. "Give me your hand. Now feel here and here and here. Now give me your mouth. Can you feel me here close to you? That

is right. Hold me so. You may have me closer than
this if you will. You know I am young—as young as
you are. Don't you think it would be worth a little
danger?"

"To-night, to-night," he implored.

"No, not to-night. To-morrow night or never at all.
What a trifling danger. This is England, a civilised
country. The danger is worse for me. Suppose Henry
should find us like this—or to-morrow night. How
would he find us then? He will be working late. You
may come to my room. They have given me a fine,
soft bed. You are so young, I am sure that there are
still things that I can show you. It will be fun. I shall
enjoy myself."

"To-night. I can't wait."

She released herself and stood away watching him
with a cool, amused glance. "Never unless you do
what I say," she said. "Think of that never. Will you
ever have such a rich chance again? I don't know
why I'm offering it to you. I suppose it is pity for
Henry and this spring weather. You are a likelier
man than anyone else I've seen in this hotel."

He watched her closely. Never before had he desired a woman so much—no, not Elizabeth. There was
a kind of mystery in Elizabeth, a kind of sanctity which
blurred and obscured his desire with love. Here was no
love and no reverence. The animal in him could ponder
her beauty crudely and lustfully, as it had pondered the
charms of common harlots, but with the added spice of
a reciprocated desire. It is true, he thought, what

danger can there be? This is a civilised land. I will go to London and I shall not be lonely without Elizabeth for I shall have many other such adventures as this.

"Do you agree?" she asked.

"Yes," he said. "And you—it shall be to-morrow night?"

"Unless the court sits too late. Nothing will make me stay awake for you." She yawned. "How naughty of me it is. Henry would be furious with me," she murmured with a smile of very faint amusement. "But I am so deathly bored. It is a mistake to live with a man for three years. He almost regards me as his wife, is virtuous with me, continent. I can't bear that. Good night." She held out her hand, but he ignored it. "I have bought her," he thought, "why should I be polite? I have touched a better hand."

"Good night," he said.

She shrugged her shoulders, grimaced at him and passed through the door. Shadows swept around her, drowned her dress and body in darkness, so that for a brief moment her white face alone was visible and seemed to be floating disembodied in the dark. Then that too vanished and he heard the stairs creak under her running footsteps.

"To-morrow we face the guns." He was doing for a wrong reason what he had refused to do for a right. He had turned a deaf ear to what his heart, supported by the critic within, had asked of him, but he had capitulated at the first hungry wail his dirty, lusting body had uttered. His body had feared death and shrunk from danger. "If you had conquered that fear," the reproachful critic murmured, "when Elizabeth spoke, I would have upheld you. Now your body has chosen and your body shall stand alone."

CHAPTER VIII

A LITTLE after midnight it began to rain, a dull steady dripping rain which never ceased. The sun rose, but not into sight. Grey banked clouds slowly appeared, and that was the one sign of day. Along Lewes High Street there was no sound save the regular drip, drip of water from pipes and gables and sign boards. Water streamed from the hair, the robes and the sword of the fat stone Justice on the Assize Court, as though she had just risen from the leaden waves of a "pleasure resort", like Venus out of the Mediterranean. Unperturbed by cold and damp she stared across the street at the windows of the White Hart with an expressionless gaze. A blind was raised and a young man looked out for a moment at the street. Through another window the fading light of a candle could be seen moving upwards, as an elderly, sharp-featured man mounted the stairs to bed. The flames of the two street lamps ceased to be bright gold breaches in the dark and became finally a faint yellow smear on a grey page. Presently an elderly man shuffled along the pavement and

turned them out. By order of Lewes Corporation day
had officially begun.

For several hours yet there was no movement of
human beings in the street. A thin grey cat trod delicately along the gutter in a kind of dignified despond-
ency, and a dog came trotting from a side turning,
tail erect in spite of the rain. The cat leapt up three
steps of a house and stood with bristling curved back,
spitting defiance, while the dog, crouching close to the
ground, barked in short, sharp bursts, more for amusement than for any real enmity. The blind of the White
Hart was again raised and the same young man looked
out, watching the by-play with an intent interest. He
was fully dressed and his eyes were strained as though
he had been unable to sleep. The cat, suddenly conscious that she was a show for two male creatures,
leapt on a railing and disappeared. Dog and man
watched in disappointed boredom the steps on which
she had stood.

About an hour later a gang of men appeared with
brooms and attempted the impossible task of cleaning
the street in preparation for the coming of the judge.
Sir Edward Parkin was a man of the utmost fastidious-
ness and the Mayor had learned at a previous Assizes
the unpleasant results of displeasing him. While the
men scrubbed and brushed and the falling rain defeated their efforts, the clock of St. Anne's Church
struck seven and the High Street sprang automatically
to life. A milk cart rattled down the road, blinds clat-
tered up, the smell of cooking foods crossed the street,
maids came out of doors and emptied pails of water on

the steps. As the day advanced little knots of people collected on the pavement and turning their backs on the Assize Court stared up the street. They were waiting for the judge.

In his lodgings Sir Edward Parkin buttered his toast deliberately. He was a short, plump man with a very white face and very white hands. It was rumoured in London that he powdered them like a woman. His voice, when he spoke across the table to his marshal, was high and affected. It played tricks at an empyrean height, curvetting like a skittish mare. He complained peevishly of the breakfast which had been laid before him.

At the White Hart Sir Henry Merriman breakfasted with his papers before him on some dry toast and coffee. Lucy was still in bed, and Mr. Farne at the other end of the table was silent and thoughtful.

Sir Henry looked up. "Is he still in the hotel?" he asked.

Mr. Farne nodded.

"Will he stay the course, I wonder?"

Mr. Farne shrugged his shoulders.

Outside, the javelin men marched along the street to the judge's lodgings, their bright uniforms shining dimly through the grey veil of rain. They were followed at a short interval by the trumpeters of the local militia. They formed up outside the lodgings and Sir Edward Parkin rose, dusting crumbs from his knees. He had timed his breakfast to a minute. He sent his marshal out to find snuff. "It must be Bentley's."

At the prison they were fastening the irons on six

men. Five were big bearded fellows who cursed, defiantly but in the best of humour. Their lawyer had seen them the previous day and he was supremely confident in the jury. They only needed a loophole for an acquittal and that loophole he had devised. The sixth man had not understood what the lawyer had said. He dimly realised that a man was dead, and he was in the dock for murder. He was white and shaken by sudden bouts of terrified tears. He was the half-witted boy Tims.

Some time before this a maid had knocked on Andrews's door and offered him breakfast. He had refused it. He had no appetite. He felt that it was he who was about to enter the dock and be tried for his life. His mouth was so dry that he wondered how he would be able to answer counsel's questions. "I am doing the right thing," he told himself over and over again. "This is what Elizabeth would have me do." But the answer was too obvious. "This is not for her." If only it were. He remembered how the day before he had seen her cottage from the down and had taken the smoke for turning, twisting birds. His heart too had flown that now felt as though it must drag in the mud for ever. He was afraid to raise her image, since it had been so easily and completely defeated by a courtesan. If it had not been for that, for the bargain he had made, he felt that he could have faced his trial, if not with courage, at least with an echo of a resemblance to it.

Somewhere from a long way off there came a broken blare of trumpets. It meant, he knew, that the judge was entering his carriage. Any moment now they would be coming for him. It was not fear so much as disgust and regret that filled his mind to the exclusion of any clear thought—disgust at his actions and his words the night before, disgust at the young lustful woman who had come between him and a strange, purifying dream, regret that he was going to face death for so mean a reason. He heard someone moving on the stairs. Was it too late? He flung himself on his knees beside the bed and prayed for the first time for many years, with a disjointed passion. "O God, if you are God," he implored, "give me courage. Forgive last night. I will try to forget it. I will try not to see that woman again. I will not take her reward. Give, give me back the old motive."

Mr. Farne's face appeared in the doorway. "You must come along," he said. He looked puzzled, embarrassed and therefore a little angry.

Crowds lined the pavements, and a long queue had formed up in front of a side door for entrance to the public gallery. Andrews turned up the collar of his coat, lest he should be recognised. There were many in Lewes who knew his face, innkeepers to whom the smugglers had sold their goods, housekeepers with convenient cellars in which to store barrels.

In the Court was a buzz and movement, which made Andrews feel dizzy and confused. His brain was tired with the constant wakefulness of the previous night, and it was indistinctly, as though through a mist, that he picked out Sir Henry Merriman where he sat at the counsel's table. Mr. Farne had joined him and there was a third man whom Andrews did not know, as well as the two counsel for the prisoners. From where he stood he could not see the occupants of the dock and he was glad. His time would come in the witness box only too soon.

Outside the Court was a clash and rattle as the javelin men grounded their weapons, and then, heralded by a blare of trumpets and the usher's cries, Mr. Justice Parkin entered and took his seat. As though engaged in some children's game of musical bumps the Court bobbed up and bobbed down. Mr. Justice Parkin helped himself to Bentley's snuff, and the buzz of conversation began again, as though the Court were a glass tumbler containing a number of irritated and heated flies. Already the solicitors had begun to yawn.

The Clerk of the Arraigns arose below the Bench and in a tone of intense boredom informed the six men in the dock that the good men whom they would hear called, and severally that did appear, were to pass between them and the King, upon the trial of their several lives or deaths: and that, if they meant to challenge them, or any of them, they must challenge them as they came to the Book to be sworn, and before they were sworn, and they should be heard. He then sat down again, closed his eyes and apparently went to sleep. Mr. Justice Parkin smoothed his hands and gazed at the public gallery, where a number of young women sat.

The panel was then called over. There was a challenge by the Crown to the name of an innkeeper of Southover, and then the Court settled once more into inertia while the jurymen were sworn. Afterwards the Clerk of the Arraigns, rousing himself from his sleep, charged the jury on the indictment against the prisoners and on the Coroner's inquisition. Mr. Justice Parkin, sighing faintly at the necessity of removing his attention from his hands, ordered the witnesses out of Court. A police officer pulled at Andrews's sleeve and led him into a small room marked on the door with a large label in bold vulgar lettering "Male Witnesses only." In the middle of the room was a big, shiny red mahogany table, now covered by hats and coats and sticks. Round the four walls ran a narrow wooden seat tightly packed with people, who stared at him with hostile curiosity. They made no effort to move closer and find him room to sit. Andrews walked to the end of the room and leant against the window, watching his companions out of the corners of his eyes. One side of the room was entirely given up to men in the blue uniforms of the revenue. They commented on his appearance loudly amongst themselves till he found himself blushing scarlet.

"Who's this young child?" said one.

"Can't even dress decently to appear before his lord high mightiness."

"Look at the mud on him. Street scavenger I'd say he is."

An elderly man with a benevolent face called out to him. "What's your name, young fellow?"

Andrews rose trustingly to the kindness in the voice. He felt very alone, standing in an isolated position, stared at and criticised by every man in the room. He longed to make an ally and so he answered promptly and truthfully, "Andrews."

The elderly benevolent man turned sharply to his colleagues. "Andrews," he said, "that's one of the men we've been looking for these last days." He got up and stood in front of Andrews with his hands on his hips. "You ought to be in the dock, you ought," he said. "What are you doing here, eh, contaminating this company? Aye, you've cause to blush, you have. You are among honest men here."

"Can't you leave me alone?" Andrews said. "I'm tired. I haven't had any sleep."

"Nor you ought," the man said. "What are you doing here, aye? Sneaked on your comrades, aye?" He turned to his companions and raised his hands protestingly. "I wouldn't mind now if he was an honest smuggler," he said. "But a sneak thief, a damned informer. It's too thick. Are we going to let him stay in this room among honest men?"

"Hi, boy," called a man from the opposite bench, "is that true? Be you a bloody informer?"

"O' course he is," the elderly revenue man continued, twisting round again to face Andrews. He danced from one foot to the other. "Can't you answer an honest question—you rat?"

Andrews clenched his fists and half closed his eyes. "I'm not low enough to take an insult from a gauger," he said.

"Not, aye?" the benevolent faced man asked and struck Andrews on the face with the palm of his hand. Andrews raised his fist and then let it sink again to his side. O God, he silently implored, let this be my penance for last night. Now do your part and give me courage. Aloud he said, "You are an old man if you are a gauger. I'm not going to fight you," and he turned his back on the room so that no one might see that his eyes were filled with tears. This is not the worst, he thought. How can I go through with this to the end?

"O let him alone, Bill," someone said. "He's only a kid."

"He stinks," said Bill abruptly. "Why should we be put in the same room as an informer? Either he clears out of here or else I clear out."

"You'll clear out anyway," an officer said, putting his head through the door. "Your turn in Court. Get along now. Hurry."

One by one they went, dropping out of Andrews's sight like the sands of an hour glass. He waited nervously for his own name to be called, but still he remained free, free to stare through the window at a rain-lashed sodden yard, with the knowledge that he had not yet finally put the seal upon his treachery. At last the moment came. "Andrews, Andrews," he heard his name called very faintly from the door of the Court, taken up louder and carried along the corridors, till it broke on him where he stood by the window cold and sick and frightened.

The Clerk of the Arraigns sat down and without a moment's interval apparently subsided again into sleep. Sir Henry Merriman rose. "May it please your lordship, gentlemen of the jury . . ." His voice showed no sign of the past sleepless, hard worked hours. Clear, cold, vital, it taunted the minds of all the idle spectators in court. The subdued murmur of conversation in the gallery ceased. The phrases with which he addressed the jury were time worn but were lit with new life by the fire of sincerity in the man himself. "You are to pronounce your verdict on the evidence and on the evidence alone. You are to forget all that you may have ever heard or read on the subject, for it is probably erroneous and is, at all events, unsupported by proof. You are to come to the consideration of this case with pure and dispassionate judgment, to hear the evidence, and give, on that evidence, a true verdict." A true verdict! Watching the twelve men opposite him he searched in vain for one answering spark of sincerity. They watched him back with cow-like, unintelligent and hostile faces. "You are trying to trick us into hanging our friends," they seemed to say.

"Gentlemen, the crime with which the prisoners stand charged is one of great enormity, the death of a man." He was flinging his words against a wall of prejudice. To them he knew very well it was not the death of a man, but only the death of a gauger, the modern publican. It was useless to try and convince them that the life lost had any value. The only way in which he could get a conviction was by leaving them no loophole for acquittal.

"The murdered man, Edward Rexall, was a revenue officer for the County of East Sussex and was stationed at Shoreham. His superior officer, Mr. Thomas Hilliard, acting on certain information, proceeded with Rexall and ten other men on the night of February 10 to a point on the shore three miles east of Shoreham. The officers then concealed themselves behind the sand dunes which at that particular point fringe the shore. This was at 12.15 a.m. At a little after one a red light appeared to seaward hung apparently from the mast of a small lugger. Mr. Hilliard then exposed a lantern found on one of the pack horses. Seven minutes later a ship's boat grounded on the sand. In it were ten men, six of whom we hope to satisfy you are the men now in the dock. They were on the point of unloading a number of casks, when the quietness of the beach and the absence of their friends apparently aroused their suspicions, and they began hastily to re-embark. Mr. Hilliard then showed himself and called upon them to surrender. The smugglers thereupon scattered and ran in various directions along the shore. Mr. Hilliard had, however, so posted his men that they were able to drive the smugglers together again, when they would undoubtedly have captured the whole band, if the smugglers had not opened fire. In the momentary confusion which followed three of the smugglers escaped in the boat. Six, however, were captured, and it was then found that Edward Rexall had been shot dead. From start to end of the struggle no shot was fired by the revenue officers, and if there should be any doubt in your mind on this point, I propose to bring evidence to show that the bullet found in Rexall's body was of a type carried by the smugglers and not of the type served out to officers of His Majesty's service. It is not necessary for the prosecution to prove which of the men in the dock fired the fatal shot. It is not even necessary to prove that it was fired by one of the prisoners and not by one of the band who escaped. It was fired by one of the smugglers, whether he at this moment is standing in the dock or is flying for his life a hundred miles from here, and every member of the gang who took part in the resistance to His Majesty's officers is as guilty of murder as if he was himself seen to fire the bullet which killed Rexall. It is seldom, gentlemen, that murder is committed under circumstances which enable us to bring forward eye-witnesses of the crime. This case, therefore, is an unusually simple one for you to decide. I have detailed to you the principal facts which it is now my duty to establish by competent evidence. I have forborne to state anything which I do not believe will come out in that evidence. If any doubts should arise in your minds, sincere doubts quite apart from any personal knowledge you may have of the prisoners, you will, as you are bound in conscience to do, give the prisoners the benefit of them; but if the case shall be established clearly and satisfactorily, you are equally bound by the oath which you have taken before God, to find that verdict which the well-being of society and the demands of justice require."

Mr. Hilliard was called. His evidence seemed to leave no loophole for acquittal. Sir Henry Merriman, watching the jury between every question, saw them stir restlessly, uneasily. Mr. Braddock, who led for the defence, rose to cross-examine. He was a large man with an apoplectic face which might well have been formed by an undue consumption of contraband liquor. His hair was black, just mottled with grey, but his eyebrows made a continuous dead white streak like a scar across his face. He scowled at Mr. Hilliard, leaned a long way backward, as though the better to spring, wrapped his gown tight round his arms by a fierce cirular movement and pounced.

"Are you considered by your superiors an efficient officer, Mr. Hilliard?"

Mr. Hilliard flushed crimson and gazed appealingly at the judge.

"Is that a relevant question, Mr. Braddock?" said the judge.

"It is, my lord." Mr. Braddock returned briskly. Sir Edward Parkin was visibly put out. "The witness cannot be asked what his superiors think, Mr. Braddock."

Mr. Braddock glared and gulped and turned again on the witness.

"You have been in command of the revenue post at Shoreham for over four years?"

"Yes."

"Have you or have you not received complaints from headquarters that you are not properly fulfilling your duties with regard to the prevention of smuggling?"

"Mr. Braddock," the judge again interrupted, his eyes on the young women in the gallery, "that is not a relevant question."

"My lord," Mr. Braddock fired up, "I am very well

aware of what is relevant and what is not relevant. If the defence is to be hampered . . ."

"That is not the way to address the Bench. You must learn to keep your temper, Mr. Braddock. I am anxious to give the defence every latitude. Well, Mr. Hilliard?"

"I have received complaints, my lord."

"He has received complaints, Mr. Braddock. There you have your answer. Will you proceed?"

"Did you receive a complaint within the last month?"

"Yes."

"Did you say in the hearing of a number of your men that unless something was done quickly you and they would be dismissed from the service?"

"No."

"Now, Mr. Hilliard, think carefully upon that point and remember that you are upon your oath."

"I cannot remember saying so."

"Yes or no, Mr. Hilliard."

Sir Edward Parkin fluttered a white hand impatiently. Attention in the public gallery was becoming too centred on counsel. "The witness has already answered you, Mr. Braddock. He cannot remember."

Mr. Braddock snorted and shrugged his shoulders with an eye on the jury.

"Now, Mr. Hilliard, listen very carefully. I suggest to you that there was urgent need, if you were not to be dismissed from the service, for—shall we say a *grand coup?*"

"I don't know."

"I suggest Mr. Hilliard that your whole story, and the story your men will tell, is a complete fabrication?"

"That's a lie."

"These men are known to be smugglers. I suggest that you arrested them not on the shore but in their homes?"

"That's another."

"Don't laugh at me, Mr. Hilliard. This is a serious matter for you. The jury have only your word and the word of your men against the word of these prisoners in the dock."

"Counsel for the defence," Sir Edward Parkin interrupted, "cannot address the jury. Confine yourself to cross-examining the witness, Mr. Braddock."

"Can I say something, my lord?" Mr. Hilliard asked. "It's not only our word. There's the body."

"I shall come to the body in good time," Mr. Braddock said. "In the last three years, Mr. Hilliard, are these the first successful arrests you have made?"

"Yes."

"I suggest to you that it is curious that after three years of apathy you are able suddenly to hit on the exact portion of shore where these men landed?"

"I acted on information."

"Information is a vague word. Do you mean your imagination?" Mr. Braddock grinned fiercely at the jury and they tittered nervously back.

"No, I received an anonymous letter."

"Have you made any attempt to trace the writer?"

"No."

"Is that letter going to be produced in court?"

"Are you asking for it to be read, Mr. Braddock?" the judge asked.

"No, my lord."

"Well, then, you know as well as I do that it cannot be produced. It's not evidence."

"Your source of information then was an anonymous letter?"

"Yes."

Mr. Braddock laughed. The sound was like the clang of iron gates. "An anonymous letter!" With a rough sweep of his hand he seemed to brush away incredulously the whole story. "I have no more to ask this witness, my lord," he said, and sat down.

"Do you wish to re-examine, Sir Henry?"

Sir Henry Merriman with a faint smile shook his head. Mr. Braddock was behaving exactly as he had foreseen.

The next witness was the elderly gauger with whom Andrews had had his encounter. He repeated the same story as his chief. Mr. Braddock rose to cross examine. He adopted a friendly, insinuating manner which sat on him less naturally than his previous bullying ways.

"Have you been at all afraid of dismissal during the last year?"

"We been all afraid of that."

"Thank you. Did you know the dead man, Rexall, well?"

"Middlin'."

"Are you aware of any quarrel he has had during the last year?"

"Lots."

Laughter broke out in the gallery and the usher had to call for silence several times. Mr. Farne spoke rapidly in Sir Henry Merriman's ear.

"He was of a quarrelsome disposition?"

"Middlin'."

"Did you know personally any of the men in the dock?"

"All of 'em."

"Did Rexall?"

"Aye."

"Thank you. That is all."

Sir Henry gave a nod to Mr. Farne and Mr. Farne rose.

"Are you aware of any quarrel which Rexall may have had with any of the prisoners in the dock?"

"No. We got on middlin' well wi' 'em all."

Mr. Farne sat down.

One after the other the gaugers were called to testify to the truth of Mr. Hilliard's story. Mr. Braddock let them troop in and out of the box without stay, until the last had given his evidence. Then he rose again. He smiled triumphantly at Sir Henry Merriman as he did so, and Sir Henry returned the smile, for he had kept back a trump card, of which Mr. Braddock was unaware.

"Do you know," Mr. Braddock asked, "of any quarrel which Rexall had with one of the prisoners?"

"Aye, it was that scared-looked one in the front row," and the witness, a wizened rat-like man, raised a finger and pointed at the boy Tims.

"Can you tell us about it?"

"Why, 'e met the boy in the street and 'e started a teasing of 'im. An' the boy up an' slapped 'is face."

"And what did Rexall do?"

"Nought. That's only a mad boy."

"Thank you."

Mr. Braddock sat down. Sir Henry turned to Mr. Farne and spoke under his breath. "The swine. They are going to throw suspicion on that half-wit. Shall we re-examine?"

"No need," said Mr. Farne. "Our next witness smashes their whole tale."

"Andrews." The name, his own name, overwhelmed him where he stood by the window. He turned and faced the officer who called him as he would face an enemy, with clenched fists. "Get on, you sneak." A voice came to him from the benches. He wanted to stay and explain, to tell them that he was about to stand in greater danger than did the prisoners in the dock—"betraying them thus openly I stand above them." But bowing his head so that he should not see their contemptuous faces as he passed from the room, passed down the long corridor into the Court. As he went he fingered his cheek, which smarted where it had been struck.

He allowed himself to be pushed forward into the witness box, "the whole truth . . . nothing but the truth," but still did not raise his eyes. He was afraid of the anger and astonishment on the faces of the prisoners. He knew too well how each would look, how

Druce would finger his lower lip, how Hake would pull at a particular portion of his beard. He knew, as though he heard them, the words they would whisper to each other. Haven't I lived with them, eaten with them, slept with them, for three years, he thought. He was afraid to look at the gallery. There would be young, desirable women there who would watch him with contempt—"The informer, traitor, Judas." Not even honour among thieves. And he was afraid, too, damnably afraid. Suppose that he should raise his eyes and see Carlyon there, the ape-like face he had seen transfigured with an ideal, the face which, during three years of misery, he had come near to worshipping, now filled with loathing. It was not incredible. It was just the kind of quixotic, romantic, foolish thing that Carlyon loved—to venture his neck voluntarily into the noose for the sake of his companions.

"Are you Francis Andrews?" It was Sir Henry Merriman who spoke, but the question struck the witness like an accusation, like another blow on the cheek. His blood quickened to meet it. Elizabeth had said to him, "Go to Lewes, go to the Assizes, bear your witness and you will have shown yourself to have more courage than they." You are here for lust for your body, the inner critic murmured, but with a gesture of the hands visible to those in Court, he renounced that motive and that reward. "No," he whispered, his lips moving, "for Elizabeth." The sound of her name gave him courage. It was like a trumpet blown a long way off by a pale courageous spirit. He raised his eyes.

"I am," he answered.

Imagination had steeled him to meet the expected gestures. They did not affect him. For the unexpected he was not ready. Tims leant forward with a smile of recognition and of relief. His smile said as clearly as though he had spoken, "We are all right now. Here's a friend."

Andrews turned his eyes hastily away and watched the gallery.

"Where were you on the night of February 10?"

"On board the *Good Chance*."

"What were you doing there?"

Thank God! Carlyon was not there. "I was engaged in smuggling. We were to run a cargo that night."

Mr. Farne smiled triumphantly along the table at Mr. Braddock and Mr. Braddock scowled back. His purple face turned an unpleasant shade of blue. He rose and began to speak hurriedly to one of the men in the dock.

"How long had you been engaged in this—profession?"

"Three years."

"Do you see any of your companions in the Court?"

Still watching the gallery in fear of seeing a familiar face Andrews nodded. "Yes."

"Will you point them out to the jury?"

Out of the vague turmoil of unfamiliar faces, faces old and young, fat and lean, fresh and faded, swam towards him a man's face, thin, livid, cunning, with receding chin and squinting eyes. The eyes avoided his, but presently returned with a kind of terrified fascination.

"Will you point them out to the jury?" Sir Henry Merriman repeated with impatience. The face knew that it was seen and recognised. A tongue appeared and moistened the lips. The eyes no longer avoided Andrews's, but clung to them in apprehensive appeal. Andrews knew that he had only to raise his finger, point to the gallery, "there," and another of his enemies would be rendered powerless. Only Carlyon and that blundering giant Joe would remain. The face knew it also. Andrews began to raise his hand. It was the safest course. If he let Cockney Harry go free, Carlyon would know for certain who their betrayer was.

"There," he said and pointed to the dock. You fool, you fool, you sentimental fool, he taunted silently in his heart, and his heart marvellously, miraculously, did not care. It was light and drunken with its triumph over his cowardly body and carried with pride like a banner the name of a girl. This will cost you your life, he told himself, but that distant trumpet and that close banner at his heart gave him courage. I will win through, he answered, and she will praise me. This is the first foolish thoughtless thing which I have ever done.

Because he looked no longer at the gallery, Andrews did not see a stout old woman, with flippant streaks of yellow hair, struggling towards the door, and when two minutes later Mr. Braddock, a scrap of white paper in his hand, left the Court, he was answering a question from Sir Henry Merriman. "And what did you do there?"

"I helped load the boat with the casks of brandy.

Then I got in with them and rowed to the shore. They began to unload the cargo, and while they were doing it I slipped away. There was no moon. It was very dark and they did not see me go. I got away among the dunes and hid."

"Why did you slip away?"

"I didn't want to be there when the gaugers appeared."

"How did you know that the gaugers were there?"

"Two days before I had sent an anonymous letter to the officer in command at Shoreham stating the time when we intended to run the cargo and the exact place where it was to be run."

"You went and hid among the dunes. What happened then?"

"There was suddenly a lot of shouting and the sound of men running. Then there were shots. I waited till all the noise was over and then I crept away."

"Now, be careful in answering. Can you tell the jury who were with you when you landed?"

"Yes." He named without hesitation the men in the dock.

"Were there any others?"

"Yes. Carlyon, the leader, a man we called Cockney Harry and Joe Collier."

"Do you know where these men are now?"

Again his eyes met the eyes in the gallery. Again his enemy's eyes were full of terrified appeal. Andrews smiled. He was sure of himself now. "No," he said.

"While you were hiding how many shots did you hear fired?"

"I don't know. They were all together and confused."

"More than one man was firing in fact?"

"Yes. Several."

"It has been suggested that one of your companions had a personal quarrel with the man Rexall. Do you know anything about that?"

"No."

"Thank you. That will do."

As Sir Henry Merriman sat down. Mr. Braddock re-entered the Court.

He smiled a little maliciously at Sir Henry and began his cross-examination.

"How long have you been associated with the crew of the *Good Chance?*"

"For three years."

"Have your relations with them been friendly?"

"In a way."

"What do you mean by 'in a way'?"

Andrews narrowed his eyes and answered not to counsel but to the men in the dock. "I was on sufferance," he said, "treated with contempt. My opinion was never consulted."

"Why didn't you leave them?"

"Mr. Braddock, is this relevant?" Sir Edward Parkin asked, with a note of petulance.

"My lord, in my submission, highly. If your Lordship will have patience—"

"Very well then, go on."

"Why didn't you leave them?" Mr. Braddock repeated fiercely. Andrews turned his eyes away from the familiar faces in the dock and gazed at the red choleric face of counsel. It amused him to think that a man with a face like that should question him on such shadowy things as motives. Facts, hard and firm as chips of wood, were the only things that he would appreciate.

"I had nowhere to go," he said, "and no money."

"Did it ever occur to you to work honestly for your living?"

"No."

"Did you have any other motive in remaining with the *Good Chance* for three years?"

"Yes, friendship for Carlyon."

"Why did you first join?"

"Friendship for Carlyon."

"The man whom you have betrayed?"

Andrews reddened and felt his cheek with the tips of his fingers. "Yes."

"What were your motives for laying information with the Revenue?"

"Do you really want to know that?" Andrews asked. "Isn't it wasting your time and the time of the Court?"

"Don't make speeches," Sir Edward Parkin snapped in his high, supercilious voice. "Answer the questions put to you."

"It was because I had a father whom I hated and he was always being put before me as a model. It made me mad. And I'm a coward. You all know that." Andrews gripped the edge of the box and leant forward, his voice angry, his face red and ashamed. "I was afraid of being hurt and I hated the sea and the noise and the danger. And unless I did something it would have gone on for always and always. And I wanted to show those men that I was someone to be considered, that I had the power to smash all their plans."

"And to hang them?"

"I never thought of that. I swear it. How could I tell they'd fight?"

"And your friend, the man Carlyon? Did you do nothing to warn him?"

"It was a case of him or me."

A bearded man called Hake in the second row of the prisoners sprang to his feet and shook his fist at Andrews. "It's him or you still," he cried. "He'll get you for this." A warder pulled him down.

The Court was growing unbearably stuffy. The judge and the ladies in the gallery were fluttering scented handkerchiefs. Andrews's forehead was hot and sticky with sweat. He wiped it with the palm of his hand. He felt as though he had been standing for hours exposed to the gaze of the Court. His lips were dry and he longed for water. Give me strength to go through with this, he implored silently—not of God but of the image which he carried in his heart and behind which he tried to hide the faces that watched him.

"Where is your father?" Mr. Braddock asked.

"In hell I hope," Andrews answered, and a burst of laughter from the gallery came like a breath of cool spring wind to a tropic night. No relief of cool winds was allowed in a court of justice. Laughter was suppressed by the usher's cries.

"Do you mean that he is dead?"

"Yes."

"And it was jealousy of a dead man which impelled you to betray comrades of three years' standing?"

"Yes."

"Do you expect the jury to understand that?"

"No." Andrews's voice drooped wearily. He felt a sudden longing to explain to this red-faced counsel who plagued him so with questions that he had not slept all night. "I don't expect anyone to understand," he said. In his heart he added—save Elizabeth—and Carlyon.

"Do you expect the jury to believe it?"

"It is true."

The red face came at him again with the persistence of an insect.

"I suggest to you that your whole story is untrue?"

Andrews shook his head, but he could not shake off that voice which came at him again and again and again.

"That you never laid any information?"

"I did."

"That you are telling this story to save yourself from the dock?"

"No."

"That you never landed with a cargo on the night of February 10?"

"I did, I tell you."

"That you were with a woman, a notorious woman?"

"No. It's untrue."

Andrews's weariness grew on him. He held the sides of the witness box as a support. I could sleep now, he said to himself.

"Will you stand there on your oath and tell the jury that you have not been keeping company with a loose woman?"

"No, I refused," he said wearily. He could not understand how this red bladder with the bullying voice was so well aware of his movements.

"What do you mean you refused?"

"I was in the Sussex Pad at Shoreham when the girl came up to me. But I wouldn't have her. Carlyon came in to drink and I was afraid that he'd see me. So I said 'No.' I said 'No. I won't sleep with you. Not tonight.' And I slipped out. And I don't know whether Carlyon saw me or not. I was afraid and I ran for miles, for miles up over the downs."

"That is no doubt another woman. There's no need to tell the jury of all the women with whom you have consorted." Mr. Braddock sniggered and the jury tittered. Sir Edward Parkin allowed himself a faint smile as he watched the young women in the public gallery.

The faces in front of Andrews, the solicitors at the table, the usher, the now soundly sleeping Clerk of Arraigns, the bearded prisoners in the dock, the spectators in the gallery, the twelve hostile cow-like jurymen, were becoming rapidly an indistinct blur, one large composite face of many eyes and mouths. Only Mr. Braddock's face, red and angry, protruded very distinctly out of this mass, as he leant forward to shoot

out his questions, which seemed to Andrews absurd
and meaningless.

"Do you still persist in saying that you landed with
the prisoners on the night of February 10?"

"But it's true, I tell you." Andrews clenched his
fists and longed to beat back that red aggressive face
into the grey mists which surrounded it. Then I could
sleep, he thought, and his mind dwelt with longing on
the cool white sheets and warm clean blankets which
had been wasted on his restless mind and body the
night before.

"Carry your mind back two days. Were you not in
the company of a notoriously loose woman?"

"No. I don't understand. I haven't been with a
woman like that for weeks. Can't you take my answer
and have done?" Staring at the face of Mr. Braddock,
as it darted back and forth, Andrews was surprised to
see it apparently disintegrate under his eyes. It softened
and collapsed and reformed itself into a kind of tiger-
ish amiability.

"I don't want to tire you. This must be a very trying experience for you." Mr. Braddock paused, and
even in his weariness Andrews smiled, remembering
the weaver Bottom—"I can roar you as softly as any
sucking dove."

"I think we are talking at cross-purposes. I am sure
that you don't wish to hinder the course of justice.
Only tell the jury where you were staying two nights
ago."

"At a cottage out Hassocks way."

"Not all by yourself, surely?" The red face creased

itself into a sneer, the coarse mouth with two great grave-stone teeth sniggered out loud, seeming to give a lead and a cue to laughter from gallery and jury. The usher, grinning himself, called perfunctorily for silence.

"What do you mean?" The laughter confused Andrews. It was like a mist between himself and any clear thought.

"Answer the question." Mr. Braddock snapped at him. "It was plain enough. Were you alone?"

"No. Why? I was with—"

"With whom?"

He hesitated. He did not know her name, he realised.

"A woman?"

The word woman seemed too general and too coarse a name to describe the banner under which he now fought. A woman? He had known many women, and Elizabeth was not like one of them. She was something more remote and infinitely more desirable.

"No," he said, and then seeing Mr. Braddock's great mouth open for another question, he grew dismayed —"at least . . ." he said and stood confused, hopelessly barren of words.

"Don't jest with us. It must have been either a woman, a man or a child. Which was it?"

"A woman," and before he could add some qualifying phrase he was struck by a wave of laughter from every corner of the Court. He came out of it, as though half drowned, red, gasping, blind to everything but the face of his questioner, which was already darting forward for another question.

"What is her name?"

"Elizabeth," he murmured indistinctly, but loud enough for Mr. Braddock to hear. He gave it to the Court with the air of a jester. "Elizabeth. And what is the young woman's surname?"

"I don't know."

"What was that the witness said?" Sir Edward Parkin tapped the sheet of paper in front of him with his pen.

"He doesn't know her surname, my lord," Mr. Braddock replied with a grin. Sir Edward Parkin smiled, and as though his smile gave an awaited sanction, laughter again swept the Court.

"My lord," Mr. Braddock continued, when silence had been restored, "the witness's ignorance is not as astounding as it may seem. Opinion on the point differs a great deal among her neighbours."

Andrews leant forward and banged the edge of the box with his clenched fist. "What are you insinuating?" he said.

"Be quiet," Sir Edward Parkin turned on him, fingers poised in the act of taking snuff. He turned and smiled ingratiatingly at Mr. Braddock. The case was proving more amusing than he had foreseen.

"Well, my lord, I shall bring a witness to show that the girl is the daughter, probably illegitimate, of a woman called Garnet. The woman is dead and no one knows whether she ever had a husband. They had a lodger staying with them and he took over the farm when the woman died. It is a common idea in the countryside that the girl was not only the daughter of this man, but also his mistress."

"Where is the man?"

"He is dead, my lord."

"Do you propose to call the girl as a witness?"

"No, my lord, the information has only this moment come into my hands, and in any case the girl would not be a witness in whom a jury could place any credence. The whole story is a very sordid one."

"My God, do you know what's beautiful?" Andrews cried.

"If you cannot keep silent," Sir Edward Parkin said, "I shall commit you for contempt of court."

"My lord," Andrews appealed, and hesitated, trying to shake off the mist of weariness that clung round his brain and clogged his words.

"Is there something you want to say?"

Andrews lifted a hand to his forehead. He must find words in the mist which shrouded him, words to express the gold which suffused it from the light of candles lit in a far place behind the brain.

"Say what you want to say or be silent."

"My lord, it's not sordid," he muttered very low. It seemed hopeless to find words until he had slept.

"Mr. Braddock, the witness says that it is not sordid." The laughter beat upon Andrews's head, till it felt physically bruised as though by hail.

Mr. Braddock felt himself riding to victory upon a gale of laughter.

"Take your mind back to two mornings ago. We

will leave out the night," he added with a snigger. "Do you remember a woman coming to the cottage?"

"Yes."

"Is it true that your friend without a surname, Elizabeth, told the woman that you were her brother?"

"Yes."

"Why?"

"I can't remember."

"Did she say that you'd been staying with her for a week?"

"I think so. I can't remember anything. I'm tired."

"That is all I want to ask you."

Can I at last sit down and sleep? Andrews wondered incredulously. His doubt was justified. Sir Henry Merriman rose.

"Did you stay at the cottage for a week?"

"No. Two nights. That was all."

"Think hard. Can't you remember why she told those lies? They were to help you?"

"Of course. She'd never lie for herself. It was because I was afraid that the woman would talk in the town. I was afraid of Carlyon."

"Why were you afraid?"

"He knew that I'd betrayed him. He was after me. He came to the cottage while I was there. But she hid me. She fooled him. She was brave like a saint. She drank out of my cup. How can he say there was anything sordid? It's all lies they tell about her. If I wasn't so tired I could tell you all."

"Why did she do all this for you? Were you her lover?"

"No. It was just charity. I've never touched her, I swear it."

"Thank you. That is all." Andrews stood where he was, unbelieving that the end had at last come, that he had done what Elizabeth had urged him to do, that all was over now and he could sleep. He felt a hand pull at his sleeve. He stumbled down the steps to the floor of the court, still under the influence of the guiding hand, which now pulled him gently and insistently towards the door.

As he passed the dock a voice called to him. "Andrews." He stopped and looked up. It took him a moment to focus his eyes. Then he saw that it was Tims. "Let me out, Andrews," he implored.

There was a hostile murmur from the gallery and Andrews flushed. Anger, unreasoning and undirected, against himself, against his father, against this boy who held him for one moment from his sleep, tossed back an answer. "You fool, I've put you there." Then he was outside the Court.

"I want to sleep," he said. "Can I go?"

He found that he was speaking to an officer. "Not outside I shouldn't," the man said. "There's a crowd there. You ain't too popular. Better wait till the case is over. They'll look after you then."

"Anywhere—a chair," He put his hand against the wall to support himself.

"There's the witness's room."

"I can't go back there. They won't give me any peace. Isn't there anywhere?"

The officer softened a little. "Here," he said, "you'd

better sit here." He pointed at a bench against the wall. "It's against orders," he added grudgingly, but already Andrews had sank down on it and had let sleep come, instantaneous, dreamless sleep, that carried for one instant only a confusion of faces, bearded angry faces, sniggering red faces, one pale face, a gold mist and then nothing at all.

"That is the case for the Crown." Sir Henry Merriman's voice, filtering through the big double doors of the Court, came too softly to disturb Andrews, where he slept. To him in a state of content, of unknowing, without dreams, weeks might have passed and not hours. The voice was a clear whisper. That was all. And he had not wakened, when, a long time previously, the Court had risen for luncheon. The whispers of the witnesses had then ceased to sound in the corridor. There had been silence, a shuffle of persons rising to their feet and then, as the doors of the Court swung open, loud voices and a roar of conversation which burst like a bomb. Andrews slept on, slept on through the heavy reluctant return of feet, weighed down by a good meal eaten, slept on as the doors closed and the whispers of the witnesses began again.

The officer in the corridor leant his ear against the door and listened, avid for any excitement to conquer boredom. He cast an eye towards Andrews in the hope of conversation, but Andrews slept. The prisoners inside were making their defence; so much the officer could gather from the broken sentences that reached him. Each man's defence had been written out for him by his solicitor, and it was read in a toneless stumbling voice. Through the glass front of the door the officer could see the prisoners. The trial was reaching its final stages and so was the light. The Court was veiled depressingly in grey, not yet sufficiently dark to justify the lighting of the candles. The prisoners, in spite of their confidence in the jury, felt the gloom and were a little touched by fear. Each as he read from the sheet of paper in front of him felt the constraining presence of a dead man rise to refute his arguments. A man had been killed. A hundred alibis could not turn that fact into a falsehood. As though by mutual consent, bent on the sacrifice of an unwanted Jonah, they edged a little away from the half-witted youth, until he sat in a little cleared space, which in that crowded Court took on the dimensions of a desert.

Each man's defence was a little subtly changed. This man at the supposed time of the affray had been drinking with a friend, this man had been in bed with his wife. All would bring witnesses to prove their stories and only the perorations were similar, "So help me God I am innocent."

Four times the stumbling, mechanical stories were repeated to set the officer yawning, and then there was a change. It was the turn of Hake, the large black-bearded man who had threatened Andrews from the dock. When he rose the candles were being lighted in Court and his shadow swung across the ceiling in the manner of a gigantic bird. His voice boomed into the corridor like struck metal deeply toned.

"My lord, the gentlemen of the jury have a responsibility on them to-day the like of which will never come their way again. Whose word are they going to take? Those gaugers, afraid of losing their jobs the whole lot of them, ours—men they've drunk with—that sneak's, that Andrews with his loose woman, or ours? If they hang us and the truth comes out who'll speak for their souls in the day of Judgment? Who'll defend their bodies here?"

"Prisoner," a high petulant voice, "are you threatening the jury? The jury have nothing to do with the punishment. They have only to decide whether you are innocent or guilty."

"I only warn them . . ."

"The jury will be protected in the performance of their duty. Threats do not strengthen your case."

"Are you going to hang us?"

"I am anxious to be fair, but unless you proceed with your defence, you must sit down."

"My defence is the same as these others. I wasn't there. I'll prove it with witnesses as these will. But a man's been killed, you'll say, you can't get over that. Well, I'll tell you who killed him. He did," and his finger pierced across and emphasised the desert which surrounded Tims. Tims leapt to his feet. "You don't mean it," he said, "you are lying. Tell them you are lying." He sank down again on his chair and covering his face with his hands began to cry with a peculiar moaning sound like a sick animal's. Mingled with the booming voice it made a peculiar orchestral effect in the corridor.

"I've heard him, I tell you, talking about it. He's a

half-witted loon, you can see that for yourself, more
fitted for the asylum than for the gallows. He used to
tell me many a time what he intended to do to Rexall.
Rexall used to tease him in the street. You've heard a
gauger say so himself, but there's more evidence than
that to it. I wouldn't expect you to take a gauger's
word. But listen here—you are honest men and will
bring us in innocent."

"You are not addressing the jury, you are addressing the Court."

"I'm sorry, my lord, what I mean to say," he leant
forward over the edge of the dock towards the jury.
"the jury will want to know what's to happen to that
Judas and his woman. Let them leave it to us, I say,
let them leave it to us."

Before Sir Edward Parkin could speak he sat down.
The officer stole a glance at Andrews. He slept on.

The Court seemed peculiarly silent when that booming voice was still. They were waiting for the last
prisoner to make his defence, but he remained seated,
his face covered by his hands which shook spas-
modically in time with his moans.

"Richard Tims, this is the time that it becomes your
duty to make your defence."

He made no reply, no sign even that he had heard
the judge's voice.

"Mr. Braddock, you represent the prisoner, do you
not?"

"I, my lord," Mr. Braddock rose, sweeping his gown
round him, as though to escape pollution. "This prisoner? No, my lord. I represent the other prisoners."

"No one ever seems capable of making out the lists correctly. You are put down for all the prisoners, Mr. Braddock."

"I was never so instructed, my lord."

"Which of you represents this prisoner?"

There was no reply.

"Has this prisoner had no legal advice?" Sir Edward Parkin protested with a faint note of annoyance.

"If he had wished, my lord, he could have had counsel."

"This is very trying. The case has gone on long enough as it is. I don't want any delay. The Assizes is a very full one."

"My lord," an elderly little man with blinking eyes rose to his feet, "I will represent the prisoner if you so wish it."

"Thank you, Mr. Petty. Will you explain to the prisoner that he must make his defence?"

Mr. Petty stepped delicately to the edge of the Court and holding a handkerchief to his nose spoke to the boy.

"It's no use, my lord, the prisoner is not in a fit state to make his defence."

"The jury will take it that he merely asserts his innocence. Mr. Braddock will you call your witnesses?" Sir Edward Parkin leant back and dabbed his fingers furiously in his snuff-box. He was annoyed. The case had been held up for at least two minutes. His breakfast had been a bad one, his luncheon worse, and he was hungry. The trial showed no sign of reaching an end, but his hunger, far from leading to an adjournment, only confirmed his obstinacy. He would sit till midnight if necessary, but he would finish the trial.

One after another men, women and children filed into the witness box and committed mechanical perjury. This woman was in bed with that man at the time of the murder, this man was toasting another in whisky, a child had heard its father undressing upstairs. Sir Henry Merrivale shrugged his shoulders at Mr. Farne. "They have us," he seemed to say. "That man Andrews," Mr. Farne whispered, "was worse than useless." Only occasionally did they trouble to cross-examine. The witnesses had been too well-primed in their stories. Mr. Petty, having magnanimously undertaken the task of representing the half-wit, closed his eyes and went to sleep.

Mrs. Butler scrambled up the steps of the witness box and allowed her ample breasts to flow over the edge. Yes, she had seen Andrews at a certain woman's cottage two days previously. Yes, there had been every indication that he had slept in the place. The woman had told her that Andrews had been there for a week. Yes, the woman was a notoriously loose liver. All the neighbourhood knew it.

"What the neighbourhood says is not evidence."

"No, my lord, but what my eyes have seen is evidence."

Sir Henry Merriman's voice stabbed itself into the corridor, sharp and clear as an icicle. "Did you hear this woman call the man Andrews her brother?"

"Yes."

"Was that true?"

"No, of course it weren't true. They didn't take me in, I can tell you." Her hand unerringly sought the thin strands of gold in her hair and she stroked them lovingly. "I know what it is to love," she said in her sweet, damp voice. "I could tell the love light in 'is eyes.

"What does the woman mean?"

"She means, my lord," Mr. Braddock explained with unction, "that the man Andrews appeared to be in love with the woman."

"How on earth could she tell that?"

"A woman's intuition, m' lord" Mrs. Butler's hand stroked one capacious breast. "And I can tell you something else, m' lord. Only one bed had been slept in."

"If the woman lied with regard to her relationship with Andrews, have you any reason for believing her other statement that he had been with her for a week? I suggest that he had arrived only the night before."

"Well, I don't know anything, sir. But 'e must 'ave made quick time with 'er mustn't 'e?" Mrs. Butler leered ingratiatingly at Sir Edward Parkin. "Men are very shy, my lord. I've known many in my time, my lord, and I speak with conviction."

Sir Edward Parkin turned away his face, screwed up a little as though he suffered from nausea. "Have you finished with this good woman, Sir Henry?"

"Yes, my lord."

Mr. Braddock rose. "That, my lord, is the case for the defence."

"Have you any witnesses to call, Mr. Petty?"

"No, my lord."

"Gentlemen of the jury, it is growing late, but by the law of England I am not allowed to discharge you until the case is finished. I am obliged to keep you together, though, no doubt, proper accommodation will be afforded you. But I am for myself perfectly willing to go on to finish the case before we separate. I have been accustomed to bear fatigue of this kind and am willing to bear it. The foreman will consult with his brethren and collect their wishes."

There was a brief nodding of heads and the foreman intimated that they wished to finish the case. Sir Edward Parkin leant back in his seat, took a liberal helping of snuff, smoothed his white hands with some complacency and began his summing up. The officer with an impatient sigh removed his ear from the door. He had in past assizes experienced the bitter boredom of Mr. Justice Parkin's meticulous care and accuracy. Only occasionally did he put his ear to the door to gain some indication of the progress of the judge's charge.

"If you accept the evidence of the revenue officers that these men landed with a cargo on the night of February 10, and that in a fight which ensued Rexall was killed, it is unnecessary to fix the guilt of firing the shot on any one man. By the law of England they are all equally guilty of murder. The prisoners, in answer to the charge, have returned a complete denial and five of the prisoners have brought evidence to show that they were in a different place when the fight, described by the officers of the Crown, took place. Gentlemen, with regard to the credibility of the prisoners' witnesses I would have you bear in mind. . . .

"The evidence for the prosecution rests not on the bare word of the officers alone. One of the prisoners' companions, on whose information the officers are said to have acted, appeared in the witness box. You must decide for yourselves upon his credibility, but I would point out that his story is similar in every point to that given by the officers. . . .

"There remains, gentlemen, the body, and here an unexpected line has been taken by five of the prisoners. They have accused one of their number of having committed the murder as a climax to a series of quarrels with the officer Rexall. They have adopted part of the evidence of the prosecution in their own defence. Medical evidence leaves no doubt of the cause of Rexall's death, and the bullet found in his body is similar to those in the possession of these men. No evidence has been brought by this prisoner in his defence, but until a late stage of the trial he was unrepresented by counsel, and you can judge for yourself of his mental state. I would point out to you that it is for the prosecution to prove a case of Guilt. The prisoners' statements are not evidence, and the prosecution have not attempted to prove the man Tims guilty alone. He and his companions in this respect must be judged together. . . .

"You are not concerned with the past, and the evidence of the witness Andrews dealing with the life of crime lived on the ship *Good Chance* must not be taken into consideration. You are not to try the prisoners on their bad characters, nor are you to try them

on the good characters which have been given to them
by certain witnesses for the defence—you are to try
whether they be guilty of the crime with which they
are charged. It has been stated that they are good
fathers, good husbands, good sons, but if they were
angels and if the evidence as to the crime were clear
and satisfactory, it would be your duty to return a verdict accordingly. . . .

"An ill-advised attempt has been made by one of
the prisoners to influence your verdict by threats. I
can promise you, gentlemen, that whatever your verdict you will have the full protection of the law. . . ."

The officer drooped like an undignified and top
heavy flower. The candles in the Court were burning
low in their sockets, but Mr. Justice Parkin, with the
stage all his own, talked on. . . .

Through Andrews's sleep came first a hum of talk,
then a distant burst of cheering. He opened his eyes.
Through a window he could see that it was dark.
Groups of talking people passed him and paid him no
attention. The door of the Court stood open. He sat
up and cleared sleep from his eyes with the back of a
hand. Sir Henry Merriman and Mr. Farne came from
the Court. Mr. Farne was talking with gentle insistence, his hand on the older man's arm. "We shall never
put down smuggling in the Courts," Mr. Farne said.
"There is only one way—to remove the duty from
spirits."

Sir Henry Merriman stared at the ground. "No," he

said, "I am growing old. I must retire and give room for younger men. You, Farne."

"That is nonsense," Mr. Farne said. "No man could have made that jury convict."

Andrews slowly rose to his feet. "Do you mean to say," he said, "that those men are acquitted?"

Mr. Farne turned. "Yes," he said shortly. "Listen. The whole town's cheering them."

"Don't go," Andrews implored. "Tell me what am I to do. Have they been released?" Mr. Farne nodded.

"You've cheated me," Andrews cried. "You got me to give evidence and now—don't you understand that you've let them loose on me?"

Sir Henry raised eyes that seemed blurred with weariness. "I have already promised you," he said, "that you shall be protected as long as you stay in this town. I should advise you to leave for London, however, as soon as you can. I admit that certain threats were made against you. Give Sussex a wide berth and you will be safe."

"How can I get to London? I have no money."

"Come to me to-morrow," Sir Henry said. "You shall be given money." He turned his back on Andrews. "Farne," he said, "I am tired. I shall go to bed now. Listen. Isn't it rather bitter, that cheering? If we had won there would have been less enthusiasm. You remember the Duke of Northumberland, who declared for Jane Grey—'the people press to see us, but not one saith God speed'?"

"I won't let you go like this," Andrews cried. "That

cheering only means defeat to you. It will be death to me if I'm seen. How can I get away from here?"

"I have given orders to the Runners," Sir Henry said. "They will see you back to the hotel. Two men will be stationed there to accompany you at any time through the town. If I were you I should catch the first coach to London in the morning." Mr. Farne pushed Andrews on one side and the two men moved away.

Andrews turned to the officer. "You see," he said, "that's their gratitude. I did my best for them, didn't I, and I've risked my life, but what do they care?"

"And why should they care for an informer like you? I'm sure I don't," he beamed at Andrews genially. "I'd let your friends get you, but orders is orders. Come this way."

Escorted by way of a back door and a succession of dirty lanes Andrews reached the White Hart through the stables.

CHAPTER IX

ANDREWS stood in the room where the previous night he had held Sir Henry's mistress in his arms and watched with tired curiosity one star. He held in his hand a note which a winking waiter had given him. It was from Lucy and read "Henry has gone to bed. You can come to me. You know my room." He had done what Elizabeth desired him to do, and in spite of the note he held, he told himself that it was for Elizabeth's sake that he had done it. Didn't I, he thought, renounce this morning with perfect sincerity this very reward? I did what I did then for Elizabeth and why should I not take any small benefits which come after? I had no thought for this when I stood in the witness box. It was an interesting moral point.

Carlyon now could come and go where he liked. Nothing, Andrews thought with apprehension, could prevent him strolling that very evening into the White Hart. It was so exactly the kind of thing for Carlyon to do that Andrews looked with a sudden start behind him. The door was shut. He longed to bolt it. As for this letter it could not be denied that he would be safer that night in Lucy's bed than in his own. That was a reason which no one could deny. It would be to save myself, he told the star to which he instinctively addressed words meant for Elizabeth, for no other reason. I do not love her. Never will I love anyone but you. I swear to that. If a man loves one, he cannot help still lusting after others. But it was love not lust, I promise, that strengthened me this morning.

After all, he said to the star, I shall never see you again, and must I therefore never know another woman? I cannot come to you, for they will be watching for me there, and you do not love me. I should be a fool . . . and he stopped speaking to himself, struck by the astonishing knowledge of how deeply his heart longed to be a fool. Reason, reason, reason. I must cling to that, he thought. Reason and his body seemed to act together in a somewhat evil partnership. In

fear of his own heart he began to play on fear for his
own safety, and that fear seemed strangely less strong
than was its wont. And then he turned to the thought
of Lucy and the feel of her body pressed to him and
her close promises the night before. He imagined her
naked and in disgusting attitudes, and tried to whip his
body into a blind lust which would forget for a time
at least the dictates of his heart. Yet strangely even his
lust seemed less strong. What have you done to me?
he cried despairingly at the lonely star.

It was then that he heard someone twist cautiously
the handle of the door. He forgot star, Elizabeth, Lucy,
everything but his own safety. In one stride he reached
the oil lamp which lit the room and turned it out. The
room was still too light or seemed so to his hammer-
ing nerves from the wash of moonlight which entered
at the window. It was too late to get behind the door,
so Andrews pressed his back against the wall and
cursed himself for being weaponless. What a sentimental fool he had been to leave his knife behind him
at the cottage. Where were the two Runners, he wondered, who were supposed to guard him? Drunk in
bed in all probability. He watched the door handle
with fascination. It was of white marble and glimmered, touched by the crest of the moon's wave, with
deceptive distinctness. Again it twisted round with
surprising silentness and then flew outwards like a
thrown ball. An oil lamp stood in the passage outside
and its light cast a kind of mocking halo round the
head of the cockney Harry, who stood in the door-

way, his face thrust forward and moving from side to side, like that of a snake.

Andrews pressed himself still harder against the wall, and Cockney Harry sidled into the room. As though he was aware that the light in the passage put him at a disadvantage he shut the door behind him. "Andrews," he whispered. His eyes were not yet used to the dark, and the silence made him uneasy. He too put his back against the wall, opposite the place where Andrews stood, as if he feared attack. Then he saw Andrews. "So there you are," he said. Andrews clenched his fists in preparation for an unexpected spring but the smuggler saw the movement and flashed a knife warningly in the moon's ray. "Stay where you are," he whispered, "unless you want to squeak to a new tone."

"There are Runners in this hotel," Andrews also lowered his voice. "What do you want?"

"I'm not afeared of the Runners now," the man said. "But look 'ere," he added plaintively, "why d'you want to quarrel. I'm 'ere to do you a service, strite I am."

"To do me a service?" Andrews repeated. "Do you forget who I am?"

"Oh, I don't forget 'ow you squeaked on us, but one good turn deserves another. You didn't squeak on me this afternoon, and you might 'ave done easy."

"It wasn't for love of that face of yours," Andrews said. His fists remained clenched against any sudden attack.

"You ain't very griteful," Harry complained. "Don't you want to 'ear my news?"

"What news?"

"Of Carlyon an' the others."

"No, I've finished with them," he said and added, as always with a curious aching heart, slowly, as though in an effort to overcome with finality each ache, "I never want to see that man again."

"Ah, but 'e ain't finished with you. Nor with yer ladybird."

Andrews started forward. "What do you mean?"

"Now keep back," Harry flashed his knife again. "What I mean is they feel they been cheated by 'er—cheated shimeful."

"Carlyon wouldn't do anything to her, I know he wouldn't."

"Ah, but there's Joe. 'E says she ought to 'ave a fright, an' Carlyon agrees to that, but 'e don't know what Joe and 'Ake calls a fright. They are all off to give it 'er to-morrer or the next dy."

"You are lying, you know you are lying," Andrews panted a little like a dog thirsty or out of breath. "This is a trap to get me to go back there, so that you'll catch me. But I won't, I won't go back I tell you."

"Why, that's why I'm 'ere—to warn yer against goin', in case you were thinkin' of it. They'll all be there. Carlyon'll kill you as soon as look at you. Though 'Ake says as killin's too good. 'E says they oughter 'ave some fun with you first."

"Well, you can tell them that I'm never going back there. It's no use laying that trap for me."

"Good. Now I've warned yer an' we're quits. Next time," Harry spat on the floor expressively and again flashed the steel of his knife in the moonlight, "don't you expect me to be friendly." He gave the impression of sliding across the floor. The white marble handle again flew outwards and the smuggler disappeared. Up the street the clock of St. Anne's Church beat out with irritating deliberation the half after eleven.

Like a dream the man had entered and like a dream he had gone. Why could he not have been one more degree a phantom and become a vision only? Now inevitably a turmoil was roused in the mind. Carlyon would not harm a woman, Andrews thought. It is only a trap to catch me. But then was it likely that they would plan such a trap for me, a coward? They could not expect to do anything but repel him by danger. Again he repeated to himself that she was safe, that Carlyon would see to that, but still he could not dispel from his mind the thought of Joe and Hake. To-morrow or the next day. If he were to leave to-night he could warn her in time, and they could both escape. But that was only if it were not a trap. Perhaps even now Harry, Joe, Hake, Carlyon and the rest were preparing to meet him on the downs. And yet how good, how glorious it would be, to be coming down the hill at dawn, to wait perhaps for the first sign of smoke to show that she was awake, to tap on the door and see recognition lit in her eyes. She would have to welcome me, he thought. I have earned that, for I have done all that she told me to do. In a medley of the stories of his childhood he imagined—"I have climbed the hill of glass and Gretel waits." And then, he thought, I would help her get some breakfast and we would sit together in front of the fire. And I would tell her everything. His momentary exhilaration died and left the cold truth, danger to himself and her and more than that the knowledge that she would greet him as a not too welcome friend. Neither I nor any other man will ever approach her. What was the use of risking his life—miserable, debased it might be, but only he knew how infinitely precious—in return for what? A kind word. He did not want kind words. Let them give her a little pain. He had suffered. Why should not everyone in the world suffer? It was the common lot. Carlyon would see that they did not go too far.

As his fingers tightened in perplexity he felt still in his hand Lucy's note. Here was someone who would give him more than kind words and yet exact no sense of responsibility. All his reason commanded him to go to her, only his heart, and that hard abstract critic for once allied to his heart, opposed. I shall be safe with her to-night, he thought, and to-morrow Carlyon and the others will have gone off over the downs and the road to London will be safe. Why, if he went to Elizabeth now, he would have no money for their escape. You mustn't be dependent on her money, reason added, striking a noble attitude. That decided him. Why, even honour forbade the dangerous course.

He passed through the dark passage and up the stairs, slowly, still a little doubtful and reluctant. In one of the rooms which now faced him Sir Henry Merriman slept. There was even a little danger, he now realised, in this course, danger of being stranded without money in this perilous Sussex. He knew which was Lucy's room and cautiously he turned the handle and went in. He still held her note, as though a passport, in his hand.

"Here I am," he said. He could not see her, but one hand stumbled on the foot of a bed.

There was a small sigh, a yawn, and through the darkness a sleepy whisper, "How late you are."

His hand felt down the bed till he reached a cool sheet and beneath it he felt her body. He snatched his hand away as though it had touched a flame. The note fell from it to the floor. Oh, if he could surrender to his heart for once and not his body, and if he could go now before it was too late. Three hours' walk over the downs beneath the moon and he would be home again.

"Where are you?" she said. "I can't see in the dark. Come here."

"I only came to say . . ." he said and hesitated. His heart had spoken, given courage by an image of Elizabeth as she had faced Carlyon, his cup raised to her lips, and his body had cut his words short, for his hand retained the feel of her body.

"That you were going again?" she asked. "You fool."

He felt his flesh rising to her whisper.

"Will you ever get a chance like this again?" she murmured with an air of unfeigned carelessness. "You know what you are missing, don't you?"

He took a step away from the bed. "How common

you are," he said. His hand felt behind him for the door handle, but he could not find it.

"You know you enjoy that," she answered. She did not seem to argue but rather to advise him gently and dispassionately for his own good. Her quiet irritated and attracted him at the same time. "I'd like to make her squeal," he thought.

"At least before you go," she said, "strike a light and see what you miss. Put out your hand." He obeyed her reluctantly. He felt her fingers touch his. "How symbolical," she laughed a little. "Here's a flint and steel. Now strike a light. There is a candle here," and she guided his hand to a table beside her bed.

"I won't," he said.

"Are you afraid?" she asked curiously. "You've turned very pure since last night. Have you fallen in love?"

"Not fallen," he replied more to himself than her.

"And you boasted so of all the women you've known. Surely you aren't afraid. You ought to be more used to us."

He turned his back on her. "Very well," he said. "I'll strike a light and then I'll go. I know your sort. You won't leave a man alone." Without looking in her direction he struck a light and lit the candle. It made a small yellow patch on the opposite wall and in that radiance he suddenly saw with extraordinary clarity the face of Elizabeth creased by fear till it was ugly, almost repulsive. Then it was blotted out by two other faces, that of Joe, the black bearded mouth open in a laugh, and that of the mad youth Richard Tims, red and angry. Then there was only the yellow radiance again.

"I can't stay," Andrews cried, "she's in danger," and he swung round candle in hand.

The girl was stretched on the outside of the bed. She had flung her nightdress on the floor. She was slim, long legged with small firm breasts. With a modesty which had no pretence of truth she spread her hands over her stomach and smiled at him.

"Run away then," she said.

He came a little nearer and with his eyes fixed on her face, so as not to see her body, he began to make excuses, reason, even plead. "I must go," he said, "someone came to warn me to-night. A girl—I've got her into danger. I must go to her. Just now on that wall I thought I saw her scream."

"You are dreaming."

"But sometimes dreams come true. Don't you see— I must go. I got her into this danger."

"Well go. I'm not stopping you am I? But listen. What difference will it make if you stay here just for half an hour." She turned over on her side, and his eyes could not help but follow her body as it moved. "She's cool now," he thought, "but I could make her warm."

"Go then," she said. "You won't have another chance, but I don't care. I'm feeling restless—this damn spring. I'll go in to Harry. He's old and tired, but I believe he's more of a man than you." Although she spoke of going she did not go, but watched him with faintly amused eyes. Andrews moistened his lips, which were dry. He felt thirsty. He no longer tried to keep his eyes off her body. He knew now that he could not move away.

"I'll stay," he said. He put his knee on the bed, but her hands held him away.

"Not like that," she said. "I'm not a harlot. Take off those things." He hesitated for a moment and glanced at the candle.

"No there must be a little light," she whispered, a little run of excitement in her tone, "so that we can see each other."

He obeyed her unwillingly. He felt that he was raising a barrier of time between Elizabeth and any help which he might bring. Even now he could not forget the dream, vision, fantasy, what you will, which he had seen in the candle's light, it was conquered only when he felt the girl's body stretched along his own.

"Closer," she said. His fingers closed on her, pinching the flesh. He buried his mouth between her breasts. He could see nothing but he heard her laugh a little. "You cannot hurt me like that," she said. . . .

He opened his eyes and thought at first how strange it was that a candle should burn with a silver flame. Then he saw that the candle was out and the light was the first of day. He sat up and looked at his companion. She slept with her mouth slightly open, breathing hard. He eyed first her body and then his own with disgust. He touched her shoulder gingerly with his hand, and she opened her eyes. "I should cover that," he said, and turning his back, put his feet over the side of the bed.

From her voice he judged that she was smiling, but her smile which in the dark had seemed the beckoning of a passionate mystery, he considered now a shallow mechanical thing. He was disgusted with himself and her. He had been treading, he felt, during the last few days on the border of a new life, in which he would learn courage and even self forgetfulness, but now he had fallen back into the slime from which he had emerged.

"Have you enjoyed yourself?" she asked.

"I've wallowed," he said, "if that's what you mean."

He could imagine her pouting at him and he hated that pout. "Aren't I pleasanter than all the other women you've boasted about?"

"You've made me feel myself dirtier," he answered. But is there no way out of this slime? he thought silently. I was a fool and imagined I was escaping, but now I have sunk so deep that surely I've reached the bottom.

"I could kill myself," he said aloud.

The girl laughed contemptuously. "You haven't the courage," she said, "and anyway what of that fair one who's in danger?"

Andrews put his hand to his head. "You made me forget her," he said. "I can't face her after this."

"How young you are," she said. "Surely you know by this time that the feeling won't last. For a day we are disgusted and disappointed and disillusioned and feel dirty all over. But we are clean again in a very short time, clean enough to go back and soil ourselves all over again."

"One must reach an end some time."

"Never."

"Are you a devil as well as a harlot?" Andrews asked with interest, but without anger. "Do you mean to say that it's no use trying to be clean?"

"How often have you felt sick and disgusted and resolved never to sin again?"

"I can't count them. You are right. It's no use. Why can't I die?"

"How curious. You are one of those people—I've met them before—who can't rid themselves of a conscience. How talkative one becomes after a bout of this. I've noticed it often. I thought you were going to rescue that girl of yours from danger. Why don't you go? It's ridiculous to sit on the edge of a bed naked and philosophise."

"It may be a trap and they'll kill me."

"I thought you wouldn't go when it came to the point."

"You are wrong," Andrews stood up, "that's the very reason why I'm going."

When he left the hotel he took no precautions whatever, but walked down the street with his eyes fixed straight in front of him. He felt no fear of death, but a terror of life, of going on soiling himself and repenting and soiling himself again. There was, he felt, no escape. He had no will left. For certain exalted moments he had dreamed of taking Elizabeth to London, of gaining her love and marrying her, but now he saw that even if he gained that high desire, it would only be to soil her and not cleanse himself. When I had been married to her for a month, he thought, I would be creeping out of the house on the sly to visit prostitutes. The cool air of early morning touched him in vain. He was hot with shame and self-loathing. He longed with a ridiculous pathos for the mere physical purification of a bath.

He reached the downs as a first orange glow lifted above the eastern horizon. Its fragile soaring beauty, like a butterfly with delicate powdered wings resting on a silver leaf, touched him and increased his shame. If he had not seen Lucy but had started direct for the cottage some hours before, how that glow would have heartened him. What a prelude it would have been to his return.

From where he walked it was not yet light enough to see the valley clearly. Only at intervals the red spark of a lighted window would make a crevice in the grey veil, and after he had walked some miles a cock crew. The downs were bare of life, save for the occasional brooding hunched form of a dark tree. He walked, and as he walked the first poignancy of his shame departed and the events of the night slipped a little way into shadow. When Andrews realised this, he stayed for a moment still and strove to drag them back. For this had happened many times before. It was the first stage towards a repetition of the sin, this forgetfulness. How could he ever keep clean if the sense of shame was so short lived? After all I enjoyed myself, he thought

against his will, why repent? It's a coward's part. Go
back and do it again. Why run my head into danger?
With an effort he clenched his will and ran, to stifle
thought, ran fast until he had no more breath and flung
himself down upon the grass.

The grass grew in cool, crisp, salty tufts, on which
he leant his forehead. If it were barren of desire and
of the need of any action how sweet life would be. If
it were only this coolness, this silver sky touched now
with green, those unfurling wings of orange. If he could
but sit and watch and listen—listen to Carlyon speaking, and watch the enthusiasm in his eyes, with no
dangerous echo in his own. I was a strange, unrealis-
able thing that Carlyon was his enemy. Carlyon was
seeking to kill him, and yet his heart still leapt a little
at the sound of the name. Carlyon, who was all the
things which Andrews wished to be—courageous, understanding, hopelessly romantic, not about women,
but about life, Carlyon who hated well because he knew
so clearly what he loved—truth, danger, poetry. If I
hate him, Andrews thought, it is because I have done
him an injury, but he hates me because he thinks I've
injured life. He tried to laugh—the man was only a
romantic fool with an ugly face. That was the real secret of his humility, his courage, even his love of
beauty. He was always seeking a compensation for his
face, as though an ape in purple and ermine were less
an ape. The qualities he had built round himself were
dreams only, which Andrews by one act had destroyed.
There remained the large body, heavy, however lightly
poised, thick wrist, misshapen skull. Strip off Carlyon's

dreams and the remainder is inferior to me, Andrews thought. A sudden longing came that he could trap Carlyon into some unworthy action, not consonant with the dreams which he followed. That would show him they were dreams and not himself.

How could one judge a man when all was said but by his body and his private acts, not by dreams he followed in the world's eye? His father to his crew was a hero, a king, a man of dash, initiative. Andrews knew the truth—that he was a bully who killed his wife and ruined his son. And myself, Andrews thought, I have as good dreams as any man, of purity and courage and the rest, but I can only be judged by my body which sins and is cowardly. How do I know what Carlyon is in private. But as he spoke he wondered uneasily whether Carlyon might not follow his dreams even when alone. Suppose that after all a man, perhaps when a child, at any rate at some forgotten time, chose his dreams whether they were to be good or evil. Then, even though he were untrue to them, some credit was owing simply to the baseless dreaming. They were potentialities, aspects, and no man could tell whether suddenly and without warning they might not take control and turn the coward for one instant into the hero.

Carlyon and I are then on the same plane, he thought, with a wistful longing for belief. He follows his dreams and I do not follow mine, but the mere dreaming is good. And I am better than my father, for he had no dreams, and that part of him that men admired came not from following an ideal but from mere physical courage. But how he longed now for that mere physical valour, which would give him the power to fling himself blind-eyed upon the breast of his dream. He sometimes imagined that if courage could be granted him for a moment only to turn his back on fear, his dreams would have strength to seize him in their current and sweep him irrevocably on, with no need of further decision or further gallantry.

He rose and with a little melodramatic gesture opened his arms as though he would entice courage to his heart, but all that came was a cold sweep of early wind. He walked on. Why could he not, as Lucy said, kill his conscience and be content? Why if he was given these aspirations, softened and blurred by sentiment as they were, was he not given sinew to attain them? He was the son of his mother, he supposed. Her heart had been trapped by vague romantic longings. His father when he desired something which could not be attained by other means had the power of showing himself a a sort of rough, genial fellow—a sea dog of the old Elizabethan tradition. He was of Drake's county and he spoke Drake's tongue. The sea had even given him a little of Drake's face and manner, the colour, lines, aggressive beards, loud voice, loud laugh, what those who did not know him in his black moods called "a way with him." Tears of anger, self-pity and some of love pricked Andrews's eyes. If I could revenge you on the dead, he thought. Is there no way to hurt the dead? Yet he knew that that foolish sentimental heart would not have desired revenge. Was it not even possible to please the dead, he wondered, and so swiftly it seemed to his superstitious mind a supernatural answer, came the thought "Do not do as your father and ruin a woman."

Still walking swiftly in the direction of Hassocks he swore silently that he would not. "I will only warn her," he said, "and go." Only by not seeing her again he felt could he prevent her ruin.

And yet how different it would have been if Carlyon had been his father. It did not seem odd to him so to think of the man who was seeking to kill him. Carlyon would have satisfied his mother's heart, and he himself would have been born with will and backbone. He remembered his first meeting with Carlyon.

He was walking by himself away from the school. He had one hour of freedom and exhilarated by it ran up the hill beyond the school, the sooner to escape the sight of the red brick barrack-like building, the sooner to see the moors stretching away, sweep beyond sweep of short heather, into the sunset. He ran with his eyes on the ground, for then he always seemed to move faster. He knew from experience that when he had counted two hundred and twenty-five he would be within a few feet of the summit. Two hundred and twenty-one, twenty-two, twenty-three, twenty-four, twenty-five. He raised his eyes. A man stood with his back to him, in much the same way as he had stood a few days before at the turn of the road beyond Hassocks. He was dressed in black and as then he gave the impression of bulk poised with incongruous lightness. He was staring at the sunset, but when he heard a step behind him he turned with remarkable swiftness, as though footsteps were associated in his mind with danger. Andrews saw then for the first time the broad shoulders, short thick neck, low receding ape-like brow and the dark eyes that in a flash tumbled to the ground the whole of the animal impression which the body had raised. The eyes could on occasion, laugh, be merry, but their prevailing tone, Andrews found later, was a brooding sadness. They were smiling, however, when he first saw them with a kind of happy wonder.

"Have you seen it?" Carlyon said with a hushed, trembling ecstasy and outflung finger, and Andrews had looked beyond him at a sky tumultuous with flame, an angry umber, rising from the grey ashes of the moor, spumed up in tottering pinnacles into the powdery blue smoke of the sky.

They stood in silence and stared at it, and then the stranger turned to him and said, "The school. I'm looking for the school." It was as though he had mentioned the word prison to an escaped convict. "I've come from there," Andrews said. "It's down there."

"One can't see the sun set from there," Carlyon remarked, and had the air in those few words of condemning the whole institution, masters, boys, buildings. He frowned a little and said contemptuously, "Do you belong there?" Andrews nodded.

"Do you like it?" Andrews hearing the tone gazed at the stranger with a peculiar fascination. Others had asked him that question as it were rhetorically, assuming a fervent assent. They generally added some jolly reference to beatings and a dull anecdote of their schooldays. But the stranger spoke to him as though they were both of one age, with a slight contempt as though there would be something ignoble in answering "yes."

"I hate it," he said.

"Why do you stay?" the question, quietly put, was stunning to the boy in its implications of free will.

"It's worse at home," he said. "My mother's dead."

"You should run away," the stranger said carelessly and turning his back stared again at the sunset. Andrews watched him. At that moment his heart, barren of any object of affection, was ready open to hero worship. The man stood in front of him with his legs a little apart as though balancing himself upon the spinning globe. A sailor, Andrews thought, remembering that his father stood so.

After a little the man turned again and seeing that the boy was still there asked him whether he happened to know a boy at school named Andrews.

Andrews looked at him in amazement. It was as though a figure from a dream had suddenly stepped into reality and claimed acquaintanceship with him. "I'm Andrews," he said.

"That's strange," the man said, watching him with a mixture of apprehension and curiosity, "you are pale. You don't look strong. Unlike your father. I was your father's friend," he said.

The past tense caught Andrews's attention. "I'm glad you are not his friend now," he said. "I hate him."

"He's dead," Carlyon said.

There was a pause and then Andrews said slowly, "I suppose you'd be shocked if I said I was glad."

The stranger laughed. "Not in the least. I imagine that he'd be a particularly unlovely character on shore. He was a great sailor though. Let me introduce myself —my name's Carlyon, skipper and owner of the *Good Chance,* your father's ship." He held out his hand. Andrews took it. The grip was firm, brief and dry.

"How did he die?" he asked.

"Shot. You knew what your father was?"

"I guessed," Andrews said.

"And now," Carlyon asked, "what do you want to do?" He suddenly made a twisted embarrassed motion with his hands. "Your father left me everything." He added quickly, turning a little away, "Of course you have only to ask. You can have anything but the ship." His voice dropped on the last word to the same hushed note which he had used in speaking of the sunset. His voice was extraordinarily musical, even in the shortest, most careless sentence. It had a concentration, a clear purity suggesting depth and tautness, which while utterly unlike in timbre, yet suggested the note of a violin. Andrews listened to it with a kind of hunger.

"Will you stay here?" Carlyon asked, making a gesture with his hand down the hill.

"I hate it," Andrews said. "It's ugly."

"Why did you come up here?" Carlyon asked suddenly.

"It's all red brick down there. And a gravel playground. Every few yards there's something in the way. Up here there's nothing for miles and miles."

Carlyon nodded. "I know," he said. "Why don't you come with me?"

That was all that passed before the decision was made. Andrews from that moment would have followed Carlyon to the ends of the world, and yet it was Carlyon who was ridiculously impetuous and desired simply to walk away then with no more said or done. It was Andrews who insisted that Carlyon must come down to the school and make arrangements.

That night Carlyon stayed at an inn in the town and Andrews, as he said good night, asked the question he had been longing to ask all the evening. "Do you want me to come?" "Yes," Carlyon had answered. "We both love the same things. They do not love them at this school, and my men, fine men, mind you, do not love them. We are made to be friends."

"Made to be friends," Andrews laughed, walking over the downs. What a mess he had made of that friendship. He wondered whether if he had the power, he would undo what he had done; have back the covert jeers, his father's example constantly thrown up, the hated, noisy set, the danger, but also Carlyon's friendship, the cabin, shut out from the eyes of the crew, Carlyon speaking, Carlyon reading, Carlyon's clear, refreshing certainty of what he followed. He had not by his act destroyed his shame nor his fear, but had increased them both, and he had lost Carlyon. And yet if he was able to return through time he must leave behind Elizabeth and this reawakened, defeated, but persistent longing to raise himself from the dirt.

Absorbed in drifting thoughts of the past an hour

had fled. The day had begun and a pale crocus yellow light had absorbed the first silver. The lights in the valley had again gone out save for a few which still burned not brightly but like dull, rusty blossoms of a wild bush. Coming to a rise Andrews was startled to see the cottage below him, small, barren of light or movement. The faint sunlight was unable to pierce the trees in whose shelter the cottage lay, so that while the world was bathed in a light shower of gold, the cottage was in shadow. But to Andrews watching from the down, his heart beating with the suddenness of the sight, it lay in the deeper shadow of danger and of death. He did not know in the confusion into which his heart had been thrown, when thus unexpectedly woken from the past, whether it was fear or love that made the beats. He gazed hard at the cottage as though by intensity he might force it to declare any secrets which it might hold. No smoke came from the chimney, no light from the windows. This absence of life signified nothing, for the hour could hardly be later than seven, yet it frightened Andrews. Suppose that Carlyon and his men had already visited the cottage and that it now hid their revenge. It was useless to tell himself that Carlyon would not allow a woman to be hurt. Hake and Joe were with him. He wondered where Carlyon had left the *Good Chance*. If he had lost the ship his leadership was over. It seemed to Andrews that centuries had passed since he had watched, with a heart exalted as compared with now, the smoke rise from the cottage chimneys.

Very slowly he walked to the brink of the down,

his eyes fixed on the cottage. There was yet another possibility to fear, that inside the cottage the smugglers were waiting for him to fall into the trap set by Cockney Harry. But was it a trap? It was his duty to warn Elizabeth, but when had he ever done anything for the sake of duty? He might in opening that cottage door find himself face to face with Carlyon, Joe, Hake, and the rest of them. He remembered the vision he had seen in the yellow candle light in Lucy's room. He stood there in what seemed even to himself a pitiable hesitation. If only he had not fallen to that woman, he thought, how easy it would have been to have gone swinging blindly down the hill. His duty fulfilled, he would have been clean, exultant, confident of the future, confident that he had risen once and for all from his past. He returned now defeated by his body, dispirited, hopeless, to give a warning and then go. Why not abandon this attempt to be better than I am and escape now and never give the warning? I'm only beginning over again this weary, hopeless business of attempting to rise. I shall be disappointed again. Why not save myself that bitterness? The cowardly suggestion drove in on him with too great a force. If it had come quietly, insidiously, it might have won, but this brazen confident attempt defeated its own purpose. His heart rose in revolt. He half ran down the hill, careless of cover, intent only on putting it out of his power to draw back.

As he reached the edge of the trees and the cottage appeared again before him, as it had appeared on his first arrival, caution returned. His eyes on the window, he ran on tiptoe across the bare space between the coppice and the wall. Pressing his body hard against the wall, as though he hoped to be absorbed into its firmness, he put one eye to the corner of the window. The room within seemed empty. Surely all was well. He took three strides along the wall to the door and gently raised the latch. To his surprise the door opened. How careless she is, he thought. She should bolt this door. Seeing the room empty he knelt down himself and drew the bottom bolt. The top was broken.

He looked round him and sighed a little with relief to see no sign of disturbance. It was not a trap then, he thought. I must get her away from here this morning. In the middle of the room was the kitchen table on which the coffin had lain. Do not be afraid, old man, Andrews said under his breath, I will not touch her. I am going to save her from the others, that is all. He shivered a little. The morning air now that he had ceased to walk was cold. It seemed to him very possible that the room might hold a jealous, bitter and suspicious ghost. I don't want any interference from the spirits, he thought, and smiled wearily at his own superstition. The room and house were very still. Should he go up and wake her? He longed, only now he realised to the full with what passion and what impatience, to see her again. If only he had returned unsullied, a conqueror of himself for her. I will try again, will try again, he thought, beating down his own self-mockery. I don't care how often I fall. I will try again. For the second time within twenty-four hours and for the second time in three years he prayed. "O God, help me." He turned hastily round. It was as though a warm draught had been blown on to the back of his neck. He found himself again facing the table and the imagined, but disquieting, presence of a coffin. Don't be afraid, old man, he implored. I am not here to make love. She would never look at me. I want to save her, that is all.

He shook himself a little, like a dog. He was becoming foolish. I will get breakfast, he thought, and surprise her. A row of cups were hanging above the sink. He took one down and then stood, the tips of his fingers caressing the edge, but his mind on the past, his eyes fixed to a key hole, his heart trembling as though at a saint. Then the small door which led to the upper floor opened and he looked up. "Is it you at last?" he said. His voice was hushed and trembling in the presence of a mystery. The room was gold with sunlight, but he had not noticed it till now.

children it was best to go for help. She also said that there was a neighbour only a mile away. Certainly he

PART III

CHAPTER X

ELIZABETH stood at the bottom of the stairs, her hand on the open door, her eyes sleepy and astonished. "You," she said.

Andrews turned the cup round and round in his hands, embarrassed now, almost wordless. "I've come back," he said.

She stepped down into the room and Andrews watched with fascinated eyes the swing of her gait, the manner in which she flung her chin up as she moved. "Oh, yes, I can see that," she said with a slight smile. "Here, give me that cup. You'll break it."

Andrews put his hand with sudden resolution behind his back. "No," he said, "I want this cup. This was the cup we both drank from."

"That's not the one," Elizabeth answered quickly, and as Andrews gazed at her in astonishment, she twisted her lower lip between her teeth. "I remember that one," she added, "because it had a chip out of the rim. Tell me—what are you doing here?"

"I've got news," Andrews said. He spoke with reluctance. A great unwillingness to tell her swept over him. For when he had given her his news what possible excuse had he to stay?

"Will it wait till after breakfast?" she asked, and when he nodded she began with no more said to lay the table.

Only when they were seated did she speak again. "You must have been up early?" He grunted assent, afraid to hear the question which would bring out his news.

"Has anything happened since I've been away?" he asked.

"No," she said, "nothing ever happens here."

"The door was unbolted. Do you think that's safe?"

"It was unbolted when you first came," she replied, and watching him with candid eyes, "I did not want you to have a less warm welcome when you came back."

He looked up sharply in a kind of poignant hope, but her candour repelled it. All her meaning seemed on the surface, none beneath it. "Did you know I would come back?"

She frowned a little as though puzzled. "But surely that was the understanding. We parted friends, didn't we?"

"You are very generous." Her voice for some reason made him bitter, but she did not notice his sarcasm. "I don't understand you," she answered. "You say very puzzling things."

"Oh, I am not like you," Andrews said. "I don't know that I want to be. You are so clear, so terribly sane. I'm twisted."

"Am I very clear?" she asked. She laid down her knife and, resting her chin on one hand, stared at him curiously across the table. "Could you tell, for instance, that I was anxious for you to return? It's lonely here. When I came down the other morning I was sorry that you'd gone. I felt guilty. I shouldn't have persuaded you to go to Lewes. I had no right to make you risk yourself. Do you forgive me?"

Andrews jumped up from the table and, walking over to the fireplace, turned his back on her. "You are laughing at me," he said.

Elizabeth smiled. "You *are* twisted," she said. "Why should you think that? No, we are friends."

He turned round with scarlet face. "If you say that word again——" he threatened. Watching her white, puzzled, yet calm, face quietened him. "I'm sorry," he said. "I have only had one friend and I betrayed him. I don't want to betray you."

"You will not betray me," she said. "You left your knife."

"I thought you might need it."

"You knew that you might need it."

He turned his back again and kicked the coals in the fire. "I was a fool," he muttered. "Just sentimentality. That means nothing."

"I thought it brave," she said. "I admired you tremendously for that."

Again Andrews coloured. "You are laughing at me," he said. "You know that you despise me, that I'm a coward." He laughed. "Why, I've betrayed you twice in Lewes, and I'm betraying you now if you only knew it. Don't mock me by pretending admiration. You women are cunning. No one but a woman would think of that turn to the screw." His voice broke. "You win. You see it's successful."

Elizabeth rose from the table and came and stood beside him at the fire. "How have you betrayed me?" she asked.

Andrews without looking up answered, "Once with a woman."

There was a pause. Then Elizabeth said coldly, "I don't understand how that's a betrayal of me. Of yourself perhaps. What other betrayal?"

"It came out in Court that you sheltered me."

"In court?" she asked. Her voice trembled for a reason which he could not understand. "Were you there?"

"I was in the witness box," he said gloomily. "Don't praise me. It was only partly you. And the other parts were drink and a harlot. What do you say to that?"

"Well done," she said.

He shrugged his shoulders. "You go on too long. You are not as cunning as I thought you. I'm getting used to that mockery. You must change your tack."

"That woman," Elizabeth asked, "who was she? What was she like?"

"She was my equal."

"I thought you said she was a harlot. Tell me—was she better looking than I?"

Andrews looked up in astonishment. Elizabeth was watching him with an anxious smile. "I'd never compare you," he said. "You belong to different worlds."

"Yet I should like to know."

He shook his head. "I can't. I could only compare your bodies, and I can't see yours for you."

"I'm like other women, surely?" she asked sadly.

"No," he said, his voice soaring in sudden enthusiasm. "Like no other woman."

"I see," her voice was cold again. "Well, tell me more of your betrayals. Why am I betrayed because you loved this woman? You are the kind of man who does that frequently, I imagine."

"Not love," he said.

"Is there any difference? Men are very fond of splitting hairs." She glanced as he had done at the kitchen table as though to her also it stood for a certain ever-present jealous spirit.

"Which did he feel?" she asked.

"Did he wish to hurt you or did he wish, even if unsuccessful, to do unselfishly?"

"Then his was both," she said. "Tell me—you spoke of a third betrayal. What was that?"

The moment had come. "I came here to warn you, and I've been putting it off and putting it off."

"To warn me?" Her chin went up in a kind of defiance. "I don't understand."

"Carlyon and the rest mean to punish you for sheltering me. They are coming here to-day or to-morrow." He told her Cockney Harry's message. "Apparently it was not a trap," he added.

"But you thought it was," she said curiously, "and yet you came?"

He interrupted her. "You must go now at once."

"Why didn't you tell me before?"

"I hated the idea of your going," he said simply, "and so I spoilt the only decent thing I've done."

"And did you think I should really go?"

"You must," he said, and then seeing her flash to meet the unwelcome word, he added quickly, "You must take what money you have and go anywhere—to London perhaps—until this blows over."

"No," Elizabeth said, "I don't see the necessity."

"Good God," Andrews protested, "must I make you go?"

'Why should I run away? I have that,' and she pointed at the empty gun where it stood in its accustomed corner.

"It's empty."

"I have cartridges."

"You don't know how to use it. You told me so."

"But you do," she said.

Andrews stamped his foot furiously. "No," he said, "no. I've run enough risks for you. You women are all the same, never satisfied."

"You mean you won't stay and help."

"You don't know what you are asking," he said. "I'm afraid of them. I'm more afraid of pain than of anything else in the world. I'm a coward. I'm not ashamed of it, I tell you."

She smiled with a sad yet humourous twist to the mouth. "Forget that idea," she said.

He stamped his foot again with childish petulance. "It's not an idea. It's a fact. I've warned you. Now I'm going." He did not look at her, lest his resolution might waver, but walked like a drunken man with exaggerated straightness to the door.

"I stay," he heard her say behind him. He swung round and said with desperation, "You can't use the gun without me."

"I had no need to use it on you," she answered.

"Those men are different. They are not cowards."

"They must be cowards," she said with unanswerable logic, "if they intend to revenge themselves on me."

Outside the sun allured him with pale gold. What woman dared to compete with the sun in the beauty and yet in sense of peace? Its colour seemed to sleep along the ground and in its sleep to glow with an untranslatable and secret dream of an exalted place. Go, go, go, reason told him, and watching the dozing countryside even his heart felt the same urge. He appealed to that critic which had so often in the past tried in vain to drive him along a noble course, but the critic was silent, stood aside, seemed to say "Here is your last and great decision. I will not influence you." Before his eyes like a shoulder turned on him in disdain rose the down over which he had first come in blind terror a century ago. If only I could be blind with fear again, he thought, how happily could I fly from here. Even the girl behind him was silent now, leaving him, as all the world seemed to leave him, to make his own decision. And he was not accustomed thus to use his will. "I'm going," he said again irresolutely, in the vain hope that Elizabeth might waver, but she remained silent. He wondered a little at himself. He was surely bewitched, for never before had his feet found it hard to leave danger behind him. To help them he tried to call up before his eyes a vision of what might happen to him if he fell into the hands of Hake or Joe, when even into Carlyon's meant death. But instead he saw again a glow of yellow candle light and Elizabeth's face contorted in a scream. It was no good. He could not leave her. The door which he had opened he again slammed to, shot the bolt and came back into the centre of the room with hanging head.

"You've won again," he said. "I'll stay."

He looked up at her with angry resentment. Her eyes were glowing, but he noticed even at that moment that the glow was on the surface only and altered the nature of the drowsing depths no more than moonlight on a pond can transmute more than the face of the dark metallic water into silver.

"Listen," he said, "since we've chosen to be fools we must make the best of it. Have you tools and wood? I want to mend the top bolt of the door." She led him into the shed, where he had slept first, and found him wood, nails, a saw, a hammer. Clumsily, for he was not used to working with his hands, he made a bolt and fastened it in place. "That helps to shut us in," he said. She was standing close beside him and he was on the point of taking her in his arms. Then a thought stopped him. I have the living against me, he thought, I do not want the dead also. To prevent a return of the temptation he tried to busy himself with means to their defence. "The cartridges?" he asked. "Where are they?" She brought them and he loaded the gun, leaving the others spread out on the table ready to the hand. Then he walked to the window, examined the out-look, entered the shed and reassured himself that the window was too high from the ground for a flank attack to be successful. "We are ready for them," he said dully. He was oppressed by a question. If Carlyon should be the first to come, could he shoot? He glanced out of the corners of his eyes at Elizabeth. It was she or Carlyon. He would have to shoot, and yet he prayed that it might be Hake or Joe who would offer himself to his bullet.

"How far is your nearest neighbour?" he asked.

"Not more than a mile," she said. "He keeps a farm —and a cellar."

"You mean he's a friend of these men?" Andrews asked. "Surely if he heard shots he would send to Shoreham."

"You have lived very much on the sea, haven't you?" Elizabeth said. "You do not know this border-land, not close enough to the coast to be patrolled, not far enough away to have no dealings with smugglers. Here we are in the pocket of the Gentlemen." She unexpectedly clapped her hands. "What fun, after all, it is," she said.

"Fun," he exclaimed. "Don't you realise that it means death for someone?"

"You are so afraid of death," she said.

"I'm afraid of extinction," Andrews said, resting his hand on the barrel of the gun, in which he found comfort. "I am all that I have, I'm afraid of losing that."

"There is no danger," she said. "We go on."

"Oh, you believe in God," Andrews murmured, "and all that." He kicked his heels in an embarrassed fashion, not looking at her, blushing a little. "I envy you," he said. "You seem so certain, so sane, at peace. I've never been like that—at least only for a very little, while listening to music. I'm listening to music now. Go on talking to me. While I hear you all this chaos," he put his hand on his head, "is smoothed out." He looked up at her suspiciously, expecting her laughter.

Elizabeth asked with a small puzzled frown, "What do you mean by chaos?"

"It is as though," Andrews said slowly, "there were about six different people inside me. They all urge different things. I don't know which is myself."

"The one who left the knife and the one who stays here now," she said.

"But then, what of the others?"

"The devil," she answered.

He laughed. "How old fashioned you are."

She put herself in front of him. "Look at me," she said. Hesitatingly he looked up and seeing her face glowing (the only word for that radiance, which gave her face the appearance of a pale crystal holding a sun or a star) the desire to take her in his arms was almost irresistible. But I must not, he told himself I will not spoil these hours with her. I have spoiled everything I have touched. I will not touch her. He thrust his hands deep in his pockets and baulked desire gave his face a sullen, hostile look. "Tell me how you could return to warn me," Elizabeth asked, "when you do not believe in immortality. You risked death."

"Sentimentality," he said with a grin.

A faint puzzled frown dimmed for a moment the radiance. "Why do you always make little of the good you do," she asked, "and make much of the bad?"

He bit his lip angrily. "If you want to know why I came," he said, "I'll tell you. Remember it's your fault if all this peace is spoiled."

"No one can spoil my peace," she said. "Tell me."

He came closer and grinned at her angrily, as though he was going to do her a great wrong and hated her for that reason. "I came," he said, "because I loved you." He looked for a smile or even a laugh, but she watched him gravely, and the increase in her colour was so faint that it might have been imagined only.

"I thought that was it," she said without moving, "but why this secrecy?"

He stared at her in amazement. The candour in her eyes struck him with a kind of fear. "Must it remain in the past tense?" she said. "You loved me. Is that all? Is it untrue now?"

He moistened his lips, but could not speak. "If you cannot say you love me," she said with a slow but not mocking smile, "say again that you loved me an hour or two ago."

"Do you mean——" he said. His hands moved out towards her hesitatingly, fingers afraid of the irrevocability of contact. Then with a leap of the heart he found his voice. "I love you," he said. "I love you." He held her now but at a distance. "I love you, too," she said, her eyes closed and her body trembling a little. He shut his eyes so that they might be together in a darkness, which would be empty of everything but themselves. Stumbling blindly through that darkness their mouths at first lost and then found each other. After a while they began to speak in whispers lest the darkness should be shattered by sound.

"Why were you so long?"

"How could I expect—I was afraid."

"Am I worse than death? You were not afraid of that." "I don't fear it any longer. You are filling me with yourself. That means courage, peace, holiness."

He opened his eyes. "Do you know they gave you a surname in court. It seemed so strange that you should have any other name than Elizabeth. A surname means to tie you down to earth. I've already forgotten it. Open your eyes and tell me that this isn't a dream."

She opened them. "How you talk," she said, "who were so silent about what really mattered."

"I'm excited," he said. "I want to laugh and shout and sing. I want to get wildly drunk."

He took his arms away and began to move restlessly round the room. "I am so happy," he said. "I've never felt like this before. What a curious feeling it is—happiness."

"This is only the beginning," Elizabeth said. "We have eternity."

"We have at any rate all our lives. Don't squander time for that 'perhaps'. Promise you'll live long and slowly."

She laughed. "I'll do my best."

"Come here," Andrews said and when she came he

gazed at her with wonder. "To think that I can say come and you'll come. You shouldn't though. I wish you could realise how unworthy I am of you. Don't laugh. I know every man says that. But it's true of me. I'm a coward. It's no use shaking your head. You can never wholly trust me. I told you that I was with a woman last night. I'm dirty, I tell you, soiled."

"Did you love her?"

"You are very young after all, aren't you? Men don't go with harlots for that."

"Then it doesn't touch me. Look," she spread out her arms and her chin again tilted upwards with that instinctive fighting gesture, "I will stand now for ever between you and them."

A shadow crossed Andrews's face. "For ever is a long word. You must stay with me always. You must not die before me. If you did I should fall away." He laughed. "Here am I talking of death on the birthday of my life." He glanced apprehensively at the place where the coffin had lain. "He won't come between us, will he?" he implored. "His must be a jealous spirit."

"Only a spirit," Elizabeth said. "We must pity him. He was kind to me in his way. He said that if he could not have me he would never let another man love me." Her fingers softly caressed the edge of the table. "Poor spirit," she whispered. "So soon defeated."

The thought of the dead man set up a chain of associations in Andrews's mind. "It was Mrs. Butler," he said, "who brought your name up in court. Will she be coming here?"

"Not for four days," Elizabeth said.

"And we'll be gone then from here. Where shall we go?" But it was not material facts of sustenance, of earning a living which passed, image by image, through Andrews's brain. He thought of the seasons they would see together; of summer, blue sea, white cliffs, red poppies in the golden corn; winter, to wake in the morning to see Elizabeth's hair across the pillow, her body close to his, and outside the deep, white silence of snow; spring again with restless hedgerows and the call of birds. They would hear music together—organs in dim cathedrals speaking of sad peace, the heartache of violins, the piano's cold dropping notes, like water split slowly down a long echoing silence. And always the music of her voice, which seemed to him in this new foolish, drunken happiness more lovely than any instrument.

"We will not go yet," she said, obstinate lines round her mouth. "What was it your Cockney Harry said? They will come to-day or to-morrow. We will face them first and then we will go."

He shrugged his shoulders. "If you will. I will pay any price, I think, for this happiness."

"You have not told me your story yet," she said.

He hesitated. "We should be keeping a look out."

She pouted her lips scornfully. "They will not come before dusk," she said. "Let's sit down here on the floor by the fire." She smiled. "I'm tired of being old and wise. I want to be childish and be told a story."

She curled into the crook of his arm and he told her of the past two days; of how he had watched the smoke from the cottage chimney and thought it a flock of

white birds round a saint ("I was thinking most un-
saintly thoughts of you," she interrupted); of the soft-
eyed cattle who drank with him at the blue dewpond
and of the bird which sang. He spread out the story of
his walk slowly with meticulous detail, unwilling, as he
had been in reality, to arrive in Lewes. But when he
reached that part of his story he found a kind of flagell-
ant pleasure in emphasising his cowardice, his drunk-
enness and his lust. "I could not draw your picture,"
he said wryly. "I was a fool to think that I could ever
draw you." He told her of Lucy, the scene in the court,
the acquittal, and of Cockney Harry's arrival. "I put
you out of mind," he said. "I was afraid to come and
warn you. I went upstairs to sleep with that woman."

"But then you came," Elizabeth said.

"Yes, but if only I had come at once, while I was
comparatively clean."

"Forget all that," she said. "Everything is changed
now. We have only the future not the past."

"I am afraid," he said, "of the past breaking in."

"Don't be afraid." She suddenly pressed her mouth
to his with a kind of vehement ferocity. "That is our
dedication. If we are very close there will be no room
for the past."

"Don't tempt it," he implored.

"You are so superstitious. It is always so with those
who don't believe in God."

He put up his hands to her face and pulled it down
to him. "How sane and even you are," he said. "I can't
believe that you are younger than I am. You seem so
wise. Dear sanity."

"Dear madness," she replied.

"Tell me," Andrews said, "aren't you afraid of this thing that has happened to us—this falling in love. It's terribly changing. So strong that I feel that it could fling me at any moment into Heaven or hell."

"I'm not afraid."

"And yet for you it's so much worse," he said. "It must bring you pain."

"I'm not afraid of that kind of pain," she said. "You exaggerate it so. When there is anger I fear the anger —the kind of turmoil in the mind—but not the pain it may inflict."

"What do you fear most of all?"

"Hate," she said.

"For years," Andrews said, "I've longed for a peace, a certainty, a sanity. I thought I could get it perhaps in music, weariness, a number of things. I have it now. You are all of that. Do you wonder I want you? It would be worse than before if I should lose you now. You remember the parable about the swept room and the devils which entered worse than the first. You must possess me, go on possessing me, never leave me to myself."

As he talked he felt his exaltation wavering on its height. You'll never stay the course, his heart mocked him. These are fine sentiments. They are not yours, you coward, drunkard, bully. These are the trumpets preparing for another betrayal. It seemed impossible, watching the peaceful depths of her eyes, to imagine that any man could give her a more permanent happiness than she already possessed within herself. He tried to imagine that astonishingly young wise face growing slowly older in a married tranquillity, lines appearing, the dark hair turning grey, the wisdom deepening. It was a blasphemy, he thought, to imagine for one moment that any man could satisfy a face with such sad eyes. The eyes were not sad, he felt, plunging deeper into a youthful romanticism, for any grief of her own. For herself there was a white tranquillity kindling into laughter round the mouth and on the surface of the eyes—laughter which could be in turn flippant, mocking, deep. It was, and he laughed at himself for sentimentality, a pity for the ways of the world and a too impetuous anxiety of the spirit to loose the body and plead for them before a divine tribunal.

Elizabeth broke his thoughts by rising with a slight shake of her body as though to dispel vague dreams. "Wake up," she said. "However much you protest I am going to be practical." She fetched the gun from where it stood against the wall. "Show me how you loaded this," she said.

Andrews took the gun in his hands, pulled out the cartridge, then looked up struck by suspicion. "Why do you want to know?" he asked. "I'm going to be here to shoot for you. Do you think," he hesitated, feeling shame-facedly the justice of such a thought, "that I may run away?"

Elizabeth coloured. "I never dreamed of such a thing," she said angrily. "Listen and believe this if you never believe another word I speak. I trust you absolutely."

"Thank you," Andrews said.

"I will tell you," Elizabeth continued, with hesitation, "what I was thinking. I can't bear you to imagine that I distrusted you. It was only this—I realised that I was being selfish again, as I was selfish when I sent you to Lewes. There's little danger for me, but great danger for you. They want your life—they only want to frighten me. If they find me alone ready and armed they will go away, but they will not give up easily if you are here. Don't interrupt, but listen. Leave me now before it is dusk. The road will be clear. Make your way to London, I can lend you money. We will arrange a meeting place where I can join you in a few days."

"I won't leave you," Andrews said. The temptation had been conquered, he was astonished to find how completely. "Either you must come with me now or we both stay."

"I won't go," she said obstinately. "Because I'm no strong walker. The two of us would move slowly and be more easily pursued. Better face them within four walls than in the open." She laughed. "Look at me. I am not stout, muscular, am I? I have always believed myself slim. Don't disillusion me. Can you imagine me running for miles, scrambling over hedges, wading through ditches? I'd be a hopeless handicap."

"Well, I stay," he said with equal obstinacy.

She watched him for a moment with a puzzled frown as if she were trying to devise some new method of appeal. "You are brave, you know," she said.

"It's not that," Andrews replied, "I haven't the courage to leave you."

He moved over to where the cups were hung in an orderly row above the sink. "Let's pretend we have been married for years," he said, "and do pleasant ordinary things, cook food, wash up, talk to each other as though we had seen each other yesterday and would see each other to-morrow. This fresh love is too heady, too exalted as yet for me, too close to pain."

"The other will come too soon," Elizabeth said, "I do not want these ordinary things. You will know me so well in a year."

"I wish I could believe that," Andrews said.

"Let's keep the freshness while we can, even if it's painful," Elizabeth whispered with sudden vehemence. "Don't you see how quickly the time is going. It's only a few hours till dusk. Oh, I know there's no danger, but I'm a little frightened all the same. It's hate again, hate coming."

"The door's bolted."

Elizabeth stamped her foot in a sudden petulance. "Have your way," she said. "We'll pretend what you wish, be indifferent now when we are fresh, have not when we may."

"I didn't say indifferent," Andrews said. He caught her in his arms. "This is how I shall kiss you in five years' time."

She laughed. "If I am sane, you are mad,' she said. "Was there ever such an alliance? Come, take that cloth and dry those cups."

It was early in the afternoon when Elizabeth declared that she must go into the village and buy food.

"I shall be gone at least an hour," she said and told him what he might do to occupy himself, what plates might be laid ready on the table, what corners swept. At first he tried to prevent her going and when she insisted that love was not enough for a young man to feed upon, he insisted that he must accompany her.

"No," she said. "You must guard the fort. Besides," she looked at him with narrowed, faintly suspicious eyes, "if the neighbourhood knows that there's a man sleeping here . . ."

He cursed the neighborhood, for under its gaze her sanity always seemed to touch earth, to grow cautious, careful, respectable. He could not somehow square her courage and candour with respectability, and this he told her.

"Do you want me to join your harlots?" she said. "Haven't I promised to give myself to you? But not to-night, not till we are married."

"How wise you are," he said in anger less against her than against his inability to value those things in which she had such faith. "Must I make a settlement also? You can't love me if you have to wait till a form of words is mumbled over us. Or are you afraid that I shall desert you to-morrow and you'll lose that precious respectability?" A sense of his own injustice made him pelt her the more fiercely with his words.

"You don't understand," she said. "It's not what you call respectability. It's a belief in God. I can't alter that for you. I'd leave you first."

"What has He done for you?"

Her candour was very evident to him in the manner

in which she met his challenge. She did not sweep it aside in a vague rush of words, as some pious women would have done. She was silent, seeking an answer. He saw her eyes sweep the bare room in a pathetic quest. Up and down they peered, up and down, and at last with a faint note of apology she brought out the brief reply "I am alive."

"Why so am I," he said. "But I'm not grateful."

"There was this morning," she said, "and the future."

"Don't let's pay gratitude in advance," he said.

"But all the same," her chin tilted upwards, "I'll do what I think is right." Without looking at him again she unhooked a basket from a nail in the wall and unbolted the door. With her back turned she said "I love you, but if you can't take my terms, you must go." She slammed the door behind her and ran quickly down the path towards the road.

It was a couple of hours before she returned, long enough for Andrews to think over his words, grow repentant, curse himself for spoiling this first rapturous time in quarrelling. He did what she had commanded and was more than ordinarily scrupulous in the fulfilment of the tasks, regarding them as a penance for his hasty words. He knew that Elizabeth would take more than half an hour to reach the village, and yet an hour had hardly gone before he began to grow anxious, to torture himself with the idea of a possible meeting between Elizabeth and his enemies on the road. It was useless to tell himself that no harm could come to her in broad daylight. He was haunted still by his first image of the cottage, when it had raised itself suddenly before him in the dark in apparent isolation.

Now that he had nothing with which to occupy himself he was restless, walked hither and thither in the room, began even to speak aloud to himself. "To let her go in anger," he said. "It was the act of a brute. Suppose that something should happen to her now before I can tell her how wrong I am. It was not respectability, it was holiness she showed." With his eyes on the place where the coffin had lain he began to address the spirit of Mr. Jennings, not in any real belief that any portion of the dead man survived, but rather as an insurance against a very remote possibility. "Look after her," he implored, "if you can. You too loved her." It seemed to him that the spirit, if indeed it existed, had an unfair advantage in guardianship. It could travel with greater speed than the lagging flesh and to places where the body could not follow. Besides, Andrews thought with a whimsicality, partly sincere, he will have the ear of either God or the devil. The thought of Mr. Jennings, however, and this play with the idea of immortality brought Andrews's errant steps to an abrupt standstill. Mr. Jennings in the flesh had sworn that no other than himself should touch Elizabeth, and he, Andrews, in the humility of his return had given the jealous spirit a promise which he had broken. Was a spirit now on the side of his enemies, he wondered, to rob him of the glorious prize he craved? There are no spirits, he told himself in scornful reassurance. He kicked with a childish petulance the leg of the table as though to put a daring seal on his disbelief, for the table now to him represented the open coffin which, as it might seem, had come between Elizabeth and him on their first meeting with a prompt, instinctive enmity.

At that moment (he had heard no footsteps) the latch was raised and Elizabeth entered. With a shame-faced grin Andrews drew back his foot, but Elizabeth had noticed nothing. He could see that she brought news. There was an excited flush on her face and her eyes sparkled.

"News," she said, "such news. Can you guess?" She put the basket down on the table and stood watching him with hands on hips.

He could not wait to hear the news however. Minutes, since she had left him, had taken on an exaggerated value. "Forgive me," he implored, "I was a fool and a brute. You were right. Be patient and try to teach me your holiness."

"Oh that," she said and with the words brushed the whole angry past to Lethe. "But I've news." Her eyes sparkled. "We've won. Wasn't I right to stay here?"

The relief, the sudden cessation of anxiety and double fear, was too much for Andrews to believe. "Not caught?" he asked.

"No, but soon. They are on the run—and away from here. That man, what did you call him, Cockney Harry has been seen near Chichester. And those men, who were acquitted, they are locked up again on a charge of smuggling. Only the half wit has escaped."

"But I don't understand. They were released. Why should they be running?"

"Ah, there's the triumph. Fresh evidence. They can't

try them again for murder, but smuggling's another matter." Elizabeth too must have been afraid, for with excited relief she piled the words on one another. "They've found their ship."

Andrews took a step forward. "Carlyon", he whispered, his voice dry with anxiety, a mad unreasoning anxiety for Carlyon's safety.

"They'll catch him soon." Her easy, careless confidence jarred on him.

"The *Good Chance*," he said softly. "He loved the ship. Now I've robbed him of it." He was silent for a moment picturing Carlyon and how he would receive the news. It would not be with tears or any loud grief. He knew that. He would see the rather too prominent chin jerked upwards, the low and too receding brow furrowed in puzzlement, while the brain sought some way of retrieving the devastating loss. Next, he knew, would come anger and the thought of revenge—punishment Carlyon would call it.

Elizabeth's voice, the triumph gone, recalled his thoughts. "I'm sorry," she said. He looked up and seeing her standing there so soon robbed of the exhilaration of her news a pity and tenderness quite alien to desire filled him. He wanted to touch her, but only as one would touch a child who was sad at some pleasure taken away. What after all was his friendship for Carlyon compared with this? Love Carlyon who dared to threaten this—child? Hate him rather.

"I'm heavy footed," Elizabeth said. "I forgot that you'd been friends."

"No, no," he protested. "But this news is not good

for us. Carlyon will be desperate. He wouldn't harm a woman, but now that he's lost his ship he'll have no authority except his strength. I know Joe."

"But the man at Chichester. . . ."

"One of them only. It may be a blind to decoy the officers away. Remember they meant to come here tonight. And look—it's not as light as it was half an hour ago." He walked to the door and looked out. The down was golden in sunlight, but a shadow veiled its base and insidiously advanced even as he watched.

"Come away from the door," Elizabeth said in a voice that trembled very slightly.

"No danger," Andrews replied. "They wouldn't trust to a shot. If it missed we'd be warned. No, they'll try and creep up when it's dark. How long before the dark?"

"Two hours, perhaps, if we are lucky."

"There's no luck where I am," Andrews said, looking out of the door. "There's a wind driving clouds towards the sun. It will be dark long before two hours have passed."

He walked slowly back and stood still in the centre of the room, watching Elizabeth but making no attempt to go to her. "Listen," he said, "it's possible that these men will get me." He spoke dully and apprehensively. "I've always left things too late, so I want to tell you now that I love you as I've never loved anyone or anything in the world before. Even myself. I was a blind fool this afternoon to quarrel in these few certain hours. I'm sorry. I think I'm beginning to understand. I'll ask for you only when we're married and that as a favour which I don't deserve. You were right. You are holy. I don't see how I can ever touch you without soiling you a little, but, my God," his voice became vehement and he took a step towards her, "I'll serve you, how I'll serve you."

With some idea of teaching death and darkness how to bear her likeness, he shut his eyes and held within his mind her image as she listened to him speak, chin raised, a slight flush upon her face, eyes flinching a little at the pain of happiness. He heard her answer him, words dropping with a soft, tender, cooling touch, into the heat of his brain.

"And I want you to know," she said, "that I've loved you or known it ever since I found the knife you had left. But I'm not holy. I'm ordinary like anyone else. I'm no fanatic. Only my heart wants to be good. But my body, this common, ordinary body, doesn't care for that. It wants you, even though it's frightened. But it must wait. Help me for just a few hours."

Andrews opened his eyes at the mention of hours and glanced at the window behind him. "I want to hear one more thing," he said. "Say that you forgive me for bringing you into this mess."

"I'm glad," she said simply. "But if it wasn't for me you'd never have gone to Lewes. Forgive me."

"I forgive you," Andrews said with a reluctant smile, "for making me do the only right thing I've ever done."

They came across the floor to each other and for a

while stood closely pressed together with no word said. Veil after veil of dusk was drawn across the room. A sudden creaking of the old table in the silence reminded them of evening on-coming. Andrews, whose whole attention had been fixed on memorising the lines of Elizabeth's face, the brow, the neck, the eyelashes, the chin, stepped back and turned with a nervous movement towards the window. "I never thought it would come so soon," he said, and both knew that he meant the dark. His heart was beating with an unpleasant insistence and his legs were weak about the knees. "Why did we stay?" he asked with a sense of disillusionment, as though he had just discovered that his past courage was bravado merely.

"Are you afraid?" Elizabeth asked with reproach.

"No, no," he protested. "It's just this dusk. It came so suddenly. As though a hand had snuffed the light." He walked backwards and forwards in the room. Magic was no bedfellow for danger, he thought. They could not lie together.

"I hate this waiting," he said slowly. "I wish they'd come," but inwardly he prayed desperately for courage and clutched the image of Elizabeth like a jewel to his heart. He saw that she was standing by the window looking out. He noted with surprise that her fingers were clenched fiercely upon her dress as though even upon her the waiting grew a strain.

He beat his hands together. "Of course there's no use in worrying." His voice broke nervously. "It's early evening. They won't come yet." He saw her lean forward and press her face against the window pane. "Do you see anything?" he cried.

"No, nothing," she said, fingers still clenched, but speaking softly as she would speak to a child fearing the dark.

"Then for God's sake," Andrews said irritably, "don't make sudden movements." It was extraordinary how consciousness of dark had robbed the room of magic, even of tenderness, and instead there was only fear and irritation. "We've been talking too long," he said, "instead of keeping watch."

With her back still turned Elizabeth said slowly, "Too long? I thought a lifetime would not be long enough?"

"I don't mean that," he protested. "Oh, we'll be lovers again soon, but now—we mustn't waste time."

She turned and regarded him with a kind of sorrowful tenderness. "Suppose we are wasting time now," she said, "we've had such a few hours with each other. We can't tell how many more we shall have. Let these men go hang. Speak to me, take no notice of the dark. The dark is made for lovers. Speak to me. Don't listen or watch any longer."

"Are you mad," Andrews said.

"You said I was sane."

Andrews suddenly sat down at the table and buried his face in his hands. O God, he prayed silently, if you are God give me courage. Don't let me start all over again by betraying her. I thought I'd won out of this cowardice at last.

Elizabeth left the window and came to his side. He felt her fingers on his hair, twisting it, pulling it this way and that in a whimsical fashion. He heard her laugh. "Don't worry," she said, "it's not worth it."

He looked up at her and said in a voice trembling on the brink of complete uncontrol, "I'm afraid. I'm a coward."

"The old story," she said mockingly, but she was watching him with half-veiled nervous anxiety. "I know it's untrue."

"It's not. It's not."

"Lewes—the knife—your warning," she reminded him.

He brushed them on one side. "I'm afraid, terribly afraid. Suppose I fail when they come, run away?"

"You won't. I tell you you are no coward. It's a delusion you've been living under." She put her fingers under his chin and forced it up, so that she could watch his eyes. "You've proved your courage three times to me," she said slowly. "You'll do it once more and then you'll know and be at peace. You've wanted peace. That's the way to it. Dear silly fool, you've worried always about your courage. That's what was wrong."

He shook his head, but she was obstinate, obstinate as though she were defending something on which she had put the whole of her own faith, and with a trace of fear, as though she were afraid to have it proved that she was mistaken. A sudden stiffening of her body frightened him. "Did you hear something?" he whispered and the trembling in his voice reached his own consciousness and showed him in a flash of despair the gap which separated two moments divided by but minutes in time—the magic seconds when they had stood together as lovers, brave and equal, and now, fear, humiliation, inequality.

"No," Elizabeth said, "I heard nothing. I only want to see how dark it gets. We must light a candle soon." She walked to the window and glanced outside. Then she turned quickly. Her fingers, but Andrews did not notice them, were clenched. "Listen," she said. "We shall need water before to-night. You must go with a pail now before it is dangerous to the well. The pail is in the corner there. Bring it." Her voice was brisk and commanding and Andrews obeyed.

At the door, watching the night which grew outside like a dark flower opening rapid petals, she directed him. "Down that path," she said, "behind those trees. Two minutes' walk, no more." Still examining the night she commanded, "Go now—now."

He hesitated a moment and she turned on him fiercely. "Won't you do even a small thing for me?" she cried and pushed at him with her hands. Dumb, caught up by her command, he made a blind motion towards her, which she repelled. "A farewell for two minutes' absence?" she mocked. "I'll kiss you when you return soon."

Pail in hand he walked down the path, but a soft, somehow imploring, echo of that "soon" brushed him on the cheek and made him turn. A white flower upon a slender stem which trembled in the dusk was what he seemed to see. Indeed the image was not fancy only, for one hand extended itself across the dark to find support against the door. It was too dark to see her face, but in her eyes he could imagine the smile well-known to him, because he could not see the fear.

CHAPTER XI

His body a little bent by the weight of the water in the pail, Andrews turned to make his way back to the cottage. A sky curdled with dark, heavy clouds had forced the pace of night. In a crack above his head a single star shone fitfully with a pale radiance between the scurry of cloud. Quenched and returning with an almost even rhythm the glow was like the revolving lantern of a lighthouse and when unseen might have been shining on another tract of land in a different quarter of the earth. In the western sky a yellow glow rapidly fading illumined the lower edge of an aerial bank of grey, soiled snow. To the south-west shadow had now completely enveloped the down and extinguished in darkness the contempt of its heaving shoulder. A frosty bite in the air mingled with physical dread to drive Andrews into a long discomforted shudder.

The path to the well was some fifty yards in length and a bend hid the cottage from view. Still staggering uncertainly from his load Andrews turned the corner. "Unwise," he thought, seeing the door of the cottage standing open, and was amazed still further at the imprudence of a candle. From within it displayed the defenceless door by its golden glow that washed outwards and lipped along the path.

Andrews put down his pail and stepped backwards, with mouth dry and lungs that seemed barren of air. Into the diminishing radiance of the candle a large man had stepped with a blundering caution which told his name to Andrews very familiar with Joe's incongruous bulk. "O God," he prayed, "help me. He'll find I'm not there and follow." Without waiting to see Joe enter the cottage Andrews ran. Only when he reached the well did the prick of conscience bring him to a halt. Elizabeth was alone in the cottage. "But she has the gun," he told himself and awaited for long seconds a shot which did not come. "Go back, go back, go back," heart told the flinching flesh, but that single reiterated message was ineffective beside the host of reason that the fearing body had at its call. "They are looking for me, they will not hurt her," he told himself, and again. "Carlyon must be there. He'll see that she's safe," and last of all a feeling of irritation against the responsibility forced on him. "It's her fault," he told himself. "Why did she send me for water? Why did she leave the door open? She was asking for trouble. If she'd any thought for my safety, she'd have been more careful." After all if he ran back now what could he do? He was unarmed.

And yet he must do something, even the grudging flesh admitted that. The wisest course for both of them without a doubt was to go for help. She had said that there was a neighbour only a mile away. Cautiously he struck sideways from the wall towards the road, eyes growing tired with a meticulous, terrified watch, ears listening for the slightest sound from the cottage behind. It remained wrapped in a complete, puzzling and disturbing silence. "She has not even called out to me" he thought and was illogically hurt even in his fear.

The flickering wings of a bat dived at him and he put up fingers, tingling and jumping with nerves, to guard his face. The wind blew past his ears and seemed to him the passage of time rushing by him. Minutes which had crawled flew. Seconds flew so swiftly that they could not be discerned but melted into one whirling belt of time driven by an engine whose beats were the beats of his own heart and the multitudinous noises of his brain. He dared not run, for to run was to abandon caution. Andrews caught a vision of himself, a small black figure lifting slow feet with the sluggish movements of a man trapped in a shallow bog, while seconds, minutes, surely hours, roared by with an accelerating speed. Once he was brought altogether to a standstill by the sight as it seemed to him of a figure which stood beneath a tree silently regarding him. With heart beating in panic brought to a climax Andrews stared back, afraid to move lest the figure had not yet observed him, trying through the darkness to fit familiar lineaments to the invisible face. Then the clouds parted for a moment to allow the passage of a proud orange moon and before they closed again the watching figure was shown to be no more than a strip of ivy hanging from a tree.

At last the road appeared, a faintly gleaming viscous

track across the matt surface of the dark. Rutted and broken as it was, to Andrews's feet it seemed hard, smooth and safe compared with the path they had left. He broke into a run. To run was comforting. He felt that at last he was really doing something to save Elizabeth. The physical exertion of trying to force more speed out of unwilling feet gave no room for any whinings of the conscience. He felt that he was back on the heels of time.

After about ten minutes a building raised itself on his left out of the dark. Low and squat it exuded on the laurel scented evening a smell of cattle and manure. As Andrews opened the gate and began to walk up the path towards a heavy nailed door, a dog, somewhere round the corner of the house, rattled its chain and broke the quiet with a hoarse sound, more bellow than bark. Before Andrews had time to knock, a window was flung up a few feet above his head and a sluggish voice asked him who the Hell he was. Andrews thought that he recognised one of the voices which had paid the last respects to Mr. Jennings a few days previously.

His voice breaking a little through lack of breath, he called, "I want help. Up at Jennings'. Smugglers. They are attacking the girl."

Andrews felt that seconds passed between the moment which the words left the farmer's mouth and the moment when they reached his ears. When they came they were not worth the time they took.

"That's a likely tale."

Andrews's breath had returned. He grew vehement.

"It's true. You must help. You've got men here. Horses."

"You said smugglers, didn't you?" the man said. "We don't meddle with smugglers." Andrews remembered then that Elizabeth had warned him against expecting any help from her neighbours.

"A woman," he begged desperately.

"Nought but a bloody hoor," the farmer returned with crushing simplicity.

Andrews unwisely lost his temper. "You damned liar," he cried.

The man above stirred with a sleepy emotion. "Look here," he cried, "clear off. Spoilin' a man's supper. Why don't you 'elp 'er yourself?"

The question struck straight at Andrews's uneasy conscience. Why indeed? it echoed with a despairing grief. She believed in me, he thought, and then remembering her as he had last seen her, when she had hurried him off down the path to the well, he wondered. He heard again that faintly echoed "soon," imploring, yes, but unbelieving. She was in a damned hurry to get me away, he thought. Until this moment fear had allowed him no opportunity for thought. He had been annoyed at the imprudence of the candle and the open door. Now for the first time he questioned the imprudence. Struck by fear as to the conclusion to which his thoughts were leading him he interrupted them. "If you won't help yourself," he begged, "at least lend me a horse. I'll ride into town and fetch the officers."

"Now ain't that likely?" the sluggish voice mocked

him. "When'd I see that horse again, eh? Why don't you help 'er yourself?"

"I'm only one man unarmed."

"Well why should I be shot for the bloody hoor?" the man rejoined in a tone of aggrievement. "Leave 'er alone. They won't 'urt 'er. Amiable lot—the Gentlemen."

Leave her alone. Why, that, naturally, was the logical conclusion; it was only this blind, restless dissatisfied love which urged him to a bolder course. Leave her alone—and in a flash of revelation he knew that that was what she had consciously given him the chance to do. She had seen Joe coming and she had sent him away. That was the reason for her impatience and the disbelief in her whispered "soon". He remembered how she had said to him, "I had no right to make you risk yourself." Cutting him across the face like the thong of a whip struck the thought. She put her trust in my cowardice. And she was right, right, right. Her sacrifice had been safe with him. And yet remembering that "soon" he knew that she had hoped, however faintly, for his return, but a return of his own will, as her lover, accepting danger voluntarily. Clenching his hands he said to the man above, his body shrinking still in panic at his own words, "I'm going back now."

He heard a movement as though the farmer were about to shut the window and played his last card. "There's a reward out for these men," he said and added quickly, "They are on the run. They've lost their ship."

The voice, less sluggish now, said, "Money's not worth a skin."

"You needn't risk that," Andrews said. "Send a man in on a horse to Shoreham to the officers."

"You'll be askin' fifty-fifty?" the man asked reluctantly.

"No," said Andrews, "only the loan of a horse back to the cottage." At his own words his heart became a battle ground between exaltation and fear.

"Stay there," the man said, "and I'll come down to you."

He was winning, winning after all, he felt, in this race to catch up time. "O God, God, God," he prayed, "give me courage to go through with this." The knife, Lewes, his return, and the fourth time, which was, Elizabeth said, to bring him the peace he craved. But it is not peace I want now, he thought, only her, O God, guard her till I come.

He allowed himself to be inspected closely in the light of a lamp. Even to the suspicious farmer his desperate impatience proved a passport of honesty. "I'll ride to Shoreham myself," the man said. "D'you know the amount of the reward?" He was opening the stable door as he spoke and grunted with approval at the prompt lie "Fifty pounds a head." Even now, however, the faint lurkings of suspicion induced him to choose the sorriest nag in the stable for Andrews to ride. But to Andrews it was a winged Pegasus compared with his weary feet.

The night for one instant, as he left the dim fluttering lights of the farm, was a pair of dark doors which opened only to enclose him. Then he was driving his horse, urging it forward with stick and passionately whispered words to knock its head against the black wall which receded always out of reach. Still in his heart was that strange mingling of exaltation, because he was doing at last what was right and dangerous, and fear. The two emotions left no room for planning. His only object was to reach the cottage as soon as might be and fling himself upon any whom he might find there. They would kill him probably and then they would go because their object was achieved. "You trusted in my cowardice to keep me safe," he cried through the dark. "You were wrong, wrong, wrong," but his heart felt sick at the thought of how nearly she had been right. "Go faster, you devil," he called to the horse, beating it unmercifully upon the flank, till the wretched animal which was old and uncertain in eyesight stumbled in its efforts to obey. With an eye rolled backwards nervously to watch the upraised stick it put back its ears and whinnied not so much a protest against cruel treatment as a pathetic excuse for being unable to obey.

A cry came from the bushes at the edge of the road a little in front. A figure shot into his path and held out both arms to stop the horse and rider. The horse shied to one side and halted. The figure approached and put one hand upon the rein. "Where are you going?" a voice asked and Andrews recognised Tims.

He put his hand down to the wrist which held the rein and gave it a sudden twist. "Who's at the cottage?" he asked.

The boy, whimpering with pain, replied "Joe and Carlyon."

"And what are you doing here?"

"They told me to keep a look-out." He suddenly creased his face up in a puzzled frown. "It wasn't true, Andrews, was it? You didn't put me in that box?"

"Why are they at the cottage?" Andrews asked.

"They said they'd meet you there. They want to talk to you."

"Let go of my rein."

"But, Andrews, you haven't told me. It's not true, is it?"

Andrews struck his horse and forced it forward.

Persistently the boy clung to the rein and stumbled with it.

"Let go," Andrews cried again.

"But, Andrews. . . ." Andrews drew back his arm and struck the boy across the face with his stick. The mouth creased with a cry of pain, the hand loosed the rein, and for a brief instant before the darkness separated them, Andrews saw a dog's eyes raised to him in pain and puzzlement. With an instinctive gesture of self-disgust Andrews flung the stick towards an invisible hedge and leaning forward over the horse's head began to implore it, "Faster, old boy, faster, faster."

Carlyon's there, he told himself, all must be well. Enmity was forgotten in the relief of that knowledge. He was riding, riding to a friend and he urged his horse the faster the sooner to see his friend. She would be safe with Carlyon. What did Carlyon's anger against him matter? He was Elizabeth's guardian now, to keep her safe from the Joes and Hakes of an embittered world. The rattle of the hoofs upon the road sang themselves rhythmically into his brain until they became a poem which he whispered aloud to the night which was fleeing past him into banishment. Carlyon reading. Carlyon speaking slowly with rapt face stunned with the shock of beauty. Carlyon, my friend Carlyon. A face in a sunset on a hill speaking unimagined things. A God-like and heroic ape. "You can have anything you want, all except the ship." The voice falling on the last word as though it spoke of something holy and unsullied. The *Good Chance*.

Then Andrews remembered that Carlyon had lost his ship. It was not to a friend that he was riding but to a man whom he had robbed not only of livelihood and sole mistress but of his only dream, a foolish sentimental blind dream of adventure. It had not needed the loss of a ship to break the dream. Betrayal had done that. The loss only made the waking irrevocable. One of us will be dead to-night, he thought, and the horse as though in alliance with the shrinking body slowed its pace. "Faster, old boy, faster." O, to be there before his courage again departed. He must not think of the future, but the advice was an impossible one. "O God," he prayed, "let it not be me. He's broken and finished. He will not mind death, but I'm only just beginning."

The cottage light. It was less than a week since, fleeing over the down, he had seen it first. Now as then he was afraid, but with what a difference. A gulf of more than time separated the two figures. One had approached with shrinking caution. The other, leaving the horse untied to stray at will, ran with a desperate carelessness to outstrip fear and flung open the cottage door. Out of a gale fashioned of the roaring passage of time and his own tumultuous thoughts and fears he stepped into a quiet so deep that it formed a a frozen block which kept him pressed against the door, unable to move or speak or for a moment feel.

At the table Carlyon sat facing him, eyes open, breathing, seeing, knowing, yet neither speaking nor moving nor showing hatred or surprise. Elizabeth's back was turned, where she sat, but Andrews did not need to see her face, for her hunched shoulders and fallen face told him that she was dead. Told him but conveyed for a little no meaning of death, spoke, as it were, in images too hackneyed or conventional to stir the mind. He stared and stared at the extreme decrepitude of the dead body, which now had no more of grace or beauty than a sawdust doll. His eyes passed on in a puzzled and still uncomprehending inquiry to Carlyon, who sat watching him without speech or movement. On the table out of Carlyon's reach lay a pistol, trigger raised.

Pushing painfully against the cold barrier of silence Andrews approached. As feeling returns with agony to a frozen limb, so a small dull pain began to throb in his forehead, with a regular and maddening rhythm. With a kind of caution he stretched out his fingers and touched the body on the shoulder. The warm answer of the flesh smote its way to his brain, cleared his stunned mind and flung it into a passionate rebellion.

She could not be dead. It was impossible, too unfair, too final. The flesh had made to his fingers an exactly similar response to that of life. There was but one difference. The face had not turned to him. He was afraid to touch the face. She is only hurt, asleep, he thought. As long as he did not touch the face so she would remain. "Elizabeth, Elizabeth," he implored but under his breath not loud enough to wake her if indeed she slept. He shut out the knowledge which lay deep in his mind like an internal sore and clung with passionate persistency to hope. He began to pray out loud in a low voice, ignoring Carlyon's presence. "O God, let her be asleep," he whispered, "let her be asleep." He felt that he could stand there immovable not for hours merely, but for days, weeks, years, never making a sound loud enough to wake her, believing that there was a chance she slept.

Carlyon said across the table. "What's the use? She's dead." The suddenness of the words made Andrews's heart leap, and for the moment he felt that it would never begin to beat again. He gasped, robbed of air he hoped for ever. But his heart started again its regular, hateful rhythm of life, and Andrews jerked himself unwillingly into motion. He seized the pistol which lay upon the table and raised it. "Be quiet," was all he said, however, in a low trembling voice.

"What's the use?" Carlyon repeated with an unfeeling voice which dropped the words slowly and heavily into the air like small pellets of lead. "She's dead."

"You are lying," Andrews whispered, but then the suspense became too great and he turned and took the body in his arms. The face fell back against his shoulder and the eyes which he had thought were faultless stared into his with an unwinking and imbecile lack of expression. "My own knife," he said slowly, tracing the red stain on her clothes to its source.

He let the body down again into the seat and stood with hands pressed to his forehead. Despair and a kind of terror were advancing towards him down a long tunnel, but as yet he defended himself from the realisation that Elizabeth would never speak to him again, that he would never feel her in his arms, though he lived for another fifty years. And then he would die and enter a blank eternity. He stared across the table at Carlyon, but his eyes were glazed and he saw him only through a shaking, hovering veil. He still held the pistol, but he felt no anger against Carlyon. Before this complete destruction of a life which had given a meaning and a possibility to holiness and divinity hatred seemed a child's game. It was in any case, he felt dimly, not an act of the living which had crumbled life but of the dead, a victory for the old man who had preceded him in this cottage and for his father. His father had made him a betrayer and his father had slain Elizabeth and his father was dead and out of reach. Out of reach. But was he? His father's was not a roaming spirit. It had housed itself in the son he had created. I am my father, he thought, and I have killed her.

At the thought the dry, stained despair in which he dwelt gave way before a kind of blessed grief. He flung himself upon his knees beside the body and be-

gan to fondle it but without tears and over and over
again he kissed the hands but not the face, for he
feared to meet the imbecility of the eyes. If I had not
run away—the thought doubled him with pain. "It
was my father made me," he said aloud. But how
could he prove it, kill that damaging spirit and show
a self remaining?

Carlyon's voice steadied him and brought him back
to his feet. "Francis, I didn't do this." It seemed in no
way unnatural that his enemy should speak to him as
Francis, for it was not his enemy. His enemy was his
father and lay within himself, confusing him till he had
struck his friend.

"Joe came here first," Carlyon said. "I wasn't here.
She wouldn't tell him, seemed to be waiting for someone. That made him nervous, he tried to find out
where you were. He began to hurt her. She stabbed
herself. He's gone."

"Do you hate me, Carlyon?" Andrews asked. A
plan had entered his head for dealing with his father,
and it was as though in fear his father's spirit had
shrunk into a small space leaving Andrews's own brain
more clear and simple than he had ever known it.

"No," Carlyon said. "You must hate me. You can
shoot if you like. If not I'll wait for the officers. They
are coming?"

Andrews nodded his head. "I'm sorry," he said, "for
what I did against you." Across the table their hands
met. "It's extraordinary," Andrews said, "we've been
sleeping. She's woken us." His voice broke and he
dropped his hand, for his words had brought up a

piercingly clear vision of what seemed to him a perfect holiness which he would never meet again. "Carlyon," he said, "will you go—now before the officers come?"

"What's the use?" Carlyon said dully, watching the dead face opposite him. "They'll find me. I shall be almost glad to hang for this. What a stupid business. She was finer than any of us."

"Go," Andrews repeated. "Don't you understand I want to be alone with her." He clenched his hands in a spasm of fear, fear of the grief which must come when there was no voice to distract him, and yet, if his father were to be slain, he must be alone.

Carlyon rose and Andrews handed him the pistol. "You may need this," he said. "Listen. Will you promise never to interfere with me again?"

"I promise," Carlyon said. "We've been fools. That's all done with."

"I didn't mean the past," Andrews said. "Promise."

"I promise." They did not shake hands again for Andrews suddenly turned and stood with his back to the door fighting the impulse to cry out to Carlyon, "Don't go, I'm afraid to be alone." His hands over his eyes he felt the touch of tears for the first time. Yet none of them was because his friend had gone and he would not see him again. As his enmity for Carlyon seemed now only a child's foolish and dangerous game with fire, so also his love. It was like a dream recalled after many hours—without reality. The two musics had fought for final mastery—one alluring, unreal, touched with a thin romance and poetry, the other clear-cut, ringing, sane, a voice carved out of white marble. One had gone out from him into a vague world, the other was silent in death, but silence had conquered.

He was alone with the body of his love and he dared not loose his hands from his face. If he had lived with her a little longer he might have come to believe in an immortality and a resurrection, but now both heart and brain denied the possibility. Spring and summer and winter might come and go through the centuries, but their individual bodies would never meet. He had hardly begun to hear her voice and he had scarcely touched her body, and now he would neither hear nor touch ever again. He knew now how a second could crawl, and he could not bear the thought of the passage of empty years.

Dropping his hands but with eyes lowered so that he should not see her face he knelt beside Elizabeth's chair. "Do you know," he asked in a whisper, "that it was I that killed you?" For was there anything of himself that was not his father? His father was his lust, and his cowardice had been fashioned by his father. He would find out. He had a plan, but he dared not think of it too closely, lest his father fearing defeat should make a last struggle and gain ascendency.

His own knife. He had left it to guard her and with it she had taken her life. What depth of terror and disillusionment must have led her to that sacrifice. He thought of her frightened, despairing, afraid of betraying him. She had whispered "soon" in unbelief, but she must have hoped, until it was too late for hope and she knew that he would not return.

He lifted her hand and put it on his mouth. "Why were you so wise?" he whispered. "My love, my love, if you had waited Carlyon would have come." Spring, summer, autumn, winter. "Did you think I loved you so little that I could go on for ever and ever without you?" He began to weep not freely but with dry, lacerating, interrupted sobs which left him breathless and exhausted. His brain felt wearied out and yet he could not rest. Sights and sounds, disconnected, many of them meaningless, trod on each other's heels, trampled across his brain till it felt aching and bleeding. A sprig of blackberries in a muddy lane, a shrill voice talking, talking in a crowded bar, a man with scrubby beard, a wheel that turned endlessly with gathering speed, a shock of stars that plunged across a great dark gap of space, voices raised in shouts, the whistle of wind in spars, the sound of water, a red face plunged at him shrieking questions, and then silence, a white face lit by candles, and darkness and an aching heart.

The fourth time. The fourth time he would find peace. He needed it now more than ever in his life before. Even extinction was not so dreaded as the continuance of this aching nightmare. He put his head upon Elizabeth's knees and said aloud between ungainly efforts to retrieve his breath, "I'll try."

Very faint through the sound of his own hard breathing he heard the gravel of the path grate beneath a number of feet. For a second time he raised his eyes to Elizabeth's face. The vacant eyes no longer horrified him. He saw them as hope, a faint hope that might be a stirring of belief. Something had gone out of them to leave them thus, and how could a tangible knife have struck so intangible a something. If there is anything of you in this room, he thought, you shall see. Again he kissed her hands and again the sound of the shifting gravel came to him.

He realised then that his time with Elizabeth was a matter of minutes only, and that he would not even be allowed to see her into the grave. Taking the body in his arms he held it to him with a greater passion than he had ever shown in life. Although he thought that he was spilling his words vainly into an unhearing silence he whispered into her ear the first proud words he had ever said, "I shall succeed." Then he closed her eyes, for he did not want so beautiful a body shamed by their imbecility before strangers, and laid her back in the chair. His hands clenched he waited for the door to open, waited but with no apprehension, clear in a double duty of salvation, of his friend from pursuit and of himself from his father.

The many feet had come to a standstill outside the door and their owners were hesitating. It was clear that they feared resistance. Presently a familiar voice shouted for it to be opened. Half sitting upon the table facing the dead girl Andrews remained silent. After another pause the handle was turned with a sudden rough resolution and the door was flung open.

There entered first with slow caution, gun at the ready, the man who had mocked Andrews when they waited together in the witnesses' room. Some other men followed him with equal caution and ranged themselves against the wall, where they stood ready to shoot, their eyes turning nervously hither and thither, as thought they dreaded some sudden attack.

"So it's you, Andrews, again," their leader said, with a grin intended for mockery. Andrews smiled back. He felt at last clear and certain of himself, happy in his decision.

"Where are you friends?"

"They've gone," he said and smiling at the association he caught a friendly echo of Carlyon's voice, "They are all gone into the world of light, and I alone sit lingering here." Into what a harsh light had they passed and in what a refreshing darkness did he stay. It touched his hot brain with cool fingers like the fingers of a woman and the ache and restless longing and despair were at an end. And the darkness soon would grow deeper and in that darkness who knew but that there was a hope to find something which no knife could injure? It was no longer despair but a whimsical reproach with which he thought—if you had waited one month more, one week more, I might have believed. Now I hope.

"They've gone," he repeated, his eyes turning not to the elderly revenue officer who addressed him, but to Elizabeth. The officer's eyes followed his and remained fixed in a gradually growing horror and disgust.

"What's this?" he said and suddenly moved round the table and came face to face with the body. "She's dead," he added, voice falling into a whisper. He looked up. "Did they do this? We'll hang them now."

"I killed her," Andrews said. "You'll find my name on the knife." You are safe now, Carlyon, he thought, not with any bitter, soured or jealous love, but with a quiet and amused friendliness. We are quits. And yet it is true—I did kill her or my father in me. But, father, you too shall die.

Leaning forward, paler than when he entered, the man drew out the knife and read the name in the rude, schoolboy attempt at engraving. "You scum," he said. He gave an order to his men.

"I'm coming quietly," Andrews said. "Didn't I send for you?" They watched him with puzzled, suspicious and totally uncomprehending eyes, but made no attempt to bind his hands.

"There's nothing more to stay for," Andrews said and walked to the door. They followed him as if he were their leader and outside formed round him without a word. It was quite dark, but the moon, like a ship on a land girt lake, sailed in a deep blue gap between the clouds, shedding a pale light upon their crumpled splendour. One star companioned her.

Andrews did not look back upon the cottage. Regret had gone, even remembrance of the graceless body abandoned there. To his own surprise he felt happy and at peace, for his father was slain and yet a self remained, a self which knew neither lust, blasphemy nor cowardice, but only peace and curiosity for the dark, which deepened around him. You were always right, he said, in the hope, not yet belief, that there was something in the night which would hear him, the fourth time had brought peace. His father's had been a stubborn ghost, but it was laid at last, and he need no longer be torn in two between that spirit and the stern unresting critic which was wont to speak. I am that critic, he said with a sense of discovery and exhilaration.

It was the men around him who seemed over-weighted with a kind of despair for the dead. They walked heavily and nervously, forgetting the prisoner in their horror of his act. They did not know how close they were treading to another deed. Aware of his safe presence in their midst they kept their eyes away from him in a kind of shame that any man could be so callous. To Andrews's sense now there were two stars or it might be two yellow candles in the night around him. One was the sole companion of the moon, the other glimmered more brightly still in the belt of the officer in front of him and bore his own name. Slowly his hand stole out unnoticed on an errand of supreme importance, for between the two candles there was a white set face that regarded him without pity and without disapproval, with wisdom and with sanity.

About the Author

Graham Greene was born in 1904 and educated at Berkhamsted School, where his father was the headmaster. On coming down from Balliol College, Oxford, where he published a book of verse, he worked for four years as a sub-editor on *The Times*. He established his reputation with his fourth novel, *Stamboul Train*, which he classed as an "entertainment" in order to distinguish it from more serious work. In 1935 he made a journey across Liberia, described in *Journey Without Maps*, and on his return was appointed film critic of the *Spectator*. In 1926 he had been received into the Roman Catholic Church and was commissioned to visit Mexico in 1938 and report on the religious persecution there. As a result he wrote *The Lawless Roads* and, later, *The Power and the Glory*.

Brighton Rock was published in 1938 and in 1940 he became literary editor of the *Spectator*. The next year he undertook work for the Foreign Office and was sent out to Sierra Leone in 1941–43. One of his major postwar novels, *The Heart of the Matter*, is set in West Africa and is considered by many to be his finest book. This was followed by *The End of the Affair, The Quiet American*, a story set in Vietnam, *Our Man in Havana*, and *A Burnt-Out Case*. His most recent novels are *The Comedians, Travels with My Aunt*, and *The Honorary Consul*. In 1967 he published a collection of short stories under the title: *May We Borrow Your Husband?* His autobiography, *A Sort of Life,* was published in 1971.

In all, Graham Greene has written some thirty novels, "entertainments," plays, children's books, travel books, and collections of essays and short stories. He was made a Companion of Honour in 1966.